Where Sunbeams Fall

Moira Yeldon

A catalogue record for this
book is available from the
NATIONAL
LIBRARY
OF AUSTRALIA
National Library of Australia

Linellen Press
265 Boomerang Road
Oldbury, Western Australia
www.linellenpress.com.au

Acknowledgments

There are many stages to steer through when writing a book and it wouldn't be possible without the support of other people. I'd like to thank the Book Editors Group at The Society of Women Writers WA for assessing the drafts of my manuscript. Thanks to fellow writers at South Fremantle Writers' Centre and Romance Writers of Australia who read various parts of this book and supported me on my writing journey.

Special thanks to the editors who helped to make my work shine: Catherine Hungerford, Shelley London, Gail Harper, and Mairead Hackett.

I am grateful for the many friends who supported me throughout and for Bryan by allowing me space to complete the task. Thanks to my wonderful sisters for their ongoing belief in my writing and the many beta readers who gave up their time to spend on my manuscript. Pauline, Debra, Christine, Frances, Anne, Natalie, and Max – I am forever indebted. I could not have survived without your tireless dedication and support.

And to the poets such as Rumi, Cummings, and Neruda whose words have inspired and enriched my writing I feel enormous gratitude. Thanks to Caroline Myss for enlightening me with the words of *A Mile from Baghdad*.

Thank you Helen Iles of Linellen Press for editing and publishing my work.

For Zoe

Contents

Prelude

Collapsing the dripping umbrella, Debra hurled it onto the back seat and reversed out of the parking space, noting as she did the surging streams of water gushing from the monsoon drains on both sides of the road. As another crack of thunder split the sky, she cringed but nevertheless pressed her foot to the pedal and pulled out onto the flooded road. Immediately she heard a strange metallic rattle coming from the wheels, and listened harder. The car started to wobble from side to side. She needed to stop but, through the torrential rain pouring over the windscreen, she couldn't see the edge of the drain nor where the flooded road stopped.

She braked, but the steering wheel wrenched through her hands, the tyres spinning, gaining no traction on the wet road. The back end skidded around, the back wheels suddenly finding grip plummeted the car into the drain of rushing water. Her chin hit her chest as a submerged log snagged the front wheels, stopping the car instantly, which tightened the seat belt sharply across her neck. She reached down, groping frantically for the release clip, and finding it, freed the clasp.

Gasping for breath, she cracked open the door and scrambled out onto a spindly branch, searching for a way back. There was only one. As she leapt across the tumbling water from her branch to the drain embankment, her foot slid out from under her, and she sank into the murky depths. Muddy weeds wrapped around her long bare legs, and she frantically kicked to shake them off. The fast-flowing current swirled around her waist as she clambered up the slippery embankment and grabbed at the busted iron grilles which normally covered the drains. Her drenched T-shirt and summer skirt smeared with thick mud as she dragged herself up onto the flooded road.

Her legs shaking, she steadied herself as she looked around. Across the road, two cars had pulled over, one was a four-wheel-drive, the other a white Fiat.

'Oh, Debra. Thank God you are alive.' Rahim rushed towards her, visibly shaken. 'When I saw you skid across the road, I thought the worst.' He took off his jacket; draped it around her shoulders; brushed a few sodden curls from her face. 'I am so glad you are okay.' He hugged her and she felt the heat of his jacket as it touched her skin.

'I heard knocking noises …' She waited for her heart to stop racing, for her teeth to stop chattering. 'It just spun out of control. I thought I was going to die.'

She pointed to her car, and he waded across to check for defects, water lapping over his feet soaking his shoes and the legs of his trousers. The man with the four-wheel drive also crouched to examine her wheels. He gesticulated as he spoke in Malay, Rahim interpreting for her.

'He thinks your wheel nuts have been loosened. Several have already fallen out,' he shouted above the falling rain.

'Oh my God! Who would do that? Imagine if Sam was in the car with me. What if his seatbelt wasn't fastened? I can't believe I'm still alive.'

'I cannot believe it either but I am so glad you are. This man has offered to tow your car to the mechanic down the road. You had better come with me.'

The Malay man parked his car closer to hers and attached a winch to the rear bumper. He gave Rahim an address for the garage, and they watched as he winched her car out of the drain.

A sleek black Mercedes slowed down, the dark thickset driver staring at her car as it passed. When he turned to look at her, gold flashed from his teeth and fingers.

'Did you recognise the driver in that car? He didn't stop,' she noted, staring after it.

'It may have been our college director. Muhammad drives a Merc.' Rahim also peered at the black car in the distance.

'Yes. I met him earlier today at the college. He didn't introduce himself, but he made it quite clear what he thought of me. A very rude man.' She shivered as water ran down the back of her neck and she choked back tears. 'Why would someone do such a thing?'

'It may have been a random attack. I believe other people's cars have recently been sabotaged. It is not that uncommon here.' He half smiled. 'But it is still frightening. Are you sure you are not hurt? I can take you to the hospital.' When he looked at her with his warm brown eyes full of concern, his expression belied the lightness in his voice. Rain dripped off his sleek black fringe, and smudges of mud deepened his brown cheek.

'My head's throbbing. I think it's the shock. I just want to go home.' She ran her hands through her long, tangled hair.

Rahim guided her towards his car, opened the door, and she slid in.

As he drove her home, her head whizzed with images from earlier in the day. She remembered the male students outside the college as they'd hung around her car. She heard Muhammad's threatening voice again and how angry he had made her feel. But it was too painful to dwell on, too difficult to believe anyone from the college would want to harm her.

Rahim parked his car down the road from her house and rested his arm around her shoulders. 'How are you feeling?' He kissed her on the forehead, and she wanted to stay with him like this, but she couldn't get the earlier events out of her head.

'Why would anyone want to hurt me?'

No sooner had she asked the question, she thought of many reasons why they would. She was a privileged stranger who came to their country yet failed to fit into their culture. She was a European woman who claimed to know more than the locals, teaching in their college, and living in her fancy house on the hill. Had she unknowingly upset someone at the college? Was it possible someone had seen her with Rahim outside school hours? Had someone been watching them … and what if they were to tell Alex? But it wasn't only about her. As a married Malay man with a family, Rahim too was risking his life, his marriage, and his career.

Two years ago, she wouldn't have believed any of this was possible. When she'd left Australia, it hadn't been her plan to live in a faraway country – it was Alex's dream to work overseas in Brunei. From the moment he saw the pictures in *Time* magazine, he was hooked. It was the seventies, a time for pursuing your dreams, and Alex was ready for a change. She was young, with no idea what she would find in this place so different from home. While Alex devoted all his time to his new job, she was left alone to manage on her own. If not for Rahim, she would have been navigating alone through this maze of unfamiliar culture with its strange customs and people.

A Thousand Half Loves

A thousand half-loves
must be forsaken to take
one whole heart home

Rumi

'Have a look at this picture, Debra. It's amazing.' Alex peered over his thick black frames and flicked a shock of auburn hair from his face.

He slid it across the table, and she pulled it closer to get a better view. Debra noted the light in Alex's eyes, the enthusiasm in his voice. She peered at a *Time* magazine dated May 1973. It wasn't a recent issue but current enough to give her an accurate picture of what life was like there. A stark white mosque with a golden dome and shimmering minarets was floodlit against a vast purple sky. An ornamental barge appeared to float on a lake where a myriad of colourful lights bounced off the water. It was an ethereal fairy tale image as if conjured with the flick of a wand.

'But why? Where on earth is it?' Debra held her breath, remembering his recent late-night phone calls, baffled by his furtive conversations, but he answered without missing a beat.

'Bandar Seri Begawan, the capital of Brunei – on the north-west coast of Borneo. Apparently, it's a fascinating place. A tiny Islamic state ruled by a sultan.'

Scanning the pictures, her interest stirred at the water village of wooden stilt houses, of oil rigs that floated out to sea, and the opulent palace of a young sultan who lived in this far away

Shangri-La. It reminded her of something from a fairy tale and she shuddered at the thought of a genie leaping out of a lamp, offering to change everything around her into something foreign and unknown.

'That's him. The Sultan of Brunei.' Alex pointed at the image of the richest man in the world. 'He has his own collection of polo ponies, grooms from Argentina, every imaginable type of luxury car.'

Biting on toast and marmalade, Debra blinked at photos of smiling Malay women in long tunics and sarongs with heads covered but faces revealed. She looked down at her own bare feet beneath a peacock blue kaftan. She fingered the gold braided neckline and lifted her unruly blonde hair, uncovered and untamed, from where it hung around her shoulders. She stared at a different image of bare-breasted women with babies strapped to their backs, as they stood wide-eyed beside simple woven huts.

'These people don't look wealthy. According to this article, they live in longhouses in the jungle.' She shook her head at the stark contrast, so different to any people she'd ever known.

'Some indigenous groups live across the border in East Malaysia. These Ibans were once the head-hunters of Borneo.' Alex stroked his long sideburns. He was pleased with his research on this mysterious country so far from home.

'Head-hunters?' The muscles around the back of her neck started to twitch as she anticipated this exotic land, so different to Australia, a land of savage natives hunting with blowpipes in deepest, darkest jungles. She looked out at her garden where magpies were stealing coconut matting from the hanging plants to build their nests in the giant arms of the lemon-scented gum. For Debra, it was a familiar scene of shelter and comfort.

But Alex frantically sorted through a pile of travel brochures on foreign currencies, customs, and creeds. It seemed he was not afraid to rub the genie's lamp.

'I've been offered a job there with the airline – a tax-free haven with generous wages, and gratuities at the end of each contract. A wonderful opportunity for us to save money.'

The kettle whistled and the smell of burnt toast lingered in the air. 'How long have you known?' She wanted to cover her ears, too scared to hear what was coming next.

'Jim Lyons rang me last night. He loves it up there.'

Aware of his secret phone calls late at night, she'd had no idea how quickly his plans had developed and fallen into place. 'And what about his wife Rosa? How does she feel about it?' She scanned his face for clues, but Alex was in another world, already in an oil-rich land where sultans in majestic palaces lived beside head-hunting jungle tribes in strange looking huts.

'I guess she's happy to go wherever his job takes him. You know Rosa. She dotes on Jim.' He grinned as if he'd just struck gold, oblivious to all around him as he pulled his passport out of its folder.

She hurried inside to make coffee and process what she'd heard. Just as she was re-adjusting to normal life, Alex was making major changes that would affect her life as she knew it. He sat on the veranda, his solid form squeezed into a canvas chair. With his long, outstretched legs, he occupied more than his allocated space at the table. Sam sat next to his father pulling crust from his toast, remnants of jam smeared across his chubby cheeks. He threw the toast at two birds dancing around the fountain where a fine mist of water sprayed onto the lawn.

Golden daffodils spilled out of wooden tubs as she carried the coffee back to the veranda. She thought of Rosa Lyons doting on her husband, but did it justify completely changing one's life? Would she be prepared to uproot this life and leave behind everything dear to her?

Heady scented jasmine snaked its way around the wooden posts abuzz with swarms of hover flies. Stray tendrils entangled her, but she pushed them away with one hand and placed the coffee mugs on the table.

'This contract … how long would it be?' She bit on her bottom lip, dreading his reply.

'Three years.'

She switched off, but he continued to tempt her – free flights home to Perth every year, shopping in Singapore. But she wasn't convinced, and three years seemed an eternity. Inhaling the heady scent of the lemon gum where a laughing kookaburra called to its mate, she wished she had something to laugh about. The bird swooped for the toast Sam had thrown on the lawn.

Accustomed to the security of her own home, she couldn't imagine living anywhere else, especially in a strange country she knew little about.

'Is it safe there? It seems awfully close to Vietnam.' Her stomach muscles tightened as she recalled the impending threat of national service, the relief when Alex didn't get called up to fight in someone else's war. She was terrified of him going to Southeast Asia then and feared for him going away now.

'Safe? The Sultan has an elite Gurkha regiment – part of the British army, best fighters in the world,' he said, another topic he'd researched well.

She tried to visualise Nepalese fighters so far from home, as they protected others in a remote land. Hard to comprehend as she looked around their garden, her place of refuge. A screeching pair of rainbow lorikeets, invaders from the eastern seaboard, drowned out Alex's last sentence. They crashed through the golden grevillea, claiming it as their own. If Debra should agree to live in Brunei, would she too feel like an invader living in another's land? Brushing the yellow pollen from her messy hair, she massaged the tension around her neck. A grey day threatened to overwhelm, where previously a cloudless blue sky beckoned.

'I just want to make sure Sam will be safe. I couldn't bear

anything to happen to him. Do they have good medical facilities there?' She wanted to tell him of her disappointment at his sudden decision, not consulting her, but her head throbbed, and she couldn't find the right words to express how she felt.

'Yes, there's a hospital and doctors. You can also have an *amah* to help look after Sam. He will love it there.'

'Perhaps we could wait until Sam is at school.'

'I can't afford to wait. This is a great career opportunity. A promotion, better income, great lifestyle.' Alex bent to retrieve a travel brochure that had slid onto the chair, his shock of hair falling over his eyes. He brushed it away before staring at her. 'Why would you not want to go there?'

'It's just … since Mala … I worry more about Sam.' She swallowed, her throat constricting as she thought of Mala, never far from her thoughts.

'You need to move on, Debra. I miss her too, but worrying won't bring her back.' Alex moved in closer, peering over his glasses. He snatched the magazine and added it to the pile he was sorting.

Her real fear was letting go of any last thread that tied her to their baby daughter. She would be leaving the house where only last year she'd held that precious bundle in her arms. As the tiny coffin was lowered beneath the cold damp earth, it wrenched away a part of her. How could she abandon Mala with only the tall magnolias keeping vigil, showering her with their fragrant tears?

According to Alex's mother, grief was an individual experience with no simple panacea. When her husband Ted lay dying, it was a volatile period with mass demonstrations in the street not far from the hospital. As a WWII survivor, it upset Ted to hear the people protesting the Vietnam War and abusing Australian soldiers who fought there, failing to understand they too were physically and emotionally affected by the conflict. He hated that veterans like him were spat on and called killers or child murderers.

Ted, who'd lost his right arm in the second world war, liked to leave his ill-fitting prosthesis lying around the kitchen. Elsie threatened to throw it in the bin if she found it lying on her chopping board one more time. But when he died, she'd turned to Debra with red-rimmed eyes.

'They leave behind a huge empty space after they're gone.'

Debra's mother's response to grief was different. She believed life was meant to be tough and there was no use complaining. With her deadpan expression and stoic manner, she spelled it out. 'We have no control over many things including death. It's a matter of learning to endure, to move on.'

That's how her mum dealt with her own tragic life, wanting to keep the peace at any cost. She enjoyed going to the drive-in movies but while Debra complained about broken speakers with crackling dialogue, it didn't seem to bother her. She focused on the larger picture screen, her face fixed and impassive.

'How can I possibly move on when I'm stuck in this intolerable grief?' she asked her mum after Mala's life was cut short five months after her birth. She could find no sense in her death, and no meaning in her own life at the time.

'You'll find a way,' her mum had said.

After Mala's death, friends had rallied around and brought comfort food, endless casseroles, bowls of soup. Did they think by eating more she would feel better? Perhaps the food was designed to fill the gigantic void inside. But it was an emptiness that couldn't be filled by anything other than the one who had left a shape uniquely hers. Friends offered platitudes. 'There will be more children,' they said. 'You can try again.' But no end of trying or procreating was going to bring Mala back. It was Mala she missed and craved with all her senses – the chubby rolls of flesh around her knees, the soft nape of her neck, the intoxicatingly sweet smell when she buried her face in Mala's skin. It was her uniqueness that she desperately wanted. No other person was going to fill that void.

Alex had made up his mind about going to Brunei, but Debra was uncertain and needed guidance in her decision. Her guru would no doubt say, look to the heart, life is a journey. One must follow one's *dharma*, our duty or purpose in life. While there were times when Debra had chosen the exciting ephemeral journey, she now preferred the permanency of safer paths with dependable outcomes. Finally, it was her mother-in-law Elsie who convinced her to go. No doubt she meant well when she said, 'You may lose him if you let him go alone.'

Debra thought of the bare-breasted women in the magazine. Would Alex be lonely up there? She sometimes caught him looking at the framed photos of Mala and knew he grieved silently. She should have recognised his restlessness, his search for something more. For ten years he'd been happy working at the airport where his engineering job brought him the satisfaction he sought. It was a career he excelled in, but since Mala's death, he'd been unsettled, as if searching for something bigger and better. She remembered his words when he'd first learned about the job prospect. 'A wonderful opportunity. A new way of life.'

Lately, he'd been complaining about incidents at work that would previously not have bothered him. At home, he was reluctant to talk, to share his feelings. Maybe the slow sultry days and exotic tropical nights mentioned in the magazine might fuel unexpected passion in him.

That night as she reached out for Alex, he rolled away, but she snuggled in behind him.

'I love you.' She tested the words on her tongue, sliding her hand down his arm, wanting him to turn and hold her.

He shrugged her hand away. 'Too hot,' he grunted, sliding

across to the edge of the bed. She soon rolled onto her own side where a gap that felt as wide as the ocean threatened to separate them.

The following day he suggested he'd go on ahead to find them a house in Brunei and get settled before she and Sam arrived. Over the next few days as Alex made plans, his mind made up, Debra stalled. It felt like acting in a fantasy without a script, but she continued to go through the rituals of everyday life, focusing on Sam. Each day, she took him to the park where he loved to play on the seesaw and swing. Each week, she visited the cemetery, sitting in solitude, remembering Mala, sensing her presence. As she retraced her steps, she imprinted each tiny detail, picturing the tiny headstone with its butterfly motif and words of love. She smelt the fragrant magnolias and heard the crows calling from above. If she must leave Mala, she wanted to remember the sunbeams falling on the shiny paving stones that led up to her tiny grave.

With her mind riddled with doubt, she thought of how lonely she'd be if she didn't join Alex in Brunei. Finally, she succumbed to his wishes and prepared herself for this journey to a new life, so full of promise. When they said their goodbyes, Alex appeared exuberant, his spirit already in Brunei, ready to begin the adventure of a lifetime. As he was flying via Singapore, he had his long hair neatly clipped to guarantee his visa entry wasn't denied. With his hairline above his collar, he looked fresh-faced, like an eager teen.

At Perth airport, she lingered, admiring the black swans gliding across their ornamental lake. She envied their serenity, so unlike her own turmoil. As her spirit struggled to connect with her body, she felt nauseous, needing to purge her inner conflict. Sam hung onto her legs and the few remaining threads of their fragile family web. She clung to Alex, before kissing him goodbye.

'I hope we are making the right decision.' She tightened her grip on Sam's hand.

'It's the seventies, Debra. A time for change.' He waved as he dashed across the tarmac. 'An amazing time for change,' he called out, waving once more.

***

The 1970s were certainly a time of change for her mother-in-law, Elsie, widowed at sixty. Ted, who had been her whole life, was morose and laconic. He had no need of cheer as Elsie had enough for them both. She loved and missed him dearly when he died, but Ted wouldn't have survived if she'd gone first.

'He couldn't boil a kettle, let alone an egg,' she lamented as she continued to cook for two. But now it was only one plate, one cup with no one to nurture or cherish. As she clung to her only son, Alex resisted the unwanted responsibility she thrust upon him. Encouraging Debra to go to Brunei was a generous gesture and she knew how much Elsie would miss them, living alone. But as a wife and a mother, she'd been making sacrifices all her life. What did one more matter?

Not wanting to endure the same loneliness as Elsie, Debra tried to create an independent life for herself. Before Sam was born, she'd immersed herself in a teaching career, tutoring adults in literacy. While originally seeking relaxation, she'd discovered yoga, but her life changed when she found in its ancient wisdom, deeper insights into the meaning of life.

When he wasn't working shifts at the airport, Alex liked to fill his free hours playing golf and squash. He couldn't sit down to dinner each night unless he'd been for a long run. He talked about the ecstasy as he hit his stride, his body releasing endorphins, giving him that runner's high.

'You know that deeply euphoric state you get following intense exercise?'

'No. I have no idea what that's like.' Obviously, she'd never run fast enough to understand this state of bliss. Recently, she'd had more lows than highs in her life. She searched for that peaceful state in between.

Soon after Mala died, Debra found a guru and through her, gained a greater awareness of yogic philosophy, particularly, *Tantra*. A diminutive energetic woman, Swamiji trained in India under the tutelage of her guru. 'It's the role of the guru to ensure the disciple transcends from the dark into the light,' she said.

It was Debra's darkest hour when she found her guru, and she resolved to spend the rest of her life searching for the light. She chose this spiritual, mystical path of Tantra to expand her consciousness while liberating the divine within. Through her yogic practice, she became aware of the different aspects of self. With her outer world in turmoil, she garnered some semblance of peace within. Exploring the union of body, mind and spirit, she was desperate for anything to help bring sense to the loss of her baby girl. In poetry, she found meaning in words that triggered emotions she was finally able to express.

Before Mala, Debra first discovered love through Sam. From the moment he gripped his tiny hand around her finger, she was hooked. For the first few days after his birth, overwrought with love and awe, she couldn't sleep. Lying awake at night, she felt his warm sweaty body, the milky smell of his breath, and it was enough to keep her in a constant state of ecstasy. As she gazed at Mala's bright blue eyes, her angelic baby face, she cherished the same moments of love, the endless days of contented bliss. There was no reason to believe they wouldn't last, and she was bereft when these precious moments were ripped from her life just as she was beginning to enjoy them.

Sam and Debra prepared for their journey of a lifetime, sad to be leaving friends and family, especially Mala. At night she rolled over in bed, expecting to find Alex's warm familiar body lying beside her. She slid one hand up under her pillow, and the other she reached out tracing the shape where he used to be. Touching the cold empty space on the bedsheet, she experienced the familiar sensation of loss as it played tricks with her emotions, trying to sift reality from dreams. Unlike Mala, he was gone but was coming back, the comforting closeness of his body and the noisy sound of his laboured breathing absent, but it was only a temporary loss.

Now fully awake, there was no way she could get back to sleep. Missing his solid shape and earthy smell, she threw back the bedding. She needed a cup of tea, something to take her mind off the many worries whizzing around in her head. So many decisions to make about what to take to Brunei.

'Bring all the kitchen gadgets, crockery, cutlery, and cookware but not the furniture,' Alex said.

But she kept thinking about every other tiny detail. Should she take plenty of bedding or towels? Would it be easier to buy them over there? She wandered from room to room, opening and slamming cupboard doors. Finally, she sorted through the shelves of the linen closet using the opportunity to cull a lifetime of bedding. Pulling out a set of sheets and a few towels, she thought at least they'd have something to remind them of home.

Later that morning, after hearing the postman's shrill whistle, she raced to the letterbox and was rewarded with an aerogram from Alex. Tearing the perforated edges, she ripped it open, thrilled to read Alex's large unruly script.

> *Dear Debra,*
>
> *It was great to receive your letter and learn you're missing me. I've been busy checking out everything for you, I haven't had much time to write. Some things here are rather old-fashioned, but others appear quite modern. It's an interesting mix of old and new.*

When you arrive here you will also have to get an identity card with a photo of you but also a record of your fingerprints. How's that for security? I keep mine in my wallet ready to flash it, if required.

I'm just about to pick up the new Range Rover, thanks to an interest-free loan from the airline. The price of petrol here is incredibly cheap, and there's a road full of car sale yards. I've never seen so many new cars. Apparently, there are plans to build new supermarkets and a couple of modern hotels in town so lots of changes taking place. I'm sure you'll enjoy looking around the quaint old shops and markets.

There's an open-air cinema in town where they occasionally show English films but according to Jim Lyons you don't want to put your drinks on the ground because of the rats running around your feet. (Perhaps I shouldn't have told you that).

Overall, I'm impressed with Bandar, and I hope you will be too. I must dash as there's an aircraft that needs to be signed off. Give Sam a big hug. I can't wait to see you both.

Alex xxx

Alex continued to write more regularly, his letters full of positive first impressions. He talked about the local people he'd met and the ex-pats he worked with. 'A smattering of Aussies and Kiwis,' he said, 'but most of the pilots and engineers are Brits. All the engineering apprentices are young Malay guys.' Some of his colleagues, like him, lived in a hotel, awaiting the arrival of their families. He was pleased with his salary and the house the airline had allocated to him.

He posted Debra swatches of fabric so she could choose the

soft furnishings – a mass of brightly coloured samples of brocade, damask, and chenille spilled out of the large envelope. He'd included photos of curtain designs and window dressings and, as she ran her fingers along the soft fabrics, she pictured exotic valances with swathes of cloth hanging from large picture windows. 'All the furniture is provided by the airline,' he reassured her, 'so you don't need to bother about that.' Later when he telephoned, his voice was full of enthusiasm, comforting her like a well-worn cardigan.

'I have checked out pre-school for Sam and the International School looks great. I've also looked at the hospital in town where there are a few resident doctors. All medical treatment is provided free by the government.'

When she asked about shopping, he quickly told her he'd found a great Chinese Emporium he thought she would enjoy. 'They have lots of women's clothes, knick-knacks, and jewellery – the type of stuff you like.'

As Alex's phone calls became more frequent, he told her how much he was missing them. He'd moved out of the hotel in town and was settling into the new house. The swimming pool was being cleaned, and the new furniture about to be delivered. He spoke quickly as if excited and she felt her shoulders relax, happy to release some of her former tension. Maybe Alex is right, she sighed. This may be a bright new future for us both.

On Alex's recommendation, she bought herself a book called *Teach Yourself Malay*. It had an accompanying tape which she popped into her portable cassette player so she could listen to the pronunciation of these strange new words, as well as the rhythm of the language. According to Alex, it was an easy language to learn although he'd struggled with it himself. He assured her with her flair for language, she shouldn't have any problems.

From her research, she learnt that since oil was first

discovered in 1929, Brunei had flourished but was only a quarter of the size of Perth where she'd lived all her life. Somehow, she found that comforting, being able to find her way around a smaller city instead of disappearing into the void of some far-flung metropolis.

When she told Elsie about the school and hospital in Brunei, she said it was indeed a comforting thought, reassuring for Debra too until Elsie suggested she take with her various remedies to treat mosquito bites, heat rash or anything else she was likely to encounter.

'You don't know what tropical diseases they have up there,' she said.

Debra's shoulders tightened again as she imagined these strange ailments awaiting them. It wasn't the mosquitoes she worried about as much as the scorpions and snakes she'd read about. While Alex promised there were Chinese grocery stores that stocked the type of European food they liked to eat, Elsie was not convinced.

'You might not be able to buy the necessary ingredients for your baking.'

'Bandar is a city of 50,000 people, Elsie. I'm sure they will have everything we need.'

Her bulging suitcase now held a fruit cake Elsie had baked especially for Alex's birthday. Her macramé-addicted sister, Liz, had just perfected the latest craze and spent twelve hours converting three balls of string into a three-tiered plant hanger as a parting gift. Debra squeezed it in amongst the clothes in her case, careful not to squash the cake.

'I love the heavy, tropical rain which falls mainly at night. It helps me sleep,' Alex told her. 'There are often incredible storms with lightning and thunder,' he added, but then quickly changed the subject.

When Debra told Liz about the annual rainfall in Brunei, Liz enthused about the exotic tropical plants Debra would be able to grow in her new macrame plant hanger. Debra thought of the much-loved plants in her existing garden. Would the new tenants render her roses the same love and care she had. The night before they were due to leave, Debra tossed and turned in bed thinking of the family and friends she was leaving behind. When Sam crept into her bed in the middle of the night, she was glad of his warm cuddly body. Tuning into his breath, she finally slipped into his land of dreams.

The next day, as they stepped onto the aircraft, she waved goodbye to her home and the people she loved, wondering what life had in store for her.

The Dragon and the Pearl

If I were yonder conch of gold,
And thou the pearl within it plac'd,
I would not let an eye behold
The sacred gem my arms embrac'd.

Thomas Moore

Like most excited three-year-old boys, on the aircraft Sam explored every button that could be pressed or clicked. Debra pitied the woman in front as he jerked the food tray up and down. Now absorbed in the colouring book the flight attendant had given him, the small coloured pencils he scribbled with clattered down the gaps between the seats. A young man sporting an afro, sitting in the seat behind, kindly retrieved the first few that landed near his feet but, when the flight attendant offered him complimentary wine, the young man soon forgot about the pencils.

Debra too accepted a glass, enjoying this rare relaxing ritual. After a few mouthfuls, the wine worked its magic as it moved through her body, and she started to doze, lightly aware that Sam had become engrossed in the inflight movie and hopefully, would soon be asleep. She'd just finished her beef stroganoff when he said he needed the toilet. The second time in the last hour, she suspected his sudden urges were more about novelty than need. He was fascinated by the loud whooshing noise as he flushed, and the suction noise as he drained the vanity basin. They left the cubicle with clean, moisturised hands, and his blond curls reeked of the cologne he'd rubbed into his hair.

As she drained the last of her wine, she felt excited they'd soon be arriving in Kota Kinabalu.

Zig zags of lightning illuminated the sky as she peered through the aircraft window, straining to catch a glimpse of Mount Kinabalu below. Sam grabbed her arm tighter and asked why it was so bumpy as they rocked and bounced above the State of Sabah.

'It's the turbulence. We're flying through the clouds. Nothing to worry about,' she soothed him, but he looked around the cabin, wide-eyed, and she wrapped her arm around his tense shoulders. 'We'll soon be meeting Daddy. Are you excited?'

He nodded, and nestled his soft hair into her chest.

The elderly Chinese man sitting next to Debra provided a timely distraction. 'Have you heard the legend of the Dragon and the Pearl?' He leant towards Sam, smiling a toothless grin.

'No, but I'd like to. Tell me more.' Debra moved in closer so she could listen to what he was saying.

'Three brothers sailed from China in search of a pearl guarded by a dragon on top of this mountain –' He pointed out the window. 'The two eldest tried in vain to fight the dragon but only the youngest, Li, survived. While in town, Li married Sukiah, a local Kadazan woman. He climbed the mountain, found the pearl but told Sukiah he had to take it back to China.'

Sam had lost interest in the story by now, but Debra continued to listen, pondering what elusive pearl she might be chasing in life? The man appeared to be reading her thoughts.

'There are many searching for something more in their lives. The young ones … they believe in happiness at any price. We who are older know the real cost. Pleasurable moments are always diluted with equal measure of pain'. Then he proceeded with the tale. 'Every day, Sukiah climbed to the top of the mountain to await the return of her husband's ship. Finally, she died of a broken heart and disappeared into the rock. Her husband never returned. Nor did he appease the spirits of the mountain.'

So, he sacrificed his love for the pearl. There are probably many willing to do the same, she thought. *Would I be willing to sacrifice love? Probably not.*

'Some believe the name Kinabalu is derived from *Cina balu*, meaning Chinese widow. According to the legend, people have seen her ghost in the clouds. The thick mist surrounding the mountain is from her tears, they say.'

'Wow, that's quite a story. Thanks for sharing it.' She nodded as she gazed out through the clouds. Immediately, the flimsy stage curtains parted and she was rewarded with unhindered views of Mount Kinabalu.

'Sam, look!'

While it was only a glimpse, a thrill ran her through as the transient image of the mysterious craggy peaks rose out of the mist. *Could this be the image of the old woman?*

Sam peered from his seat long enough to take in the wondrous sight before the curtains of cloud closed once more. She fixed her gaze on the fading image now imprinted in her mind, hoping for another glimpse, but it was not to be. The young English couple in front, looked downcast at their cameras before consoling each other. They had missed the magical moment.

'That was worth waiting for. It's amazing to view it so close.' She gazed at the Chinese gentleman, 'especially after hearing the legend.' With its swirling mist of clouds, it was easy to imagine a dragon guarding a pearl, hiding in one of the many rocky crevices on the mountain.

'You will find it more impressive from the ground,' said the Chinese man. 'It's the highest mountain in Southeast Asia.'

The pilot jokingly asked if any climbers would care to exit the aircraft now to forgo the climb to the summit. A tall German

man stood to get something from the overhead locker and a ripple of laughter spread through the cabin.

She looked at Sam. 'We may get to climb it one day, when you're older.'

He bounced on his seat. 'When will we see the monkeys?'

'Soon, I hope. When we meet up with Daddy.'

Alex had promised to take them to the orangutans in nearby Sepilok where they would spend a couple of nights before taking a shorter flight to their new home in Bandar Seri Begawan. Sam's eyes started to droop, and she wrapped her arm around him, drawing him closer to her.

Three months had passed since she'd last seen Alex, and a shiver ran up her spine. Was it excitement or fear? She hoped this new life would strengthen their relationship, that they would be united as strangers in this faraway land.

At Kota Kinabalu Airport, she smiled on spotting Alex's wavy auburn hair in a sea of darker, sleeker styles. Frantically waving with one hand, she lifted Sam so he could see his father. A familiar sensation rushed through her as she anticipated the romantic evening ahead. Alex hugged Sam, then kissed her and, as he adjusted the glasses on his nose, she saw he was wearing new amber frames that matched his eyes and shirt.

'Happy Birthday. Are you ready to celebrate?' She hugged him again.

'Unfortunately, I'm needed at work, so we won't be able to stay here or visit the orangutans.' He picked up their heavier suitcases. 'We can have dinner in the airport lounge though while we wait for the next flight.'

Debra's shoulders slumped as she bent to pick up her carry-on bag. Her legs felt heavy, and hard to shift. While they waited, Alex filled her in on the latest happenings with his job and the new house.

'I hope you like the house. It's two -storeys with a large garden for Sam. There's a servant's room downstairs if we choose to get an amah. Right now, we have problems with borer beetle in the flooring, but they promised to fix it today.' He looked down at his wristwatch.

'It certainly looks nice from the photos. You said in your letter we might also get a dog.' She thought of Cougar, the cat they'd left behind who, at fifteen, was too frail to travel, too old to begin a new life. 'I'm sure Sam would love having a puppy, a playmate to share this new life.'

'Many of the locals keep dogs for security reasons. I'll be working away some of the time …' He squinted at the departure times on the board behind her before checking the boarding passes in his hand.

'Oh! I thought you said there was no problem with security?' The habitual knot tightened in her stomach.

Before he could answer, a female voice announced the departure of their next flight in Malay then in English. As they prepared to embark, she noted there were fewer passengers on the aircraft. This flight was much shorter in duration, barely long enough to consume an orange juice and a bag of salted peanuts. It seemed that she had only just reclined her seat, when the next minute she was pushing it upright again, preparing for landing. Looking out the window, she focused on the tiny circle of lights as the aircraft began its descent into Bandar Seri Begawan. Beyond the lights, rooftops faded into the dark jungle. As she gazed into the vast unknown, she wondered what she would discover in this strange new land.

Sam slept through the aircraft landing, and Alex carried him over his shoulder as they descended the aircraft stairs. Debra instantly felt she had stepped into a sauna as the sultry night air wrapped around her like a suffocating wet blanket. She gagged on the humidity and gasped in a breath. The competing scents of fragrant frangipani, and musty dampness confirmed they'd arrived in the tropics. After piling their luggage into the boot of a taxi, Alex jumped in the front with the driver and Debra stretched Sam's body across her lap in the back seat.

Driving along poorly lit deserted roads, the dark surrounding jungle swallowed the scattering of small houses along the roadway. Up ahead, water glimmered in a clearing where white scarecrow shapes fluttered above paddy fields. Behind them, small wooden houses teetered on stilts. A lantern hanging from a roadside stall cast shadows on an old man smoking a pipe, the only visible sign of life. While on a nearby hillside, the glint of a shiny spire or minaret suggested a mosque or prayer house. The road veered to the left, up a hill, and around a steep bend until their house finally appeared, bathed in light, at the top of the road. The house and garden looked just as Alex described them in his letters.

Vibrant magenta bougainvillea framed the front porch, illuminated by the porch light swarming with moths. Driving up the steep driveway, she caught glimpses of the gloomy jungle on the far side where it hadn't yet been cleared for housing, separated by a narrow lane from the local village *kampong*. Alex pointed to a house on the other side behind a tall wire fence. 'That's our neighbours, Gareth and Jo McKenzie.'

As they entered the main living area, the wooden flooring and furnishings were covered in a thick layer of dust. 'Borer beetle,' he said. 'What a mess.'

Sweat gathered on her forehead and upper lip, and she guessed no chore would be easy in this humidity. After a long exhausting day, Sam snuggled down in his new bed, and she kissed his sweaty brow and pulled a sheet over him before turning on the overhead fan. Then she wandered around their bedroom, admiring the fashionable drapes made from the fabric she'd chosen, the vibrant tones of pink, peacock blue, and purple matching the bed cover.

'I think you were a little over-exuberant in your choice of colours,' Alex thought aloud as Debra admired the room. 'I think you'll agree now you see them up that it's too vibrant, much too psychedelic for my liking. I prefer the bedroom to be bland. Slightly more restful.'

She sighed, and looked down at the creased clammy layers of her lime green dress. The boutique owner guaranteed it would impress any man with its flared skirt and halter neck style. She had hoped it would work on Alex, but he wasn't impressed by the dress or the matching accessories. His cursory glance simply served to remind her it was not appropriate attire for a Muslim country.

'You must remember to cover your legs, armpits, shoulders. Wear long sleeves. You don't want men staring at you,' he muttered as he brushed his teeth and spat out mouthfuls of watery paste into the basin.

Perched on their bed, Debra's shoulders sagged. This was not how she'd imagined their reunion. She rolled her wedding band with her right hand until the protruding point clicked into place with the notch in her diamond ring, a habit that served to distract her when she was flustered, nervous or annoyed; she had a different technique when dealing with sadness or pain. Pressing the thumb pad of her right hand into the sharp diamonds helped redirect her pain and she tried it now while she fought back the lump forming in her throat.

A faint clicking noise shook her out of her reverie as a small translucent gecko ran across the floor and up the wall in search of an insect. Another gecko joined its mate clicking in unison, performing their mating ritual of chase and catch. She sat transfixed by this rare display of romantic union.

'*Cicaks,*' Alex said, and it was the last word he uttered before he fell asleep. Propped on his pillow, the noise coming from his mouth sounded like someone sawing wood.

'It looks like romance is off the menu tonight,' she muttered with disappointment. Unlacing her lime green espadrilles, she kicked them onto the floor, then peeled off her clothes and lay next to him. Succumbing to the invitation of soft downy pillows, she stretched out relieving the cramped muscles from hours confined to a narrow aircraft seat. Her eyes felt dry and scratchy, and she removed the contact lens, and lay them in the soaking solution before closing her heavy lids.

***

In the dark hours of early morning, Debra woke to the sound of a rooster crowing nearby, but must have dozed off again for when she opened her eyes blinding sunlight streamed through the wooden shutters. Unfamiliar swishing sounds and the smell of fresh cut grass filtered in, while a whiff of spicy curry caught in the humid air. She sat up, slowly taking in these strange, new surroundings as she tried to remember where she was. The ceiling fan clanked and whirled overhead as she glimpsed vibrant drapes and bed covers through blurred vision. When she tried to open her right eye, it didn't respond. Instead, it wept tears, perhaps of a life left behind or a fear of what lay ahead. Intense pain forced her to keep that eye closed, and she stumbled around the rattan furniture towards the bathroom.

A long-legged young woman with a messy blonde mane squinted back at her from the bathroom mirror. Once bright blue, her eyes, now half-closed, streamed tears and she tried to remember what might have contributed to her current lack of vision. Her right eye was stinging as she returned to the bedroom and reached across the bed to wake Alex. At the touch of her fingers on his arm, he bolted upright and flung back the sheets.

'What's going on?' He rubbed his face before groping for his glasses.

'I can't see. Look at me.' She wiped at the tears running down her cheek.

'What on earth have you done?' Adjusting the glasses on his nose, he peered closer at her swollen weeping eye. 'I'll have to take you to the hospital.'

'Mummy, where's the toilet?' Sam tiptoed around our bedroom, staring wide-eyed at the unfamiliar furnishings.

She pointed to the bathroom behind him. 'Use that one, darling. I'll find some clothes for you.'

Grabbing a small pair of shorts and shirt for Sam, she then slipped into a wraparound skirt and long-sleeved top.

Sam roamed from room to room, exploring his new surroundings and while she dressed, carefully dodging the mess of open suitcases on the floor, Alex made tea and toast in the downstairs kitchen.

'The tea has been tasting strange lately. Not sure what it is,' he shouted up the stairs. Using a strainer, he poured two cups from the pot.

'I'm so desperate for a cuppa, I don't really care.' She sat on a kitchen bar stool and Sam sat beside her eating his buttered toast. She hardly had time to brush her teeth before Alex grabbed his car keys from the sideboard and rushed them into the car.

'Let's go,' he prodded Debra as she ran a hairbrush through Sam's unruly hair.

As she stepped outside, her sunglasses did little to protect her from the intense sunlight. She pushed back strands of her long contrary curls wondering how she would survive this interminable humidity. Alex gave her quick instructions as he drove into town, telling her how she could get home again from the hospital.

Blurred images of golden domes with minarets morphed into a gilded dragon sitting atop a Chinese temple. She squinted as bustling markets with bright umbrellas like beach balls flashed past. Sam absorbed the changing scenery with his nose pressed up against the car window, his endless questions drawing her concern from the tooting horns and revving engines.

'Why are those houses built on the water?' He pointed to a cluster of wooden stilt houses erected in the middle of the river.

'That's the water village, Kampong Ayer. Many Brunei people live there. See those little water taxi,' Alex said, pointing as he overtook a slower car and manoeuvred into a small gap between two cars in front. 'That's how they get into town.'

Debra peered at the blurred image, the water village appearing as a jigsaw puzzle with its multi-coloured rooves catching the sunlight. For a small town, there were many cars on the road, all noisily competing for space, and she worried about finding her way home again.

'I'm not too sure about the street names. They all look so strange.' Her lips twisted with worry. 'I hope I don't get lost.' Her good eye now wept in sympathy with the right.

'It's impossible to get lost. There are only two main roads out of town. Besides, I wrote down our address. Did you bring it with you?

She rummaged in her handbag for the scrappy piece of paper as Alex found a parking space outside the dilapidated hospital building. The entrance looked more like a cattle market with its main waiting area divided into wooden stalls and rows of benches. Dodging malodorous monsoon drains, Debra clutched at Alex's arm as she lurched up the front steps, resisting the urge to throw up.

As she shuffled away from the heat and stench, she felt squashed by the sea of covered heads and colourful sarongs of women queuing to consult one of the resident doctors. Men dressed in long white tunics queued on the opposite side of the railing. Surrounded by a throng of sweating bodies, she gagged at the assailing odours of chili and garlic. Alex pushed her towards the waiting queues, and she chose the shortest one; lined up behind two younger women. They looked at her then turned away giggling. As other women joined the queue, they too stared, tittering amongst themselves. After waiting at least ten minutes, a woman handed Debra an empty jar that had once held baby food. When she shook her head, the woman said, 'pee' pointing towards a toilet sign. This resulted in more giggling from the local women.

Growing impatient, Alex strode over to ask what was happening. Sam clung to his father's hand, uncertain of all the unexpected attention he'd been getting in this crowded space. Women kept touching his hair, squeezing his chubby cheeks. Although they smiled while chatting to him in Malay, he didn't know what to make of it all. Alex prised him away from another adoring fan.

'What's going on? Why are you taking so long?'

'Going on the Haj?' said a female voice from somewhere behind.

'Good God, no!' Alex shrieked. 'Debra's certainly not going on the Haj.'

'What are they saying? Why are they laughing at me?' Suffocating from the lack of air, her head throbbed and sweat beaded on her upper lip.

Alex pulled her away from the queue of women – Muslim pilgrims going to Mecca. 'They need to have vaccinations and medical checks before they go,' he told her. He then positioned Debra in the correct female queue, and she progressed to the front of the line. A woman behind a glass partition thrust a cardboard square into her hand before shooing her away with a flick of the wrist. Debra scuttled across the floor like a pawn on a chessboard; shuffled along the wooden railing until she could make out Alex's large solid frame standing next to Sam. Alex peered at the piece of cardboard in Debra's hand bearing the number eight. '*lapan*,' he said.

They missed hearing the Malay number when the receptionist called it, but she soon waved at Alex, and they followed her into the doctor's room. The doctor thought Debra's lack of vision was likely due to her new contact lenses having scratched the cornea. After a nurse taped wads of cotton wool over the offending eye, she walked out of the hospital looking like a pirate but lacking the expected courage or pride. They exited the building, squeezed past long queues of people and out into the stifling humidity.

'I'm going to have to rush into work. It's probably easier if I take the car. If you walk down the street a couple of blocks, you can pick up a taxi. Do you remember where we passed the market and mosque? You can't miss it. You might need groceries too.' He pressed a pile of Brunei money into Debra's hand, before pointing her in the direction of the taxi stand. Patting Sam on the head, he gave her a quick peck on the cheek, then he was gone.

It was Friday, noon, and staccato sounds reverberated from a loudspeaker as the *muezzin* called Muslims to prayer. She followed the sounds in the direction of the mosque, remembering what Alex said about the market nearby. Stumbling down the street, she dodged the loose concrete slabs on the pavement. As she lifted Sam across a monsoon grille, she shrieked in horror; the wrap-around cheesecloth skirt she wore had started to unravel, revealing her long, bare legs. She clutched the skirt; shuffled with smaller steps as Sam's whimpers grew louder.

Men in white tunics with black *songkoks* on their heads bustled towards the mosque. The crush of the swarming crowd buffeted her towards the smelly drains, and Sam, panicking, grabbed at her legs while his sweaty hair dripped onto his beet-red face, no doubt mirroring her own. Her pulse racing, she tried to reassure him as sweat dripped down her spine and gathered under her breasts. Confronted with a maze of narrow winding laneways that had her fearing they would never find their way, she wrapped her arms around Sam's trembling body and tried to comfort him.

'It's okay, darling; we are nearly there,' she said, but deep down she knew they were lost.

Sam wailed, and stumbled as she shuffled to the end of the street. The stink of fish and rotting vegetables trapped in the humid air wafted past their noses, and she lifted Sam onto her hip and staggered down a side street in the direction of the market smells. A mangy dog lay on the pavement chewing what looked like a fish. Veering away from it, she tripped on a woven basket of ripe mangoes lying outside a market stall. Before she could regain her balance, a tall dark-haired man ducked out from behind an awning and crashed into them.

Debra fell face down with Sam on top of her, but scrambled to her knees as the man's bag of red fruit scattered all around them.

'I'm so sorry.' She fought back tears as she tried to comfort Sam who now wailed inconsolably.

'It's okay. It's my fault. May I help you?' He held out his hand, helping her to stand. 'What have you done to your eye?' he said in a clear Oxbridge accent.

'I've been to the hospital. My new contact lens scratched the cornea. I should've taken them out during the flight.' As she squinted, a brown angular face with warm dark eyes looked back at her.

'So, you've just arrived then?'

'Yes, we flew in last night.'

'I am Rahim. Can I offer you a rambutan?' He held out the red furry fruit. 'They taste like a lychee. Here, let me peel it for you.'

Sam took the peeled white flesh and popped it into his mouth.

'Just suck it, don't swallow the stone,' Rahim laughed.

'I'm Debra and this is Sam. We're from Australia. This is all very strange to me. I've never lived anywhere like this.' *I can't believe I'm confiding in this stranger, but he's attentive — he's actually listening.*

Rahim's brows arched in concern. 'Yes, it is difficult adjusting to another culture. I grew up in England. When I came to live in this part of the world everything was different for me too. The weather, the people, the food.' His voice revealed his concern and understanding.

'Really? I assumed you were from Brunei,' she replied, trying to control the quaver in her voice. 'It is a bit overwhelming.'

She stifled a sob as she rummaged through her handbag for the scrappy piece of paper Alex had given her. 'My husband wrote down our address, but I'm not sure where to go. Would you mind showing me where I can get a taxi?'

'Certainly. It is no problem. The taxi rank is not far from here. Come, I'll show you.'

He guided them down the street where he helped them into a taxi, and explained in Malay to the driver where they needed to go.

'He will take you home. I hope you feel better tomorrow. Sometimes, it takes a few days to settle in and get your bearings.'

'I can't thank you enough. You've been very kind.'

When they arrived home, Debra felt embarrassed on realising the stranger had also paid her taxi fare.

After an exhausting day, she and Sam sat on the veranda, surrendering to the cooling, overhead fan. Sam dozed, stretched out across her lap, and she stroked his warm silky curls. The sweaty smell of his tiny body evoked a wave of love and sadness. She kissed his sweaty brow and as he stirred, and smothered him with words of comfort.

'You'll be okay, sweetheart. I promise I'll keep you safe.'

When she closed her eyes, images of a warm handsome face flashed through her mind and she remembered his gentle voice, his impeccable manners. But she couldn't remember his name and it seemed important somehow that she did. She breathed in deeply to dispel the thoughts that were threatening to frighten yet excite her.

When she'd first met Alex, he too had been like this attentive, caring stranger, but he'd changed. While he seemed to enjoy his new job and meeting new people, he'd shown little interest in her since she arrived. Coming to Brunei in search of a new life, she assumed that his new life would include her. As she gazed up at the unwelcoming tangle of jungle canopy, the vast cloudless sky that extended forever, she doubted whether he noticed her at all. She thought she'd made the right choice coming here, but now she questioned her decision.

Touching the Sky

Only from the heart
Can you touch the sky.

Rumi

Debra paced slowly back and forth along the verandah, occasionally letting out a sigh. On any normal day, she would have been visiting her friends, or at least sitting on the end of a phone, but her friends and family were so far away, and their telephone in Brunei was a party line, shared with several neighbours. Even then, Alex had told her the phone didn't always work due to flooding or lack of maintenance. As her friends had promised to write regularly, she couldn't wait to receive their letters from home.

On another big sigh, she flopped into a chair, the humidity and demanding events of the day knocking her flat; she sat listening to the whir of the fan, and forced herself to unwind. Breathing in deeply, she tried to focus on the rhythm of her inhale and exhale, but her mind wandered in a mosaic of moving pictures, thoughts sliding into images of strange faces and places she'd seen earlier in the day, at the hospital, at the market.

When she focused on calming energy, a familiar image again flashed across her mind. He was the first person to speak kindly to her, offering help without relegating her to the 'helpless female' status. She opened her eyes; squinted at the blinding glare, and immediately grabbed her sunglasses. Sam sat up and slowly gazed around the garden and surrounding jungle. Debra fetched two large glasses of cold water from the kitchen, which they drank on the veranda, both staring out across the landscape.

Debra's childhood dream had been to live in a place where monkeys swung from the trees and bananas grew in abundance, but she'd never expected the gods would grant her wishes. The jungle around their house appeared to be replete with both. Sam squealed when a monkey leapt onto a clump of bamboo that creaked under its weight; he jumped off the sofa, mimicking the monkey by waving his arms as he shrieked with laughter. His levity helped lighten her mood and she became absorbed in the unfamiliar noises around her. She tuned into the gentle hypnotic sounds of a bamboo wind chime, its repetitive melody wafting down from the rafters.

At the nearby kampung, a village rooster crowed loudly, unaware of time or custom. Birds and insects joined in a shrill chorus of chirping trills, reminding her she was not completely alone. Even in this new land, so far from home, life continued, though set to an unfamiliar rhythm, and a slower unconventional pace.

Her nerves leapt as the neighbour's side gate slammed, and someone in heavy boots stomped down the path towards them. Soon, a tall woman with cropped brown hair, dressed in navy drill pants and matching shirt, appeared. A young girl of about seven trailed behind her, the child a smaller image of her mother.

'Josephine McKenzie,' Debra's neighbour introduced herself as she settled onto the sofa beside her and nonchalantly rested her feet on the potted hibiscus. 'But call me Jo. Josephine sounds too feminine or genteel,' she laughed.

Her daughter Kali asked Sam to take her upstairs to play with his toys.

'How did you get on at the hospital? Alex told me about your eye.' Pulling out a tobacco pouch, she rolled a cigarette and offered Debra the pouch.

'No, thanks, not for me.' She shook her head. 'The doctor said my contact lens scratched the cornea. It's been such a hectic morning. I still haven't unpacked, and Alex wanted me to buy groceries. I'm so exhausted.' Debra reattached her eye patch which was coming unstuck. 'I hope I acclimatise soon. This humidity is killing me.'

'You'll get used to it. It's great to have another Aussie, living nearby. Most expats here are Brits. They come here chasing the sun and end up staying on for years; they don't want to face another English winter.' Jo appeared at ease in these tropical surroundings as she eased back on the sofa. 'I can take you shopping if you like ... show you where to go.'

'That would be great. I'm so glad you're living next door. I've been worrying about security,' Debra admitted, absently turning the rings of her finger. 'In fact, I worry about everything, especially Sam. I only came here to please Alex.'

'It takes time to settle into such a different culture. It took me a couple of weeks to adjust. Is there anything I can help you with?'

The concern in Jo's deep voice triggered the surge of tears Debra had been fighting to suppress. 'I feel so alone ...'

'I know what you mean.' Without hesitation, Jo slid a comforting arm around Debra's shoulders and they shared a companionable silence. 'Having an amah will make life easier for you,' Jo finally said. 'We couldn't survive without our Tina. Housework is no easy task in this humidity. It's also great having a live-in babysitter.'

'I'm not used to leaving Sam, but I guess a live-in amah would be like part of the family.'

Jo then told her about an expat family who were leaving Brunei and were keen to find a new employer for their Filipina amah. 'Apparently, she's great with young kids – I'm happy to contact them if you're interested.'

'I'd really appreciate that, Jo. I'll discuss it with Alex, and see what he thinks.'

'Alex told me you're a teacher. Do you intend teaching here?'

Debra half-shrugged. 'I'm not sure. It would probably be good for me to work but we came here for Alex's career. He thinks I shouldn't need a job now, but Sam will be going to pre-school soon. I'll have more time on my hands.'

Jo smiled. 'Too much time on your hands is not always a good thing. Here, school finishes at midday. In the tropics, students begin earlier in the morning to avoid the afternoon heat. And Friday is the Muslim holy day, so schools are closed but there's school on Saturdays, then off again on Sundays.'

'So, I could spend the afternoons with Sam.'

'My sailing buddy, Mike Jasper, teaches English at the Sixth Form College. I could arrange an interview for you if you're interested.'

'Really! That sounds great. Perhaps I can convince Alex …' For a moment Debra worried about what Alex might say, then quickly put it out of her mind.

'I can draw you a mud map. And I'm happy to mind Sam if you want to check out the college or organise an amah.'

'Thanks. I do appreciate your help.'

So much was happening so fast Debra's head felt ready to burst. After listening to Jo, she believed there was nothing Jo couldn't handle. Pulling out the pen and small notebook from her shirt pocket, she jotted down a few notes.

'It's a good opportunity to become immersed in the local culture – it will give you a sense of purpose in life. Many wives become lonely or bored with their husbands working away.'

'I know I must keep busy.' Debra nodded,

She remembered the days after Mala died when she wasn't working; the days and weeks dragged on forever. It was one of the loneliest times of her life.

While making coffee, Debra asked Jo about her career. The woman grinned widely. 'I'm a flying instructor at the local aero club. Some of the larger companies engage me to fly their executives to offshore oilfields … but I'm also available to take people on joy flights.'

'Sounds like an interesting job. I bet there are not many women working there – surely you are in a minority.' Debra couldn't imagine ever having the courage to fly or to compete in a world of men. *It would be great to have that much confidence though.*

'You're right. I'm the only female pilot in the whole company. Maybe because I believe there's nothing women can't do.' She laughed. 'My husband – Gareth – is also a pilot but no longer flies. He works as security manager at the airport. It's probably his last job before he retires. But I'll be flying for many years to come.' Her laugh was infectious, and within no time, Debra was laughing along with her.

'You've inspired me, Jo. I'm determined to go out and find myself a job.'

'And what about Alex? What will he think?' Her eyebrows lifted. 'Husbands can be a bit funny about their wife's career. I know Gareth isn't always agreeable when it comes to my job.'

'He'll be okay. I won't tell him until I get the job. Besides, he's always telling me I should be more independent.'

Debra pondered what independence would look like for her. A personal income. An interest that stimulated and absorbed her. The freedom to follow her own path. It sounded empowering. As she gazed across their garden of exotic tropical plants, she could already visualise new vistas expanding beyond the fence line.

'Are you ready to go shopping?'

***

Jo drove them to the nearest Chinese grocery store. Down the hill, she pointed out small roadside stalls with crudely erected plastic awnings, and rough wooden benches where vendors displayed their wares. She pulled off the bitumen and parked on the dusty roadside. Bunches of small locally grown bananas hung from the awnings.

'Ladies Fingers,' Jo told her.

Red furry rambutans hung beside them, tied with blue plastic string. On the wooden bench lay an assortment of fresh chillis, turmeric, ginger, and purple shallots. Jo pointed out the tapered green pods of okra piled next to leafy green Bok choy. 'They taste a bit weedy, but you'll get used to them.'

The elderly Malay vendor eased herself up from the ground where she'd been squatting, and readjusted her sarong. She appeared to be chewing betel nut, her mouth stained red and several teeth were missing in the front. As Jo and Debra pointed at the items they wanted to buy, she signalled to the small boy at her feet, who handed them a plastic bag, into which Debra put some leafy greens, a bunch of bananas and some rambutans for Sam. Kali and Sam befriended a cat with no tail as it sunned itself in the dirt until the Malay boy gave it a shove and it took off.

Jo selected okra, chillis, ginger, and turmeric. 'Good for a vegetable curry,' she said. 'I'll add a few tomatoes.'

The vendor calculated the cost of their purchases on her fingers and held up five fingers to indicate the total amount they needed to pay. They placed their plastic bags in the boot of Jo's car.

Further on around a sharp bend in the road lay an unpretentious building, set off the main road on one of many dirt side lanes. Luckily, Jo knew what she was looking for, or they could easily have driven past the Chinese grocery store. Like the roadside stall they'd just visited, it had been extended to house an ever-increasing stock of food items and general household essentials. Concertina-style wooden doors could be locked or pushed wide open to view the stock displayed on the many shelves inside. Above the door hung a wooden painted sign bearing the shop owner's name, CHOP HUA HO.

Manoeuvring their way through brightly coloured plastic buckets, enamel cooking pots, a display of tools and hardware, they found an unexpected variety of processed foods from many parts of the world; jars of English marmalade stood next to stripey jars of American Goober Grape.

'Look at those bright purple stripes?' Sam squealed with delight as Debra lifted a jar to read the label, which described it as a blend of peanut butter and grape jelly. She added it to her shopping basket along with a jar of marmalade for Alex.

Kali picked up an aerosol can from the refrigerated section and waved it at her mother. 'Mum, we need more cream.' Kali tried to squirt it into her mouth, but Jo stopped her by grabbing the can.

'American,' Jo said, looking at Debra's puzzled expression. 'Artificial cream in an aerosol. We can't get fresh cream. But it's amazing what desserts we can make with this stuff. Unless it's a pavlova or souffle. Nothing collapses quicker than a pav in this humidity. Living in the tropics presents you with many challenges but you soon learn to compromise and find solutions to most of the problems you encounter.' She laughed her deep throaty chuckle.

'And if there's a particular food item you want, Hua Ho will usually have it for you the next time you call in,' Jo said.

Debra and Jo stocked up on cartons of long-life milk, fresh milk also on the list of 'cannot get'. In the freezers, many items bore little resemblance to the label stuck on the plastic wrap, which was usually a solid frozen block of indeterminate colour covered in ice crystals and therefore hard to distinguish.

'According to the label, this is a New Zealand leg of lamb.'

Debra looked at Jo to gauge her reaction then looked at the price and gasped. She settled for a cardboard box of frozen chicken drumsticks from America. At least she could recognise the picture on the box. A frozen bag of French fries looked more appealing than the wilted potatoes lying in a hessian sack on the dirt floor. Jo picked up a plastic tub of red bean-flavoured ice-cream. The only other flavour available was sweet corn. She reassured Debra the taste was not too bad, so Debra added one to her basket for Sam.

***

Alex arrived home soon after Jo dropped her off with her shopping. Sam ran out to greet him in the driveway, telling him about his first day in Bandar Seri Begawan.

'Me and Mummy fell over,' he said.

'Are you okay?' Alex kissed her on the cheek. 'What happened?'

'I'm fine. Just a few grazes.' She pointed to her knee and elbow. 'I couldn't see properly with this bandage over my eye. I tripped on some fruit at the market.'

Sam interjected. 'We were lost, and I was frightened.' He wrapped his arms around Alex's legs.

'How could you get lost? It's only a small town.' Alex peered over his glasses at her.

'It worked out all right in the end.' She winked at Sam. 'Someone helped us get a taxi home.' She looked at Alex, but he didn't seem too interested in the details. Instead, he strode into the kitchen and opened the fridge door.

'What's for dinner? I'm starving.'

She thought of what she'd been through that day and the effort it had taken to purchase groceries: nothing in this place was going to be easy. Taking a deep breath, she hauled the last of the heavy shopping bags onto the kitchen bench.

'We've only just arrived home. It's been exhausting. I haven't had a chance to check out the oven yet, but I've bought some chicken legs.'

'Well, I'll go take a shower.' And with that, Alex hurried up the stairs, Debra watching his disappearing form.

She returned to the kitchen and opened the cardboard box of chicken drumsticks, discovering one large frozen block. Taking out a rolling pin, she whacked it hard and swore as she hit her thumb. She hit it again and again and the amorphous blob finally separated into smaller identifiable shapes. She did the same with the frozen bag of French Fries. Cranking up the oven to the highest setting, she hoped it could perform miracles and turn frozen blobs into something edible. The eye patch, now hanging by one piece of tape, annoyed her and she ripped it off and chucked it across the room – it landed in a pitiful pile of bananas and Bok choy, which did little to ease her anger but at least she could focus more clearly now.

***

The next morning, Debra felt elated – she could open both eyes – and the sunlight coming through the shutters felt tolerable. She smiled in the bathroom mirror when she found her eye was no longer red or swollen. Taking out a new contact lens, she rinsed it thoroughly with saline solution before fitting it into her eye, and sighed that it no longer stung. Now rested, she felt ready to face unpacking and tidying up the house. For breakfast, as she opened a packet of Cheerios, a strange smell of dampness wafted past her nose.

Alex confirmed that most food in the pantry tasted the same way. Seeping into every entity, the humidity destroyed any natural flavour and instead replaced it with the heavy, musty odour of the tropics. She opened a packet of instant pancake mix – it smelled the same. Sam complained about the long-life milk, saying it didn't taste like real milk. The local bread tasted sweet like cake. *How long will it take to get used to these different smells and tastes?*

Jo brought over the phone number and address of the Wilson's whose amah was looking for a new employer. Debra mentioned the food smells, and Jo agreed with Alex.

'It's the humidity. It gets into everything. Make sure you put your flour, spices, biscuits, potatoes in the fridge. It keeps them fresher. The humidity also gets into leather shoes, bags, jackets, even leather-bound books. They go mouldy. You can place dehumidifiers in your wardrobe which helps to stop mildew.'

As she turned to leave, she said, 'Do you have any Tupperware?'

'Doesn't everyone?'

Most of Debra's friends had followed the trend, holding parties to celebrate the modern plastic containers in every colour with matching lids and iconic burp seal. But what Jo told her next about Tupperware shocked her to the core.

'They might lock in the freshness, but they don't keep out rats. I've found teeth marks in my lids where they have chomped their way into the food inside.'

'Rats? Oh my God.' *A lifetime warranty against chipping and breaking but they can't keep out rats!* Debra felt the hairs on her arms rise as she processed this latest information. Rats running around in her kitchen pantry distressed her far more than her disappointment in a product voted one of the greatest inventions of the twentieth century. But there was more to worry about.

'They also chomp chunks out of the foam sofa cushions, so don't let Sam drop any food on them.' Jo looked at the clock. 'I must dash. I've got to rush into work.'

Debra gulped, sitting down on the sofa before quickly rising again. She stared at the foam cushions recently covered in trendy chocolate brown corduroy. *No! Surely not. They can't possibly chew through that*. Instinctively, she brushed the surface of the cushions in case Sam had dropped any crumbs.

Later, Sam helped her unpack his clothes and toys. As they placed them into cupboards, she remembered the many plastic containers at the Chinese grocery store. The smaller ones would be ideal for sorting out his Lego and small cars. She would add that to her next shopping list. Some aspects of this lifestyle appeared easier to manage. Finding solutions for the larger problems would have to remain on hold for the moment.

When she'd finished unpacking and given the house a quick tidy, her clothes were drenched in sweat. She turned the ceiling fans on high and drank several glasses of cold water; then she rang Sue Wilson to ask her about her amah, whose name was Lena. As arranged, Sue drove Lena over to meet them. Debra suggested afternoon tea to give her time to check out the amah's quarters downstairs.

The airline had furnished the room with the basics of a small bed, wardrobe, dresser, and a tiny bedside table. She gave the room a quick clean and picked some frangipanis to put in a bowl on the bedside table. Lena would also have her own shower and toilet.

Debra talked to Sam about the prospect of having Lena live with them, and explained that Lena would help keep the house tidy and sometimes she would babysit him while they were at work or if they went out at night. She brushed a few curls back from his face, dripping sweat onto his forehead. Waving his GI Joe in the air, he asked, 'Will Lena be able to play with me?'

'I'm sure she will when she has time. You will have to help her by keeping your room tidy. We don't want her to be forever picking up your clothes or toys from the floor.'

'What about GI Joe?' Sam waved the toy in front of her.

She gave his rubber arms a tweak. 'Yes, even GI Joe will have to be tidy.'

'Does she know how to make pancakes?'

'If she doesn't, I can make them for you. Mummy will still do most of the cooking. There won't be a great change in our lives.'

When Lena arrived with Sue Wilson, her face broke into a smile at the sight of Sam. He took her hand and guided her into the house. When she asked him about the toy in his hand, he was happy to tell her about the small action figurine. It took little discussion before they all agreed Lena would come to work for them. Sue explained that Lena's visa was about to expire, and Debra agreed to take on the responsibility of getting it renewed and keeping it up to date. After seeing her quarters, Lena asked if she could move some of her belongings in during the weekend, and so it was all arranged.

Debra ticked off a few more items from her list. The next major task, her interview at the sixth form college, filled her with panic. As she prepared her resume, she tried to think of possible questions she might be asked. Could she convince her new employer she was a worthy employee? She certainly hoped so.

The Barriers Within

Your task is not to seek for love,
but merely to seek and find
all the barriers within yourself
that you have built against it.

Rumi

On Thursday morning, Debra woke early, but lay in bed rehearsing the interview questions she might be asked. She left Sam with Jo, dropped Alex off at the airport, then nervously drove his new Range Rover to the college. His many instructions included leaving plenty of space in front of her on the main road, avoiding other parents double parking as they dropped off their children and to park his car well clear of other incompetent drivers.

Debra glanced up a dirt side road Alex had told her to avoid, and caught a glimpse of paddy fields where water buffalo wallowed in the mud. On a road full of potholes from constant flooding, she swerved to miss another hole.

She looked for *Simpang* 66 but had difficulty translating the Malay signs. Simpangs, Alex had said, were the smaller turnoffs along the main road; she counted them as she drove. Some street signs shared the name *kanan* or *kiri,* and it took a while for her to realise the words meant right and left. After driving around for ten minutes and turning Jo's map upside down, she found the college, where uniformed students filed through the front gates. She parked on the verge under a shady tree well clear of drivers who might bump or scratch Alex's pride and joy. No sooner had she climbed out of the air-conditioned car than beads of sweat appeared on her upper lip and streams trickled down her spine.

It was only 7.30 but the transparent sleeveless top and long colourful print skirt that covered her legs clung to her sweaty skin. Remembering Alex's warning about acceptable standards of dress, she had also thrown on a long-sleeved silk shirt.

The humidity intensified as she stood there, clammy, until, without warning, a sudden downpour drenched her. She scrambled up the slippery, sloping lawn in lime green espadrilles now sodden and covered in mud, her umbrella still resting on the car's back seat. Seeing the covered heads of the female students, she draped a silk scarf over her head and followed them through the decorative wrought iron gate in search of the principal's office.

Jo's friend Mike had arranged an interview with his boss, and in her panic, Debra now couldn't remember his name. Was it Ramid or Harim? A group of male students amused themselves kicking a soccer ball across the yard while the female students gathered to watch from a distance. Clutching her handbag against her chest, she asked directions from a girl lounging against a veranda post. The girl tipped her head towards a nearby door. As Debra walked away, she heard them laughing. The sign on the first door she tried to translate, guessing it might be a toilet. Several other doors displayed signs, but she had no idea what they said, and had almost given up when she spied a door in an adjacent building, with the sign, 'Office'.

She hurried towards the open door, noticing through its opening a tall solitary figure standing staring out the window, his dark trousers and white shirt outlining a lean, strong physique. His back was to the door. He ran his hand through his black hair before thrusting it into his pocket.

Debra knocked twice.

He turned his head, revealing a recognisable face, and his brown eyes widened in disbelief.

'Rah…id?' she stammered, stepping in through the door.

'Rahim,' he corrected in his charming Oxbridge English. 'And you are Mrs Grainger, I believe? How is your eye?'

'It's good now. I, um, I'm sorry for the other day. You must have thought I was strange. Oh God, I mean … I'd only just arrived you know.'

'Not at all. Please come in.' He beckoned to a chair. Shuffling papers across his desk, he cleared a space as she handed him her handwritten application letter and resume, which he read thoroughly, taking time to scan each page and give an occasional nod. 'We generally like our teachers to have a master's degree.' He slowly considered what he was reading, then looked up. 'But you have lots of teaching experience, I see.'

His shy smile put her at ease, but she instinctively rotated the rings on her finger. Having reached this far, she was determined to get the job, not just for herself but to prove to Alex she could do it.

'If it's an issue, I can get the university to send an up-to-date transcript. I've almost finished my master's.' She bit her bottom lip, thinking about what was at stake.

'No, it shouldn't be a problem. May I ask why you want this job? And do you think our college will meet your needs?'

'I'm passionate about the English language and literature. Teaching gives me an opportunity to share my passion.' Her hands gesticulated and she fought to keep them still, but this was the moment to prove herself. Losing her intention to stay calm, her mouth went into overdrive, words tumbling out. She took a deliberate breath to curb the flow, not wanting to appear too eager.

'I understand.' He put down her papers, nodding, something in his voice reassuring her that he didn't need convincing. 'Do you have a particular interest in literature?'

'I love poetry,' she said more calmly. 'It resonates with me. The words sometimes trigger emotions I never knew I had. I love finding poets who bring such meaning into my life.'

She breathed in deeply, scared of getting too carried away with her passion.

'And do you write poetry?' Picking up a pen from his desk, he clicked the end with his thumb. He now appeared unsettled, not knowing what to do with his hands. He placed them on his lap.

'Yeah, I find it therapeutic,' she laughed. 'A great way to express myself. But I've never published anything.'

His face brightened as he stared at her for a moment before replying. 'I too enjoy poetry. I find it soothes my soul.' He looked as if he wanted to share more but changed his mind, focusing instead on her application. 'I see you also taught adult literacy. That must have been a rewarding experience.'

'Yes.' She nodded. 'Many students fall through the cracks, despite our top-class education system. I can only imagine how difficult my life would be if I couldn't read or write.'

He looked engaged in what she was saying. Observing his enthusiasm, she sensed he shared a similar philosophy, that he agreed everyone should have the right to enjoy communication.

'I believe by communicating effectively, we can break down barriers in the world. Otherwise, we will never understand the lives of others. I think we experience much from learning about other cultures.'

He nodded, as if encouraging her to continue.

'I'd like to learn more about the local culture here. There's so much I would like to know. Teaching at the college would give me an opportunity to do that. Apart from sharing my knowledge, I would also enjoy learning from the students, hearing their stories.'

She prattled on, too nervous to stop. *Are my words sounding jumbled, my sentences too long?* To avoid the silence, she continued. 'Everything is so new to me right now. I'm sure it won't take me long to adapt though. I'm certainly keen to give it a go.'

'Yes, I can appreciate how daunting it must be.' He paused a moment before continuing. 'It takes a while to adapt to a new culture. We won't expect you to know everything straight away. One of our teachers is about to go on maternity leave so it will be good to have another female teacher on board.'

He explained how the sixth form college students followed the British education system: students who had the necessary 'O' Level qualifications proceeded to do a two-year pre-university course leading to an Advanced Level Certificate. It was different from the Australian system, but she was keen to learn everything she needed to know. As she listened, she jotted notes in a notebook.

'You would be teaching English to the female students at the college. Mike Jasper teaches the male students. Have you met Mike yet?'

'No, not yet. He's a friend of my neighbour …'

Before she finished the sentence, there was a loud crash as a tall, fair headed man tripped on the staffroom steps. Regaining his balance, he walked straight into Rahim's office.

'You're late, Mike.' Rahim's voice reflected a playful tone.

'My God, so I am. Who on earth have we got here?' Mike stared, grinning from ear to ear.

'Mike, this is Mrs Grainger.' Rahim greeted this latest visitor with relaxed camaraderie.

'Please call me Debra,' she told the tall man with his messy beard and twinkling eyes.

'Well, Debra, welcome to the funny farm,' Mike said, shaking her hand vigorously.

'I believe you enjoy sailing with my neighbour, Jo.' She let go of his hand.

'Yes, I'm a man of many talents. Jo and I often enjoy our days out on the water. But then there are minor irritants like a job that gets in the way of social pursuits. It's a tough life we live here.'

'You might like to get Debra a coffee or a towel,' Rahim interrupted. 'Perhaps you can show her around; tell her what she needs to know.' With a slight excusing nod, he retreated to his office. 'I have some paperwork to finalise. I won't be a moment.'

'My first tip, Debra, would be to get rid of that ridiculous scarf. You look like a cross between an Amish and a hippie. And you should take off that wet shirt too,' he said as he led her towards the staffroom kitchen.

She ripped off the damp scarf, finger combed the shock of wet hair, then scrunched it into some semblance of order. She wrestled to remove the wet long-sleeved shirt.

'On second thoughts, you better keep your shirt on,' Mike added.

Debra followed his gaze to the clinging silky fabric of her transparent top, and quickly drew her arms across to cover her breasts, not knowing whether to laugh or cry but settled for the former.

'I don't seem to have made a good first impression.' She threw her hands to her face, and slowly shook her head.

'On the contrary!' Mike looked at her dishevelled state with a grin that spread into infectious laughter. 'Oh, don't stress too much – Harry is not easily shocked. He's shy until you get to know him.' He passed her a coffee mug and a hand towel. 'But he's a great boss and a loyal friend. He cares deeply about people, especially the students.'

'Harry?' she queried, drying her arms with the towel.

'Apparently, that's what his mother called him. He grew up in England you know, until his father took him to Malaysia to live. He had to leave his English mother behind.'

When they'd met that first day at the market, Rahim had

mentioned having lived in England. She remembered he said he'd found it difficult adjusting to a new culture. She'd never suspected that he'd had to leave his mother. She couldn't imagine what that would be like.

'That's why he prefers the privileges of the expat lifestyle we all enjoy here. Not too many pressures. He wouldn't get that in KL.' Mike finished his coffee and placed the cup in the sink.

Debra wanted to ask more questions about her prospective boss but thought better of it. Instead, she asked, 'So that's my interview? He didn't ask too many questions.'

'He obviously likes you. Consider yourself lucky it isn't Muhammad Osman interviewing you.' Mike looked her up and down with a scrutiny that made her blush.

'Is he the college director? Someone mentioned him. I believe he's not overly friendly.' She drained her coffee and tried to remember what she'd been told about this man.

'Muhammad is not greatly enamoured with ex-pats. He resents us taking jobs from the locals. No doubt you will meet him soon enough although he doesn't spend much time at the college. He's with the Ministry.'

'The Ministry?' Her voice sounded louder than she'd intended.

'The Ministry of Education. This job is just a bonus for him. You shouldn't have any problems teaching here, especially with the female students. They tend to be compliant, work a lot harder than the males. They need to fight for their place in society.'

'And the male students?'

'They take their privileges for granted. Some think they are entitled to good marks whether they work hard or not. They don't like to be challenged. Nor do they appreciate my British humour or the odd expletive that I drop now and then.'

She laughed, imagining Mike swearing at his students. 'So, they wouldn't appreciate my Aussie slang.'

'No, you would probably lose them with "Crikey"!' He grinned.

'Well, Mike, if that's all, it's been nice meeting you. No doubt we'll meet again.'

With his sense of humour, she believed Mike would make a great colleague.

'I'm sure we will, Debra. We are mere puppets in life's strange journey. Some other bugger out there is always pulling the strings. One simply learns to go with the flow.' He laughed deeply and heartily.

While she was trying to make sense of her interview, Rahim walked into the kitchen and handed her an envelope.

'I'm sorry we can only offer you casual employment. Because you are being recruited locally, you will be employed according to local salary and conditions. If you are still interested though, you can start at 7.30 Monday morning.'

With a slight hesitation, he held out his hand. 'Thank you for coming. I hope you will be happy here. We would love to have you on board.'

'Yes … thank you. I'm sure I will. I'll see you soon. I mean on Monday, that is.'

Debra shook his hand then looked up. They both laughed nervously and backed away.

'Yes … yes you will. I look forward to it.'

He walked back to his office. Debra looked towards the door while Mike chuckled to himself.

'What did I tell you?' He winked at her. 'I'm also looking forward to seeing you on Monday.'

'Thanks, Mike.' When she walked towards the door, Mike strode back into Rahim's office.

Once outside the door, she ripped open the envelope. Smiling, she read the acceptance letter, the terms of casual employment. For the first time in ages, she wanted to thrust her arms in the air yelling, 'Yes, yes, yes!' A group of male students stared as they walked past, then snickered amongst themselves.

'Well, what do you think of our latest recruit?'

Rahim's voice carried through the open door and Debra stopped to listen, anxious to hear Mike's reply.

Before she could fiddle with her rings, he said, 'Wow! Despite the weird outfit, she's a stunner, a great choice. I think she's the right one.'

The rain then stopped, and all around, the sun reflected on droplets dripping from leaves. Everything appeared fresher, brighter somehow. She draped the damp shirt around her shoulders and looked up at the sun. A brilliant rainbow appeared through the clouds, arcing across the sky to spread its watery colours. It offered a refreshing perspective, and the promise of an exciting new life ahead.

Sunflowers and Sundowners

And still, after all this time,
the sun has never said to the earth
'You owe me.'

Rumi

After another hectic week of teaching, Debra found it easier to relax sitting on the veranda with Jo and Gareth, sipping sundowners. Settling into these rituals of life in the tropics allowed her to enjoy the last peaceful moments of sunlight. As Sam and Kali sat on the floor with puzzle pieces spread out in front of them, she looked across at the garden, admiring the large hands of bananas and the bamboo that provided a natural screen around Jo's swimming pool.

'Look at those sunflowers. Aren't they stunning?'

Tall, truly majestic, golden blooms lined the front fence, their faces turned towards the setting sun.

'Their Malay name is *bunga matahari*. Matahari is the sun. And these are known as *bunga kertas*, paper flower. Here, feel this.' Jo plucked a spent bougainvillea blossom and handed it to her.

She scrunched the dried petal in her palm; ran her finger along its papery texture. The swimming pool reflected the last shafts of sunlight across its surface and fruit bats swooped around the mango tree, circling in and out. Dusk was short-lived and night fell swiftly. Except for the constant rhythmical drone of cicadas, a tropical tranquillity descended on the garden. Debra wanted to absorb this ephemeral moment, to treasure it while it lasted. For the first time since arriving in Brunei, she sank back into the cushions and kicked off her shoes, feeling totally at ease.

'Your friend Mike is quite a character.' Debra watched Jo light sandalwood mosquito coils in terracotta pots, and hand her one which she placed next to her feet. 'Considering his wife and children live in the UK, he seems happy most of the time.'

'His family visit occasionally. His wife is finishing her nursing studies.' Jo placed a mosquito coil next to where Alex and Gareth sat at the other end of the veranda. "She what's your new boss like?'

Debra forced a shrug. 'I'm sure I'll have no trouble working with him. He's a quiet, sensitive guy who exudes caring, positive energy.' She wanted to say how comfortable she felt in his presence, that she could trust him with her life, but Jo would think her crazy. After all, she'd only just met him. But it was as if a new world had opened and invited her in, and she was going to make the most of it.

Jo cocked her head slightly as she looked back at her, but Alex butted into the conversation before she could respond.

'How many people applied for the job? You may have been the only candidate.' He laughed, and picked up his glass from the small side table.

'I don't know. I didn't think to ask.' She noted the cutting edge in her own voice and twisted her lower lip tight to hold further words back.

'I'm sure she wasn't,' Jo came to her rescue. 'Anyway, it doesn't matter. They obviously thought you were a real asset, Debra, and well worth employing.'

'Not many people would be prepared to work for those low wages. At least if we're recruited from overseas, we get a decent salary.' Alex looked to Gareth who nodded in agreement.

'Well, it suits me. Especially as school finishes at midday. Monday to Thursday then a break on Friday. I view it as a bonus.

The wages aren't that important.' Debra's grip tightened on the glass.

'Good for Sam too,' Jo added. 'You get to spend afternoons with him. I bet the female students will enjoy having you there.'

Debra moved in closer, told Jo that, although there was a set curriculum, she had flexibility to plan as many interesting activities as she could. There was no shortage of resources. Unlike some places she'd worked, where they counted the white board markers, for any extra books or outings, she simply put in a request. She told Jo about the Royal Shakespeare company which was about to visit Brunei as part of their educational tours around Southeast Asia.

'When I mentioned it to Mike, he was keen to arrange an outing for our students. He asked which production they were doing and when I told him it was Julius Caesar, he said, "Bloody hell, Grainger! Plotting to kill the ruling monarch! No way will they agree to send the students. It will be a definite no show."'

'Yes, that sounds like Mike. He's never one to mince his words.' Jo busied herself as she talked; with secateurs in one hand, her drink in the other, she trimmed stray pieces of bougainvillea that had encroached too far onto the white wicker sofa.

On the sideboard sat a framed photo taken on Jo's parents' cattle station in northern Queensland. It showed Jo sitting astride a horse with the brim turned up on her hat. With her upturned nose, she looked as if there was nothing she couldn't handle. Gareth, with his balding pate, complained about the heat, declaring he was a cold-weather type. His pale freckled complexion looked better suited to the cooler climes of Glasgow than tropical Brunei, whereas Jo looked as if she thrived in the heat, embracing life in its entirety. She told Debra she participated in as many activities as she could: flying, sailing, scuba diving and Hash House Harriers.

'You must come along to the ladies hash on Tuesday nights,' she urged Debra. 'It's a tradition everyone needs to try at least once. Like an initiation, a rite of passage.' After listening to her description of The Hash, Debra hesitated before agreeing to give it a go.

'If it's just running through the jungle, I'm sure I could manage a few hills.'

'Depending on the weather, you might have to wade through mud or swim across streams. It's the job of the person laying the paper trail to make it as difficult as possible. Sometimes it gets mighty slippery.'

Alex, who had already run on the men's hash, agreed that Debra should give it a try. 'What doesn't kill you makes you stronger,' he said.

Yes, I've already discovered that about life. Surviving grief is not always easy. But it's the fighting instinct that gets you from the floor to your knees. Next, you are sitting. Then one day you realise you are up walking again. She now knew it was time to move on. As this was a new beginning in life, she was prepared to give it a go.

'Thanks for finding us an amah. I think we'll love having Lena. Life will be so much easier.' Debra drained the last of her gin and tonic, 'Lena is keen to get her husband a visa so he too can work in Brunei.'

'You can take her across the border to Labuan in East Malaysia to get her passport stamped. Perhaps she can also sort out a visa for her husband while you're there.'

Like many Filipinos working abroad, Lena sent her wages back to her parents in the Philippines to support them in their old age. They, in turn, looked after her five-year-old son. It couldn't be easy leaving her family, but she had a sister who also worked as an amah in Brunei.

Gareth refilled the drinks, handed out crackers with dip, then turned to Debra. 'It's great if you can find good workers. We have a young man, Azri, who does our gardening. He's brilliant.'

'Is he from the Philippines?'

'No, he's from Malaysia but came out because he has an uncle living here. We share our gardener with another family, Jim and Rosa Lyons. Have you met them?'

'Yes, I know them, but haven't met their gardener.' Debra noticed Jo flick Gareth a puzzled look.

While Jo was salt of the earth, Gareth was an enigma. Debra watched as he admired his lanky reflection in the sliding glass doors, smoothed down his purple body shirt and tucked it tightly into his white flared trousers.

'I'm enjoying teaching the female students,' Debra said, focusing back on Jo. 'They're very shy, always clinging to each other in groups but they're lovely. I think they're intimidated by the male students.'

'Debra, you think everyone is lovely. You are far too trusting.'

Before she could respond, Jo interjected again. 'It's about mutual respect. I'm sure Debra gets on well with the local people because she accepts them without judgement.'

'She should come work at the airport, eh, Alex? God knows what would happen if there was a real emergency.' Gareth launched into a history lesson about how Brunei had been in a state of emergency since '62. 'Although at the airport you wouldn't really know it. Apart from banning Indonesian aircraft flying over Brunei air space, they are complacent when it comes to many aspects of security.'

'A state of emergency? Is that something I should be worried about?' Debra drew in a breath.

''62 was the year the Brunei People's Party launched their armed insurrection,' Gareth continued, '… when the Sultan declared a state of emergency and suspended the constitution. He deemed the elections void and banned the Brunei People's Party.'

'I guess with Indonesian Kalimantan occupying most of Borneo, he was worried about a possible communist threat from Sukarno in the south. Protecting eighty miles of coastline can't be easy,' Alex added.

'The communist connection was debatable. Fortunately, the Gurkhas managed to crush the revolt. And Brunei chose not to join Malaysia in its federation.'

'Britain is still responsible for foreign relations and defences,' said Jo, 'but you can rest assured, Debra, there's no need to worry about security with the Gurkhas stationed here.'

'I hope you're right. More than anything, I want to feel safe.' Debra's shoulders relaxed as she thought of the fearless Gurkhas. Renowned for their bravery, while fighting battles overseas their own impoverished country beset with political instability. She switched back to the conversation, caught snippets about sightings in Labuan of a banned political leader.

'So, who is this guy?'

'He founded Al-Arqam, the deviationist Islamic sect.' Gareth left to refill the glasses.

'And so, what? He's currently hiding in Malaysia?' Alex asked.

'Well, let's not bother about him. Debra looks like she's about to fall asleep,' Jo said.

Alex happily changed the subject. 'How do you deal with the system of graft they use here? Is it the only way to get anything done? I'm uneasy about reprisals if I refuse their handouts.'

'It's the way they carry out business,' said Gareth. 'I'm happy to go along with it. If they want to give me gifts, I'm willing to accept them.'

Alex chose a toothpick of cheese and cocktail onion, one of many stuck into an orange. 'Bribery doesn't sit well with me. Only one company can win the contract for the new hangar. I can't possibly please everyone. There will be some disappointed contractors, I'm sure.'

The responsibility for the new hangar to be built at the airport weighed heavily on Alex. Many international construction companies had tendered for the contract. As the Engineering Manager, he'd refused offers of dinner and expensive gifts to avoid showing any favouritism.

Once again, Debra drifted from the conversation, remembering what Alex had said earlier about her being too trusting. Apart from the respect she felt for her new boss, she truly believed he was someone she could trust. Despite their embarrassing beginnings, she enjoyed his company and felt comfortable in his presence.

She listened to Alex telling Gareth he was going away again, this time organising a maintenance contract in Nepal.

'Why doesn't Nepal Airlines maintain their own aircraft?' she asked.

'They are a poor country. They can't afford training or maintenance.'

With their modern service equipment and engineering facilities in Brunei, Alex had recently been able to secure maintenance contracts with other smaller airlines such as this one. It meant, in addition to his busy role at the airport, he would be away often overseeing maintenance.

'Are you able to take your wife on any of these trips?' she asked.

'Kathmandu is not a place you would want to go. Too many drugs and hippies.'

'It's the seventies, Alex. From what I've heard about free love and flower power, Kathmandu sounds like a magical place to be. Besides, it would be nice to spend more time with you.'

'None of the other managers take their wives.'

'I miss you when you're away. It's not like being at home, surrounded by family.' She bit on her bottom lip as the old sensations of loneliness threatened to overwhelm her.

'You'll have to learn to be more independent. I'll be doing more of these trips from now on.' Alex was already planning the Sultan's VIP flight the next morning, focusing on how he would change the seating configuration to fit in the personal toilet with gold plated taps and accessories.

Brunei's oil had helped make its ruler one of the richest men in the world and the aircraft were adapted to suit his needs. If his highness wanted new cars or polo ponies flown in, the aircraft were adjusted accordingly. Debra pondered over what it must be like to have people listen to your needs and take them seriously. She doubted she would ever know.

'Tomorrow I'll take Lena across to Labuan to sort out her visa.'

As she verbalised her thoughts, Alex yawned then added a warning. 'You be careful wandering around on your own. I hope you know where you're going, what you're doing over there.'

Off the coast of Sabah, Labuan was an island two hours by ferry from Brunei. If they took the early boat across, they could be back before Sam's bedtime as Jo had offered to mind him for the day. Debra lifted Sam from the sofa where he slept and carried him through the garden gate. Lena helped carry him up to his bed. Later Debra asked Alex about the person Gareth mentioned.

'Should I be worried about that group – Al-Arqam?'

'I wouldn't believe half of what Gareth says. I know he calls himself Security Chief, but he's often distracted, not always present.'

Alex climbed into bed, while Debra thought about her plans for the next day, what she'd be doing and where she'd be going.

Crossing Over

If the sun were not in love,
he would have no brightness,
The side of the hill no grass on it.
The ocean would come to rest somewhere.

Rumi

As they drove through the town centre of Bandar Seri Begawan, Lena helped Debra find her bearings. She was nervous about parking on the iron grilles covering the monsoon drains, as they easily dislodged. She'd been told there were only two types of drivers in Brunei: those who had driven into a monsoon drain and those who were about to drive into one.

Lena had also never been to Labuan and Debra was more confident knowing they'd be making the trip together. Keen to get her husband out from the Philippines, Lena had been paying money to an immigration "official" who'd insisted she meet him in private. Debra had expressed her uneasiness about the arrangement which sounded rather dodgy.

'Mam, there's the river. I think the wharf is down that street.' Lena pointed, and Debra concentrated on finding a parking space.

She swung the wheel to the left to manoeuvre into a space outside the Post Office. As she straightened the Subaru that Alex had bought for her, she reversed into a white Fiat in the space behind her and the two cars touched. In the rear vision mirror, she immediately glimpsed the face of her new boss, and cringed.

Leaping out of the car to survey the damage, she reached Rahim, who already stood scanning the two bumpers. He looked relaxed in a pale aqua shirt neatly tucked into his jeans.

'We seem to keep bumping into each other. Luckily, there does not appear to be any damage,' he said, looked from one car to the other.

'And I seem to be forever apologising to you. This time I'm rushing to catch the ferry. Lena has paid some immigration official who's promised to give her husband a visa when she extends her own in Labuan.'

'That does not sound legitimate. I do not think it a good idea going on your own. Let me post these letters. I will come with you. Maybe I can help sort it out.'

Debra accepted his offer graciously then looked around for a parking meter before Lena reminded her there were none. The parking meters were mobile young women dressed in brown with white gloves. Lena finally spotted one half-obscured by her umbrella who wrote out a ticket, and Debra placed it inside her windscreen.

It was only a short walk to the ferry office, but they quickened their pace when the ferry started revving its engines. They jumped onboard as the gangplank was about to be pulled in but, as Debra grabbed the railings, her finger caught on a sharp piece of metal. Instantly blood dripped onto her white jeans and Rahim took her hand, examined the cut and wrapped his handkerchief around her finger.

They worked their way to a corner of the crowded deck surrounded by pineapples in rattan baskets and chickens in wooden crates. Piled in another corner of the deck, thick coils of rope lay snake-like. Choppy waves tossed the ferry's bow up and down, flinging passengers around the deck. Each time the boat lurched, Rahim tried to steady Debra, but each plunge pushed her harder against him. People stared, and she was conscious of the closeness of their bodies; she distanced herself again, but the next wave knocked her down against a rooster in a cage. Rahim grabbed her arm, helped her to stand but seemed in no hurry to let go of her. She shuffled to where Lena stood starboard and grabbed hold of the railings.

After an extremely uncomfortable journey, Debra, like everyone else, felt relieved to soon be stepping off the ferry and standing on firm ground. As a shoving crowd converged on the gangway, they were pushed back; forced to wait in line. In due course, they found their way to the immigration office by following the white painted walls, now blackened with fingerprints from those wiping off excess ink.

When they asked for Sulaiman, a woman waved her hand toward a warehouse behind the wharf. Once again, they followed the fingerprinted walls, hoping to meet this "official" and, after sliding open a small side door, saw a group of men huddled together in one corner. At the sight of the visitors, an older man with a red scarf at the head of the table rubbed his wispy beard as he spoke to the group. The other men abruptly dispersed, and a middle-aged man in a long white tunic soon appeared. But when Rahim spoke to him in Malay, Sulaiman indicated Lena must come alone. Rahim insisted on staying but was waved away with a flick of the wrist. He paced up and down outside for the next five minutes, at times shaking his head.

'Debra, I think we should intervene,' he finally said. 'I don't think we should leave Lena on her own.'

She nodded. 'I don't have a good feeling about this, Rahim. Let's go inside.' Her concern for Lena outweighed her own fears but she followed him cautiously.

At that moment, a moustache-faced man in a black songkok, peered around the corner of the door; he was one of the younger men they'd noticed earlier. He flung open the door, gave a familiar nod then hurried off down the street. Rahim stared after him as Lena stepped out, passport in hand. Debra rushed to greet her.

'Are you okay Lena? I was worried about you.'

'Yes, Mam. He has given me the visas. Can I go to the market? I'd like to get some fresh crabs for dinner?'

Though uneasy about Lena going off alone, Debra understood her need to shop and have some time alone. She reminded her of the five o'clock ferry and they agreed to meet at the terminal at four forty-five. When Lena dashed off toward the fish market, Rahim and Debra turned and walked down a quiet lane, searching for a café. As they dodged the uneven paving slabs, their stumbling steps echoed in the silence. When Debra heard another set of footsteps, she turned and caught a glimpse of a shadowy figure ducking into a doorway.

'What is it?' Rahim asked, following her gaze. 'Let's go in here.' He pointed to a small café.

The suspicious behaviour of the men Debra saw earlier made her edgy; the way men had stared at her made her feel nervous. Rahim took her arm and politely ushered her through the café door to a quiet booth at the back. A waitress brought iced water while they waited for coffee and curry puffs. Squashed into the tiny booth, Debra felt the proximity of his body which did nothing to quell the strange sensation of fear and excitement. As she lifted the icy glass to her lips, she couldn't steady her trembling hands, and the glass slipped through her shaky fingers. Cold water poured onto both their laps, and she dabbed at her soggy jeans with a paper serviette.

Rahim quickly placed his serviette on top of hers, their fingers gently and momentarily touching. Debra blushed.

'Don't worry. At least the cold water will cool us down.' He glanced at his damp jeans and smiled.

Debra's gaze moved from the puddles of ice blocks melting on the floor to the top of his wet thighs, then to the waitress arriving with the food and coffee. She gratefully accepted more serviettes and continued to mop up the water.

'How are you settling in at the college?' Rahim asked her. 'Do you think you will enjoy teaching there?'

'I can't tell you how happy I am. I think I've found my niche.' She lowered her voice, aware of the hovering waitress. 'The students are attentive … keen to learn. Some of the students I taught in Australia were a real challenge. Those with literacy issues found learning a struggle but with others it was often their poor attitude. They didn't really want to learn.'

Rahim continued to gaze at her, smiling as he nodded in agreement. 'I am so glad you are enjoying it. While not all the male staff members are friendly, you must not let them get to you. We are lucky to have someone with your dedication and experience. We could do with a few more teachers like you.'

'Thanks – that's so good to hear.' She felt the warmth of pride surge through her – it had been such a long time since she'd received such positive feedback.

By the time they finished their coffee, their jeans were almost dry. As Debra took out her purse to pay, Rahim gently placed his hand over hers. 'My treat,' he said warmly.

They sauntered down the same narrow lanes they'd walked previously, admiring old buildings and gazing into small gift shops. But when they arrived at the ferry terminal in time to meet Lena, she wasn't there. Debra's skin turned cold as she remembered the earlier gathering of men, and feared for Lena's safety. She also feared the potential scandal if they missed the last ferry and failed to return home.

'I will go and look for Lena,' Rahim offered. 'You stay here at the terminal in case she arrives.'

Debra looked in all directions but, after ten minutes of searching, there was still no sign of Lena or Rahim.

The incoming ferry drew closer, its wake rippling out like bad news. As it docked two men threw ropes around the bollards and secured it, and the disembarking crowd spilled onto the jetty and merged with the waiting passengers keen to embark. Much pushing and shoving ensued as they climbed aboard, their hands full of bulging shopping bags, some obviously duty-free.

A wispy bearded man with a red scarf raced past Debra, knocking a woman and her small child into the water as he passed. Debra spun and watched him go – he looked familiar – he'd been in the warehouse earlier. Several men standing nearby shouted and waved their arms; women screamed and grabbed their children to them. Finally, a man threw a lifebuoy ring to the struggling woman, and someone dived in to rescue the child who had sunk beneath the water. Clutching desperately to the ring, the young woman was hoisted like a sodden dishcloth as grabbing hands hauled her onto the wooden jetty. Water dripped from the pile of rose-patterned cloth as she coughed and spluttered until someone placed the crying child in her arms. Wailing women edged in closer to assist, and people gathered around her. Despite the heat and suffocating crowd, Debra shivered.

Then, out of nowhere, Lena appeared beside her, laden with bags of fresh crabs.

'Here, Mam, these are for you. I thought you might like them for your dinner tonight.' She handed Debra a plastic bag with water dripping claws dangling over the sides.

'Thanks for thinking of me. Rahim has gone to look for you.' She turned a circle, looking for him. *Where is he? What is keeping him?* Someone touched her shoulder from behind and she swung around with the bag of crabs, smashing it against the man's back. Rahim flinched from the blow.

'I'm sorry. I thought you were that man with the red scarf.' Debra instinctively reached out to stroke his shoulder but pulled her hand back. *Everyone is staring at us.*

'It's okay,' he laughed. 'At least we're safe. Let's get on the ferry.'

Lena grabbed Debra's arm. 'Look, Mam, the police are chasing him. Perhaps he has no visa.'

Debra looked to where she pointed. The man with the red scarf was now part of a blur of faces in a crowd of moving shapes. Quickly sucked into the throng pushing towards the ferry gangway, they weaved their way through disembarking passengers and piles of baggage as they scrambled onto the ferry.

The return trip was much calmer than their journey across and they found a quiet place to sit. As Rahim looked back at Labuan, he edged in closer to Debra.

'Did you know we are now leaving Malaysia's only deep-water anchorage? Labuan was once a place of refuge for seafarers travelling across the South China Sea? Apparently, the deep-water bay provided protection from monsoon winds as well as pirate attacks.' He smiled, and his shoulders relaxed.

'No, I didn't know that. I hope the pirate attacks are a thing of the past.' She preferred to think of it as a place of refuge. Having safely made it to the ferry on time, Debra didn't want anything to disturb the peace.

'As far as we know there are no pirates.' He leant back on the seat. 'Let's hope that's the case.'

Sitting quietly, absorbing his calming energy, the previous tension of the day eased as she reflected on their time in Labuan. She stole a glimpse at Rahim, who was aware she was watching him. When he smiled, which he did often, an imperceptible dimple appeared in the corner of his mouth. She'd never been this physically close to him before and she noted his long eyelashes, and arched brows. Her cheeks felt warm, and she looked away. Apart from the steady droning of the engines and the lapping of waves, it was a companionable silence.

As the sun slowly sank on the horizon, its golden sunbeams

laid a bright path across the water, lighting the way home. Lena napped beside them, her head nodding with the rhythm of the waves. As Rahim's leg bumped against Debra's, a tingling sensation coursed through her.

The hazy outline of Labuan faded behind an elderly grey-haired man who sat on the bench opposite them. His face etched with time, he tapped a white stick on the deck and muttered to himself. He attempted to stand but his glazed rheumy eyes and frail appearance suggested he might have difficulty. Debra motioned to Rahim who offered his arm to help the old man up. The ferry glided on a gentle swell towards the Brunei port, the sun now a small golden orb on the horizon. As Rahim reached out his hand to the man, the sun appeared in direct line, as if he was catching it in his palm. Leaning closer, the old man whispered something in Rahim's ear and, looking over at Debra, pointed towards the sky before he continued, his fingers speaking faster than his words. Bringing both his hands towards his heart, the old man gave them his blessing. '*Assalam alaikum.*'

Rahim returned the blessing, 'And peace with you also.'

In the distance, a flotilla of small water taxis with noisy revving outboards sped towards the water village. The twinkling lights of Kampong Ayer revealed the tiny boats and their passengers whose baggage bobbed up and down on the ferry's wake. The golden dome of the mosque reflected the first rays of the moon outlining the taller buildings of Bandar Seri Begawan. A busy and eventful day was coming to an end; people gathered their belongings and prepared to disembark, to return to their homes and regular routines. They would soon be separated by the demarcation of culture and protocol that determined their lives. Rahim extended his hand to help her stand. They both began talking at once then laughed together.

'Thanks ever so much …'   'I've really enjoyed …'

'That old man …' Debra tilted her head to where the old man

slowly moved along the railing. '… what was he saying? Why was he pointing at the sky, looking at me?'

'He mentioned the man who was being chased.' Rahim ran his hand through his hair before thrusting it in his pocket. He looked towards the gangway. 'He was also quoting Sufi poetry.'

'Oh really! I'd like to hear that. What's it about?' She moved in closer to listen above the engine noise.

He hesitated before answering. 'He was quoting Rumi. He said, *If the sun were not in love, he would have no brightness.*'

A rush of heat that had nothing to do with the sun flooded through her.

'Rumi? I think I've read some of his poems. There's one about a guest house and another I remember has something to do with a reed flute. I'd love to learn more of his work.' She looked to where the old man was stepping off the gangway. 'You wouldn't think he could be bothered making such a trip at his age. I know it's only a couple of hours, but it's a rough voyage.'

'I guess it is all about the journey. Some experiences are well worth the discomfort. It is a matter of whether you are prepared to take that first step.'

She looked down at her feet, then lifted her eyes to meet his. He took hold of her elbow as they stepped out onto the gangway and walked back to where they'd parked the car. With the darkened streets now deserted, she felt comfort in having an escort. When they reached the car, they parted with brief goodbyes.

As Debra drove home, with the words of a Sufi poet rolling over her tongue, Labuan would remain in her memory, a special port of call. It had revealed a sea of emotions in her she didn't know existed. Like its lighthouse, it also flashed out warnings she found difficult to decipher.

By the time she arrived home, Jo had already fed and bathed Sam; he was ready for his bedtime story. But when Jo asked if she'd had a nice day, Debra paused, momentarily lost for words.

'It was truly amazing – as if I'd crossed over into a parallel universe – or at least stepped into a fairytale land.' She stopped, not wanting those last moments to disappear from exposure to the mundane. 'I'll tell you about it one day. It involves the words of a Sufi poet.'

'Good. I'd like that.' Jo fixed Debra with a knowing stare. 'Will it begin with "once upon a time"?' As she grabbed her keys, she spun around. 'Or will it end with, "and they lived happily ever after"?'

As she exited through the back door, Debra's words came out before she could stop them. 'I certainly hope so'.

She read to Sam until *The Cat in the Hat* fell onto her face. When Alex arrived home much later, he looked tired, his face drawn. They'd had mechanical problems and waited hours for parts to be flown in from Singapore. As he sunk down on the sofa, Debra sympathised, knowing it had been a long day.

'That must have been frustrating. Would you like some chilli crab? Lena made us some for dinner. She bought them at the market in Labuan. They have an amazing variety of fresh seafood there.'

'I'm too tired to eat. Did you buy any duty-free booze while you were there?' He searched for signs of tell-tale shopping bags.

'No, sorry. I didn't get to do any shopping at all. I was busy doing other things.' Her shoulders slumped, her earlier joy now eroded by the demands of everyday life, the fear of not living up to expectations.

Alex frowned before picking up his papers. 'I need to go into work early tomorrow. There are lots of things to sort out.' He strode towards the stairs.

'We managed to get Lena's passport sorted out but there was an incident with a strange man …'

Alex turned, scowling. 'Didn't you listen to what Gareth said about taking extra care? Debra, you're a European woman living in a foreign country. Let Lena sort out her own problems. You need to look after yourself.'

'I was only trying to help her.' She choked back tears, wanting to justify her actions but saw his puckered brow. He had already made up his mind.

'You don't need to keep helping other people. Focus on your own problems.'

'I'm trying.' She reeled back, struggling to find the right words. 'It's just that sometimes my own problems are too difficult to face.'

But Alex had switched off; was no longer listening. Debra sighed deeply – he was not the only one who was tired. Exhausted, her head spinning, she re-lived the day's events.

That night she dreamed of Rahim gently draping a shawl around her shoulders. Then the image changed and the man with the wispy beard smothered her with his red scarf. She screamed but it was a stifled cry, muted with fear. She awoke drenched in sweat, struggling to breathe, and threw back the covers, if only to convince herself it was not real. It was only a dream.

Finding Rumi

Listen to the story told by the reed,
of being separated.
Since I was cut from the reedbed
I have made this crying sound.

Rumi

Inhaling deeply, Debra stretched out her elbows before gazing around the office she shared with a few other teachers. On her desk was a book of Sufi poetry and she opened it to where an inserted handwritten note bookmarked a poem by Rumi.

Dear Debra,

I was surprised yet delighted to hear you are interested in Sufi poetry for it has long been a passion of mine. Regarding Rumi, I thought it would be easier to explain in writing as much of the ancient text is esoteric. His poem about the reed flute, like many of his analogies, are symbolic. Rumi likens the yearning sound of the flute to grief at having been separated from its reed bed. The flute longs to return to its source symbolising man's longing for union with the Divine. We humans are also searching for our own source, for something greater than us. For that which will make us whole.

I know you are interested in meditation. You may be aware that, when Sufis practise meditation, they focus on musical sounds such as the reed flute, to stop their minds from wandering. Long after the music stops, they can sense the inner vibrations. I must say I haven't tried it myself, but I can understand how it works in theory. Maybe it will resonate with you.

Kind Regards

Rahim

She picked up *The Reed Flute's Song* and read each stanza. As she ran her fingers down the page, she reflected on the many times she'd been disconnected. The times when she'd stood in a room surrounded by people, yet often felt separated from everyone and everything, like a flower plucked from the stem prematurely, then discarded on the ground to wilt. Through meditation, she connected to music and breathed it through the palms of her hands. Eager to learn more about this ancient luminary, she picked up a pen to reply.

Dear Rahim,

Thanks for your book of poetry and your introduction to Rumi. Tantric yoga shares a similar believe that surrendering to divine love will transform us and make us whole.

I was interested to learn that Sufis believe one must chase away the ego with sorrow and tears. In Tantra, we must also try to let go of the ego instead of letting it take control.

I've been trying to let go for years but it hasn't been easy. Part of me needs to find solutions instead of accepting what is. I think I'm getting closer to letting go and one day soon I hope I will succeed!

I find it fascinating that such ancient philosophies are as relevant today as when first written centuries ago. But it takes time to come to terms with the classical text and its symbolism.

Thanks for sharing it with me.

Regards

Debra

By the time Mike sauntered into the staffroom and tucked in the ends of his wrinkled shirt, Debra was absorbed in the inspiring words of a Sufi poet. Mike headed straight for the coffee pot but not before giving her an approving glance of the expanse of legs below her denim skirt. When he asked what she was reading, she recited a few lines from a poem of Rumi's, *Stay Close, My Heart.*

Mike appeared uninterested until she reached the line, '*Only your drunken ecstasy can pierce the rock's hard heart.*' He perked up. 'It doesn't sound like Keats, but the drunken ecstasy interests me.'

'It's Rumi,' added Rahim as he quietly entered the room.

'I find it rather cramped actually, but who's the bleedin' poet?' Mike laughed.

'You might find it too refined, Mike. It's about love.'

'And what hidden insights do you have on love, Debra?'

'I'm still learning but I'm enjoying it so far.' She sensed a rush of heat to her face as she looked down at the book.

As he walked across the room, Rahim added, 'Rumi writes about the ecstasy and mystery of divine love. Love in Sufism is not simply about the erotic.' He looked at Mike, waiting for his reaction.

'Give it time. They all say that in the beginning. Look at John and Yoko. "Give Peace a Chance," they said. More likely, give sex a chance. Free love? They spent their days in a hotel bed getting free publicity and no doubt free accommodation. Did that really help those poor buggers fighting in Vietnam?'

'In this spiritual age, people are choosing peaceful protests. They prefer to find passive ways to resolve conflict.' Debra playfully raised her fingers in a V-sign.

'If Sufi poetry is about divine love, why does it use words such as ecstasy and intoxication?' Mike picked up the poetry book and flicked through the pages. 'Weren't they aware back in the thirteenth century that such intensely physical poetry could arouse lust? That such erotic metaphor might lead to sinful behaviour?'

'The relationship Sufis have with God is that of sensual lovers,' Rahim explained. 'Erotic verse was probably a useful medium for converting the masses to their mystical message. They hoped their fascination with the erotic would lead them to an interest in the Divine.'

'You should try reciting your poetry to some of our male students, Debra.' Mike said. 'Make sure you wear that tight skirt.'

'Yes, perhaps I should have worn a longer skirt. I'm trying to get everything right. I'll have to go through my wardrobe again.' She crossed her legs, smoothing down a mid-calf length skirt hoping it would miraculously stretch to her ankles.

'Sometimes we try too hard to change ourselves. Then we don't know who we really are.' Rahim sat next to her and gazed at the poetry book Mike had discarded.

But Mike continued to rant. 'Are Sufis those whirling dervishes? Perhaps you could try that in the classroom, Debra.' He stretched his arms in the air, circling for special effect and barely missing the overhead fan.

Rahim laughed and thrust out his foot, trying to trip Mike as he completed his final twirl.

'Sufism is a mystical dimension of Islam, and dancing is only one aspect. It provides a variety of paths for the follower to experience the presence of divine love and wisdom.' He closed the book and placed it back on her desk.

'I think I have enough mystique in my life already, especially while my missus is in the UK.' Mike winked at Rahim and, without waiting for a response, sauntered out of the room.

There was an uncomfortable silence before either one spoke.

'Well, I'm thoroughly enjoying your book. I find Rumi stirs my soul.' She worried that she was gushing, talking too fast. She took a breath, slowed down. 'How does Sufism sit with the local Sunni Muslims here in Brunei. Do they accept that mystical side of Islam?'

'The local government can be intolerant of what they consider to be deviationist Islamic ideals. But Sufism is also a path to truth and love.' Rahim's face lit up. 'I'm glad you're enjoying Rumi.'

She looked away before asking, 'Do you know of a Sufi group called Al-Arqam?' She wanted to learn more about this exiled political sect that Gareth had mentioned was recently sighted in East Malaysia.

'Al-Arqam is an Islamic revival group. I believe they have followers throughout Southeast Asia, but they are currently banned from entering Brunei.'

'There seems to be many aspects of Sufism. I was fascinated to learn that Sufism takes on the colour or texture of the individuals who travel in its path. In fact, the more I read of Sufism, the more I want to learn.'

'Yes, it will transform those who want to be enlightened.' He slowly nodded. 'Once I began reading Sufism, I too was inspired to know more. I guess I've been seeking for meaning most of my life.'

'And have you found what you've been searching for?' She scanned his face for clues.

'I think I have.' A comfortable stillness unfolded between them, and she tried to read his gentle mood. 'I also have other poetry books if you'd like to borrow them. You mentioned Rumi's poem about a guest house and the strange behaviour of unwanted guests. It's one of his most popular poems. If you like, I'll bring it in tomorrow.'

'Thanks. That would be great. And Rahim, I didn't get a chance to thank you for your help in Labuan yesterday. It was very kind of you to accompany us. I felt safer having you there.'

'It was a pleasure. I'm glad I could help. I enjoyed it immensely despite the bruises on my back. Do you always have so much excitement in your life?' He grinned.

'No! Only when I'm with you,' she blurted out as a flush of heat spread up her neck and face. 'You know … I mean … like the first day when I'd been to the hospital … You must think I'm clumsy, always bumping into people.'

'Not at all,' he said. He had the kind of smile that inhabited every part of his face – his eyes, his cheeks, and of course that dimple.

She glanced at the clock on the staffroom wall, and gathered up her notes. 'It's time for my class. We've been working in small groups, discussing well-known poets. One member of each group then presents their interpretation to the class. Today's poem is Elizabeth Barrett Browning, *How do I love thee?*'

'… *to the depth and breadth and height … My soul can reach, when feeling out of sight*,' Rahim completed the next few lines of the poem.

'I'm impressed.' She wanted to avert her gaze but didn't want to ruin the moment. 'So, it's not just Sufi poetry that interests you.'

'There are some poems that stay in your heart longer than others,' he said. 'The words bring new hope and meaning into your life.'

Debra nodded, knowing what he meant. 'I'd better go.'

Grabbing his jacket from the back of the chair, he followed her out the door.

The Guest House

This being human is a guest house.
Every morning a new arrival.
Be grateful for whoever comes,
because each has been sent
as a guide from beyond.

Rumi

Each day Debra searched for books Rahim had left in her staffroom pigeonhole. But what excited her most was discovering the handwritten notes accompanying them. Since he'd lent her the first book, she enjoyed a connection with the poems and the messenger who delivered them. The more she read of Rumi, the more his lyrics and images provided her with questions and insight on her path to self-discovery.

According to Sufis, for the soul to grow one must endure anguish or suffering. Previously, stuck in her personal grief she had been unable to move on, yet here was a source offering some semblance of meaning for her loss. She remembered the constant ache in her chest, the primal cry pushing up her throat, and the loud, terrifying howl that she discovered was coming from her as she mourned her baby daughter. Maybe now she was ready to heal.

Before reading his latest note concealed in a book of poetry, she looked at the bookmarked poem. As she scanned the words, she remembered when she'd first heard this poem. Her chest tightened as a dark cloud passed over her as she recalled the

Monet print on the therapist's wall. *Water lilies in Giverny. Such a tranquil scene.* At the time she longed to submerge herself in that pond, to sink beneath the still water, the weeping willows keeping vigil. Muted strains of Pachelbel's *Canon* had bounced around the therapist's room from her portable cassette player in the corner.

Debra's doctor had suggested grief therapy after Mala died, thinking it would help her deal with the loss. The yellow chair she'd sat on she easily remembered. It was one of a matching pair the therapist directed her towards; she sat on the other. Bright and cheerful, matching the sofa, which looked softer and more inviting, but with an upright back – the hard yellow chair was no doubt designed to keep her awake during her meditation therapy. *The Guest House* poem was the prompt for the meditation. The therapist's voice, her anchor.

While she acknowledged how far she'd come since that first therapy session, she felt relieved to distract herself with Rahim's note. As she read his words, contentment spread through her, like drinking a hot cup of tea on a cold winter's day.

> *Dear Debra*
>
> *I forgot to ask why you're familiar with this poem, but you were right about the interpretation. Rumi personifies our emotions and each of the unwanted guests are guides or emotions that have come to teach us. He says to welcome them with open arms. Accept them without resistance. We can learn from all these emotions, good and bad alike.*
>
> *According to Rumi, acceptance is not simply passive resignation. It's about accepting life without making judgement even if it makes us uncomfortable. Recognising some things are outside our control is often our best option.*
>
> *I haven't always found acceptance easy. There was a time in my teens when I fought against anything outside*

my control. I viewed my life as unjust and unfair. As I
get older, I'm finding acceptance is easier as I understand
there is a purpose for most things in life. Faith is often
about accepting without seeing the reason why.

Regards

Rahim

As she refolded his note she remembered when *The Guest House* was first recommended to her by the grief therapist. She thought it would be helpful as a meditation to settle her mind, to distract her from all-consuming grief. As she sat in meditation, the therapist asked her to imagine her inner world as a large guest house with many rooms and a large front door. When Debra was ready, she should open the front door to welcome in the "guests". Observing each one, she should identify who'd come to call on her. Was it sadness, anger, or fear? Debra had been overwhelmed by all of them. Next, she was supposed to note any positive visitors such as hope, gratitude, or peace. At this point, she remembered being so full of anger she didn't want any of these "happy guests" to enter. She wanted to jump up from the bright yellow chair and yell at them, 'Piss off and leave me alone!'

Resentment was what she felt towards these "guests". There was no way she could greet them, let alone invite them to stay. They couldn't possibly understand her sadness or loss. There was no way she could sit peacefully, observe her guests, or make notes in a journal as she was asked to do. In frustration, she had thrown the journal on the floor. The emotions arising within were all negative and she was glad when the meditation ended. She couldn't wait to open the door again allowing her guests to leave.

'What were your guides showing you today?' the therapist had asked her.

They were showing her how bloody angry she was. It was too

soon, her emotions too sharp-edged and raw. She was not ready to move on with her life.

Now that she had learned to treat herself with more compassion, to view life in a more positive light, she felt pleased to acknowledge how far she'd come. She happily shared this experience with Rahim and, before she left the college at lunch time, sat at her desk to write a reply.

Dear Rahim

Thanks for sharing your insight on Rumi's poem. The Guest House was first recommended to me by a grief therapist as a meditation practice. I believe this poem is often used by counsellors to teach mindfulness because it gets at the very heart of what it means to be aware. Although, at that time, I didn't understand awareness. Nor did I know about being "in the moment", aware of one's present emotional and physical state.

Now that I know more about meditation, I can recognise the thoughts as they arrive one after the other, just like house guests. I've learned that like temporary guests, they also fade away. I'm sure you're right. By facing these uncomfortable thoughts with acceptance, they will soon lose their control, and their power will diminish.

My first attempt at meditating wasn't a positive experience. I was unable to acknowledge my thoughts or accept they weren't real. I knew nothing of letting go. Looking back, I can see I wasn't ready, and had no desire to move on. Now that I've had the opportunity to practise meditation regularly, I can accept more easily.

Thanks again for sharing the insightful words of an erudite poet. I don't think we will ever stop learning if we open our minds to the wisdom of those who are wiser.

That night Debra took her favourite ginger jar from the high shelf in the pantry, an imitation green jade from Hong Kong, cheap, yet exotic. Damaged in transit, she couldn't bring herself to discard it. As it had sustained only a small crack, she had concealed it by turning the damaged face to the wall. Up until recently, it had sat on the shelf with other similar pieces but now she kept it out of sight. She slipped Rahim's folded note from her pocket, stole one last look at the handwriting she'd come to admire, lifted the paper to her nose, sniffing a hint of citrus and musk. Then, taking the lid from the jar, she deposited the precious gift into the repository. She remembered Rumi's metaphor of the fermentation of grapes into wine as he likened it to human transformation. Could it be that his poetry was revealing her identity at last? Would his words nourish the part of her that desired a continually unfolding truth? When she tried to read the Sufi poems to Alex, he squinted and his brow furrowed deeply.

'Debra, you are such a romantic, a real dreamer. It's as if you're on another planet,' he'd said. 'Why can't you just be normal like everyone else?'

'There's more to life, Alex. A higher dimension that provides added meaning to life. Why not aspire to whatever brings you joy?' She explained to Alex that Rumi's writing was something they needed to experience for themselves. 'Through divine love we learn to love ourselves. Only then will we know how to love others.'

But Alex didn't hear the sincerity in her voice. Instead, he took off his glasses and rubbed at some obstinate smear. 'Debra, I worry about you at times. Where is all this leading? Why can't you be happy like most other people?' He cast her a mere glance then continued reading his newspaper.

'I want to be happy. But I also want to be loved and accepted for who I am.'

She followed Alex's gaze to where Jo had entered through the kitchen door. She'd cooked them stir-fried pork, purchased from the local pork market, accompanied by pickled ginger.

'I've made this for you as I know it's your favourite.' She made a beeline for Alex as Kali followed with Sam.

'Thanks, Jo.' He took the dish from her, placed it with the pickled ginger on the table. 'Now you'll have something to put in your old jar.' Scanning the room, he asked, 'What happened to that ginger jar?'

'Oh, it has a crack in it.' Debra steered her gaze away from the shelf.

'Haven't we all? Life is a broken thing.' Jo laughed. 'Although, don't they say it's what we do with the pieces that defines us?'

'None of us is perfect, Alex. We all have flaws but that's what makes us unique. But we're all worthy of love.'

'In Japan, they have pottery where they repair the cracks with gold paint to make it more beautiful. I think it's called *kintsukuroi.*' Jo looked up at the ceiling, trying to recall.

'Or *kintsugi,*' Debra added. 'I believe it's to honour the cracks, to dignify the scars. Wouldn't it be great if we were all viewed in that positive light?'

Alex screwed up his face and shook his head again.

Sam and Kali sat at the table while Jo served rice into small bowls from a larger dish. Silence prevailed as everyone enjoyed their food, finishing each grain of rice, each spoonful of pork. When Debra picked up the dirty plates to take them out to the kitchen, Jo followed her.

Alex prattled on about the upcoming cricket match between the yacht club and the college, and mused whether he should be practising his bowling, questioning if he still had that magical spin. As he exercised his bowling arm, it appeared he hadn't lost his confidence. 'I can probably bowl with my eyes shut.' He changed direction, this time bowling underarm with an imaginary ball.

'I'm sure you can,' Debra shouted from the kitchen as she stacked the plates in the sink.

As Jo and Debra walked back into the living room, a brilliant flash of light split the sky followed by a deafening crack. The clackety clack of the overhead fan slowed to a gentle click. The lights flickered for a moment before the house plunged into darkness. Kali and Sam both let out a scream.

'Not another power cut. That's the third this month.' Alex walked over to look out the window, grabbing candles and matches from the sideboard left there for occasions such as this.

'Do you remember that power cut we had when we were entertaining George Perry from Boeing?' asked Alex.

'I don't remember,' Debra said. 'Was it before I arrived?'

Jo and Alex shared a grin before turning to look at her.

'Yes, the week before you came. Jo was helping me entertain. Playing hostess.'

'All I did was make the dessert. Our amah, Tina, made chilli mussels. For an entrée, we dipped croutons into cheese fondue. We also drank plenty of alcohol, thanks to the Perrys' duty-free allowance.'

'But what a dessert it was! Just as you walked in with the flaming Bombe Alaska, the lights went out.'

Jo joined in as if on cue. 'And George's wife Sal thought we did it deliberately for dramatic effect. It was very funny, and the timing was perfect. They both laughed.

'Sounds like it was quite a night. Obviously, you all enjoyed yourselves. Was Gareth there?' A tinge of envy crept into Debra's voice at a memory she didn't share. Apparently, he wasn't. Like tonight, he was working.

When Alex mentioned they had water cuts each day, their American guests found it hard to believe. They wanted to know how anyone could possibly survive without water. It was the same question Debra had asked Alex, horrified when he told her the first week she arrived. How would she survive from 8am to 8pm without water? Apparently, everyone filled up their baths, basins, or any bucket they could find.

'Doesn't that defeat the purpose of saving water?' she'd asked.

'Well, at least it provides enough water to last us twelve hours,' he'd said. 'You'll get used to showering with a bucketful of water.'

'What about when George's wife, Sal, went into the bathroom and noticed the buckets lined up near the toilet?' Jo held her stomach as she laughed.

'Yeah … she asked me which bucket she should wash her hands in.' Alex threw his hands in the air. 'She probably thought she was in some sort of time warp. It would never happen in Seattle.'

Minutes later, the children squealed with delight when the lamps flickered for a few seconds before surrounding them in light. While Jo and Debra remained seated, Alex moved towards the darkened window, his white shirt shimmering as he extended his bowling arm, exercising it over and over.

A Voice of Dark Honey

O nightingale, with your voice of dark honey!
go on lamenting!
Only your drunken ecstasy
can pierce the rock's hard heart!

Rumi

The cricketers assembled on the green for a social match between the yacht club and the college team. Debra and Sam arrived as Alex prepared to bowl for the yacht club. A lover of most sports, Alex's favourite was cricket. Sam dressed in matching whites, navy cap, and carried a smaller bat and ball. As Alex walked out onto the pitch, Debra moved into the shaded area to get a drink from the bar. Striding towards her, padded up, ready to bat, Mike greeted her with his usual friendly banter.

'Ms De Bra. You are looking spectacular as always.' He scanned her from head to toe.

Before she could think of a suitable reply, an unexpected figure appeared behind him; she halted, startled at the sight of him in this different setting. He looked relaxed in his cricket whites, cap in one hand, a drink in the other.

'You missed our hero of the day.' Mike inclined his head towards Rahim.

'Oh, did he hit a six?'

Mike grinned. 'No, I think he just bowled a maiden over.'

Embarrassed, she looked down at Sam and pointed to her colleagues. 'Sam, this is Mike, and Rahim, who we met at the market that day. Are you going to say hello?' She nudged him and he stepped forward and extended his hand to each of the men in turn.

'Have you come to play cricket?' Rahim said, looking at the miniature bat. Sam nodded.

Mike grabbed Sam's cap, and tussled his curls. 'Mummy needs to trim your hair. We can't have you looking like a girl.'

'And what's wrong with looking like a girl?' Debra asked.

'I think he looks cute.' Rahim pointed to Sam's bat. 'Would you like to have a hit? Let's go in the shade.' Rahim led him to a grassed area where he aimed the ball at Sam's bat.

'Three sixes, Debra. He hit three.' Mike's grin spread across his face. He looked over at Sam. 'He has found a new friend for life now.'

'I didn't know Rahim played cricket.'

'There are many things you don't know. He's a real dark horse.' Mike looked as if he was going to say something else, then changed his mind.

Debra thought of many things she would like to know about Rahim. She yelled good luck as Mike walked onto the pitch, then joined Sam and Rahim. As she stood watching them, stealing an occasional longer glimpse at Rahim, she realised she was fiddling with her rings, gently twirling them round and round. She forced herself to stop; put her hands down. *But why am I so nervous, so restless?*

Nevertheless, she moved in closer; listened to his gentle words of encouragement whenever Sam missed the ball. Occasionally Sam hit one, and Rahim praised him, and patiently fetched each ball.

'Have you always played cricket?'

'It was once my whole life. At school, I was team captain. I played in Under 16s for Worcester County but that probably doesn't mean much to you.'

'That sounds like quite an achievement.'

'Yes, it broke my heart when I left England. I really missed cricket and my friends. It was what I loved most about school.'

'What about when you moved to KL? Didn't you play there?' She sensed a change of mood, an air of melancholy.

'No. My cricket bat was left in a cupboard to gather dust. My father had no interest in the game. It was my English mother who always encouraged me to play, to follow my dreams.' He bowled another slow ball towards Sam's bat.

'What about you? Do you enjoy cricket?'

'I come because I know it's important to Alex. I also want Sam to take an interest in sport.'

Sam now scooted off and retrieved the ball, and Rahim rolled another low ball along the grass at him.

'Alex obviously enjoys the game. A great bowler. He took a few scalps today, including mine.'

'Yes, he's certainly competitive. Loves to win.' She looked to where Alex was about to bowl another ball down the pitch. A high-pitched refined voice under a large-brimmed hat grabbed at her arm.

'Hello, it's Debra, isn't it? I met you at the airport.' Unlike Rahim's dulcet tone, her nasal twang had a jarring effect.

Debra searched under the hat, and found a face to match the voice. The white straw hat was shading a mane of chestnut hair, a flawless English complexion, and a strong scent of *L'Air du Temps*. Peering through large rose-tinted glasses, she thrust out her hand.

'Beth Worthington. I'm here to cheer on the yacht club. What about you?'

'My loyalties are somewhat divided as I teach at the college, but Alex is out there bowling for the yacht club.' She pointed towards Alex, but Beth stared curiously at Rahim. Debra launched into introductions and Rahim extended his free hand, his tone, and manners impeccable.

'Oh, what accent is that? You don't sound like a Bruneian.' She peered at Rahim from under her hat.

'No, that's probably because I'm not.' He looked down at the ball in his hand.

'Oh. I should have known. We don't get many locals playing cricket.' She stared at Rahim; looked him up and down.

Debra didn't have the heart to remind her that expats didn't invite the locals to share this hallowed patch of turf. Instead, she told her how Rahim was once selected for the Under 16s at Worcester County.

'Really? That must have been a long time ago.' Her horsey laugh revealed a mouthful of oversized teeth. 'But, I will tell Dick to look out for you. That's him on the boundary, sledging at the opposition. Cricket is part of our English heritage you know. We need to support our men. It might be different for you Australians.'

Debra flinched as Beth peered out from under her hat long enough to steal another sideways glance at Rahim. Then, in a voice loud enough for him to hear, she asked, 'What exactly does he do?'

Debra's back stiffened. She could have told her he was a highly qualified principal of the college, but instead, she said, 'He's my boss, and a good friend.'

Beth scowled, then turned and flounced back to the match, leaving behind a lingering trace of Nina Ricci. "Her man" cheered loudly from the boundary as he clutched the ball. The latest victim was the eighth man, who'd buckled under Alex's famous spin ball. While Alex was in his element, Mike, as ninth man, faced an early demise. He slashed the first ball on the offside, but it carried to second slip, where a stumbling, grasping hand caught him out. 'Howzat!' the captain cried.

The college team was now down to the last two men. With

sixty-four runs, they were well short of the twenty runs needed to win the match. The tenth man took the crease and faced up as Alex delivered another spinner that split the offside and middle wicket. The bales shot up in the air, the umpire raised his index finger, the batter was out. Alex and his teammates patted each other on the back, jubilant at their hard-fought victory. Most of the college team headed for the bar to drown their sorrows, but Rahim stayed back.

'I'm sorry about Beth. I only met her the other day. She's no friend of mine.'

'You don't have to apologise for her, Debra.'

'I know, but she's pompous. I don't think she's in touch with the real world – probably been living in the tropics too long.'

Rahim gave a wistful shrug. 'I've learned to ignore them.'

'Well, I choose not to put up with her.'

'That's your privilege, Debra.' He handed her the bat and ball.

She lingered, not wanting their contact to end. While she'd enjoyed learning about his life in the UK, there was more she wanted to know. But she was conscious of the noisy crowd gathering at the nearby bar. Sun-reddened cricketers sculled cold beer or tipped iced water over their sweaty heads.

'Well, no doubt we'll bump into you at a few more games,' she said.

Rahim hesitated, his hands in the air as if unsure what to do with them. She had an urge to reach out and grab them, but he thrust them into his pockets.

'I sincerely hope so. I've got another poetry book in my car if you want to walk over there.' He nodded towards his car parked under a shady tree.

As he handed her the book, a piece of paper protruded from the top. She couldn't wait to get home to read it but hid the book under the towel lying on the back seat of her car. She joined Alex for a quick drink before leaving him to celebrate while she drove home with Sam to organise dinner.

Later when Alex walked into the kitchen, he quizzed her about the cricket match.

'Did you notice all the wickets I took?' He grinned.

'I sure did. You were best on field. Man of the Match.'

She handed out the rice bowls; placed a large bowl of chicken fried rice in the middle of the table. As they ate, Alex enjoyed a post-mortem of the game, relating a blow-by-blow account of his many successes as well as those where he could have bowled better.

After a brief pause, he said, 'I noticed you speaking to that Malay guy. How do you know him?' He peered over his glasses.

'He's my boss.'

'Really? I thought you said your boss was an older guy. A pommy bloke. You didn't mention he was Malay.'

'No! He's about my age. A year or so older maybe. He's only half Malay. His mother was English.'

'Where did he learn to bat like that? He's pretty good. But I managed to bowl him out.' Alex stretched out his bowling arm, reliving his success.

'He played competitively in England but had to leave it all behind when he went to live in Kuala Lumpur. He also had to leave his mother behind. That couldn't have been easy.'

Alex showed little interest. Instead, he muttered 'these things happen' before turning on the television. 'At least Sam has a father who can teach him to play cricket. I'm going to have a shower. I'm knackered.'

Once Alex and Sam were asleep in bed, Debra moved into the study and pulled out the note inside Rahim's book, eager to read what he'd written.

Dear Debra

When I was in England, I spent many wintry days

*memorising stanzas from Byron, Keats, and Yeats. But it
was Keats whose odes to melancholy and autumn consoled
me with his expressions of sorrow. When I moved to KL,
as the relentless sun burned down on me, I longed for
Keats' 'season of mists and mellow fruitfulness'. But it
was not only the lack of seasons that caused my nostalgia.*

*There were two factors which helped me survive my
first unhappy years at school in Malaysia. The first was
my love of poetry. The second was my tutor, Ali Hassan.
Poetry was a means for me to find purpose in a mosaic
of otherwise inexplicable happenings. I covered my
schoolbooks with scribbled words of pent-up rage, while
my bedroom walls bore the brunt of screwed up
declarations of yearning scribbled in moments of despair.
Through his support, Ali Hassan encouraged me to keep
writing. He introduced me to Sufi poetry to transform my
physical and spiritual practice. He showed me how the
prose could evoke moods, convey meaning to language that
I hadn't previously understood. Ali may have been wanting
to steer me away from English literature, but I am grateful
to him for igniting my passion in poetry.*

I'm so glad you are enjoying Rumi.

Regards

Rahim

All was quiet in the house; she was alone with her thoughts,
apart from two cicaks watching from the ceiling above. As the
fan clanked and whirred, she wrote her reply, and thought of the
person who would receive her musings, a person who, until
recently, she barely knew yet now felt a connection simply
through writing. She imagined him pulling out her note from his
pigeonhole at work. What would be his reaction? Would his pulse

race as hers did? Or would his hands fumble as he unfolded the note, eager to share a moment of joy, reading the words of another?

Dear Rahim

It sounds as if Ali Hassan was a wise tutor recognising your passion for literature and flair for semantics. By introducing you to ancient Sufi poetry, perhaps it wasn't simply to steer you away from Western literature. He may have wanted you to find an awareness of divine love expressed so intensely by Rumi, in the hope you would find the elixir to soothe your restless soul.

As you mentioned previously, Rumi wrote on states of longing, emptiness, and grief. You must have felt a comfortable connection with him. I believe he referred to the grief which lovers felt, the deeper the grief, the more radiant the love. I was pleased to find that Rumi also embraced the beauty of the world. So important in a spiritual age. Through Rumi's words, I hope you discovered a secret world that you could immerse yourself in, and devoured each nourishing morsel until your appetite was sufficiently sated.

P S I'd love to read anything that you've written. Do you have any poems you wrote back then?

Regards

Debra

As she climbed into bed, she immersed herself in her own secret world. Would she ever find the magic elixir to soothe her restless soul? She allowed the velvety darkness to wash over her, thinking of the states of grief Rumi mentioned. Grief was something she understood. There was a time when it occupied every waking minute of her day. At night, it consumed her dreams and was the first thought that jolted her awake, forcing her to remember when all she wanted to do was forget. Now she found it easier to remember the precious moments spent with Mala. The feel of her tiny body, the soft downy hair as she fingered the nape of her neck. She could smell the intoxicating scent of her skin.

While she understood the states of emptiness and loss Rumi referred to, she was yet to fully discover the state of longing. Was it the need to satisfy something that was missing in her life, to fill the void? Or was it a desperate need for union and belonging? The passionate desire to be whole, yet to be recognised and respected as an essential part of another? The emptiness she had known then, lurked around her now. With Alex away so often, Debra had a need to be loved, to be cared for, to be cherished but she had much to learn on this state of longing.

***

Next morning, darkness prevailed outside as Debra spread her yoga mat on the wooden floor, cooled by the aircon during the night. The air was heavy, with a restlessness she found hard to explain, a state of longing from unfulfilled desires, sensual urges that couldn't be sated. Facing towards the rising sun, she performed five rounds of Salute to the Sun.

With her pulse racing, she worked up a sweat. Outside the window, the faint pink haze would soon creep in and flood the house with heat. The oppressive humidity would eventually suck the life out of her and everything in its path. For the moment though, she enjoyed the quiet darkness split with the occasional chirping of birdsong. Each sound promised a new day. The ancient yogis experienced this same deep communion with nature, their daily discipline, a ritual of veneration to life and creation.

As she reflected on the changing signs of nature, she thought about Alex and his ever-changing moods. So different to Rahim with his calm certainty. Re-reading Rahim's latest note which he'd left in her pigeonhole, she had the same sensation as when reading his first note. Difficult to describe, it was like a thirst that needed to be quenched, a hunger yet to be filled. Consuming his letters, she felt sated in a way not previously experienced. Before placing it with the others in the ginger jar on the shelf, she took one last look.

Dear D

Thanks for your insights on Rumi. I agree with you about embracing the beauty of the world. It's so important, especially in this spiritual age. While there is much focus on seeking wealth and fame, we also need to show gratitude for the small blessings in our lives.

The recent cricket match brought back many memories for me. One image I thought I'd blocked out forever suddenly resurfaced. It was a warm day in June. Worcester County was playing Leicester in a local cricket match. It was my best innings as I carried my bat with 100 on the scoreboard. The crowd cheered and my teammates slapped me on the back as I walked off the pitch. I was the hero of the match, the toast of the club. It was the proudest moment of my life. I could not have been happier.

But as I walked off, I was surprised to find my father waiting for me. I was shocked when he told me I must leave immediately. After the euphoria of the match, I was slow to react. I could not comprehend what was happening, let alone understand what I was experiencing at the time. I just remember an incredible sense of loss, like a living branch that's been snapped and wrenched from a tree before its time.

Amidst the jubilation of my teammates, I had to make my final farewell. An unexpected force, more powerful than cricket, determined my fate. Wearing my cricket whites, I was marched into the car, whisked onto an aircraft bound for Kuala Lumpur. Unaware that this was to be my last match, I was completely bowled over and dismissed. There was no opportunity to farewell my mother and sister or explain to my teammates. I was given no explanation and my British heritage, which I believed to be my birthright, was severed in one swift blow. 'You'll never be English,' my father said.

Please forgive my woes. I didn't intend to offload on you. It was an unexpected pleasure seeing you at the cricket match the other day. I'm glad that I've been given another opportunity to play a game that was once an important part of my life.

PS   You asked if I've kept anything I wrote years ago. I will have to dig deep to find them. Most of my old poems are packed away somewhere.

Regards R

Debra quickly showered; took her coffee out into the garden where she could write a reply. Touched that he shared one of the saddest moments of his youth, she began to understand certain aspects of his life, and felt flattered that he considered her a friend worthy of his trust. In past years when she longed to share her own loss with someone who understood, there had been no friend with whom she had a close connection. She now felt confident enough to share some of her inner thoughts with him.

Dear R

I can't imagine what it must have been like for you having to give up your family, friends, and birthright. However, I do understand loss. My eleven-year-old brother, my close companion, died when I was ten. With my family traumatised by his death, Trevor's name was rarely mentioned   all his personal belongings were hurriedly removed from the house. I couldn't bear the emptiness of the house. Trevor used to hang a pair of boxing gloves from a hook above his bed. Stealthily, I would run my hands over the smooth red surface of the gloves inhaling their leathery smell which reminded me of him. I thought of keeping them after he died but I knew the sight of them would sadden my mother. When I knelt beside my parents' bed at night, I continued to include him in my prayers. Mum quietly tried to explain he was no longer there.

'But I want God to protect him,' I said.

My mother didn't understand my need to maintain his existence. Nor was she aware of my presence at that time. Nobody did and I was a poor substitute for Trevor. With my parents engrossed in their own silent grief, I became invisible.

Regards

D

Dancing Inside My Chest

In your light I learn how to love.
In your beauty, how to make poems.
You dance inside my chest where no one sees you,
But sometimes I do, and that sight becomes this art.

Rumi

As Debra sat in the garden lost in her own private world, she became aware of Lena raking leaves into small piles to burn. Lena was now like one of the family, and she adored Sam who followed her wherever she went. Unlike her own childhood where she often wandered around unnoticed, Sam got plenty of attention and was usually the centre of focus.

Over the fence came the sound of a male voice laughing, and a moustached face appeared through the hedge. With his blond streaked black hair, Azri, the young gardener, giggled once more before ducking down again. As he ran past the fence Debra glimpsed his long spaghetti legs, clad in a pair of brief orange shorts. He covered his face with his hands as Gareth, wearing a matching pair of shorts, chased him with the garden hose.

'Mam, you know he was there the day we got the visa?' Lena raised her eyebrows towards the hedge.

'Who? Azri? In Labuan? Was he one of the men behind the wharf?' she whispered.

'Yes! You didn't see him, Mam?' Lena continued raking the leaves.

'I didn't go inside. I just stuck my head around the door.' Most of the men she saw that day were wearing black velvet songkoks on their heads. She only remembered the wispy bearded man with the red scarf.

'Mrs McKenzie is a nice lady.' Lena rested on the rake. 'Maybe my sister could work for her or another friend of yours?'

'I thought Viola worked for a local family.' Debra recalled it was someone who worked for the government.

'Yes, but her boss is not a nice man. He won't give her Sundays off. She can't go to mass.' Lena wiped her brow with the back of her hand.

'That's not fair. He shouldn't be allowed to treat her like that. I'll talk to Jo.' Debra shook her head. This young woman should not be at the mercy of her employer, but, as she looked over the fence, she started to worry about Jo.

Later that day, Kali came over to play with Sam, as she was home alone. She couldn't find her father or Azri.

'You can stay here with us.' Kali's vulnerability evoked memories in Debra of her own younger self; like Kali, she too had needed to create a world of her own away from the pressures of the real world.

'Do you know what Azri put in our garden?' Kali asked.

'No. Is it a guava tree? Pineapple plants?'

Kali shook her head. 'No. He put a big box in the ground over by your fence.' She pointed towards their mango tree.

'A box? How big?' Macabre thoughts whizzed around in Debra's head as she imagined the size of a coffin, and breathed with relief when Kali stretched out her thin arms to less than a foot wide.

'About this big,' she said.

When she looked at Kali she wondered if her own daughter would have been happy or troubled. Would she have loved dancing as Debra did, driving everyone mad with her splits and cartwheels as she flitted from room to room? Or would she have been like Kali who spent most of her time in this fey state. Would she have been highly imaginative?

The day was unbearably humid even though the bamboo leaves swayed gently with the slight hint of a breeze. Kali, already in her swimsuit, jumped in the pool with Sam, and laughed as Sam splashed her; then she taught him how to jump in, swim to the edge and climb out again; she also showed him how to dive for toys she had thrown on the bottom of the pool.

Later in the day, Lena returned to the garden with a box of matches and proceeded to burn the small piles of leaves she'd finished raking. Following close behind, Sam was about to throw a plastic bag of leaves onto the small fire when Debra turned to see a trail of ash and wavering smoke enshrouding him.

'No, Sam,' she screamed. 'No!'

She ran towards him as a corner of the plastic caught fire. When he flicked it away, the bag landed on his shoulder and the melting plastic stuck to his back. He screamed as the hot molten blob burned his skin. Lena fetched ice, while Debra raced towards the scorching fire. With the garden shears, she cut away most of the plastic then gathered him in her arms, comforting him. Kali sobbed as she fetched wet towels, and they placed them over his back.

'It will be okay,' Debra soothed Sam and tried to reassure Kali at the same time. 'We just need to keep his skin cool.'

While she applied water to the burns, Lena extinguished the fire with the garden hose. As if on cue, Jo's car appeared in the driveway, and they bundled Sam into the car. Kali and Debra cuddled him while Jo drove as fast as she could to the hospital in town. When they arrived, similar queues greeted them as on their first visit. But this time a sympathetic nurse let them forego the usual process of waiting for hours in a queue. A doctor beckoned, and quickly prescribed analgesics to ease the pain.

Throughout the procedure, Jo kept up her cheerful banter,

reassuring Debra, comforting Sam. As Debra carried him out to the car, he whimpered, his head flopping onto her shoulder. When they arrived home, Jo rang Alex at work, and before long he rushed through the door demanding to know what happened.

'Why weren't you watching him, Debra? How did he get the matches?'

'I was with him. So was Lena. We were both there.' She stroked Sam's hair. 'It wasn't the matches. He was tipping a pile of leaves into the fire.' Her voice strained. 'He was helping Lena rake leaves. It was an accident.'

'He shouldn't have been near the fire in the first place.' He rushed over to Sam and knelt beside him.

'I'm sorry, sir, it was my fault,' Lena said. 'I wasn't quick enough. I shouldn't have let him help me.'

'Nobody is to blame Lena. These things happen even when you think you're protecting a child. It was an accident.' A sob escaped Debra's throat.

She sat on the edge of Sam's bed, crying into the silky softness of his hair, muttering soothing words while Alex sat beside her holding Sam's hand. When he turned his back on her, she felt the heat of his anger. He'd never forgiven her. Debra wanted to shower Sam in love, take away his pain, protect him from all hurt. But she kissed him and tiptoed away. Collapsing on her bed, she sobbed into her pillow.

When Alex finally came to bed, Debra turned to cuddle his back. She wanted him to hold her, to console her but after a few minutes, he pushed her arm away.

'It's too hot. I'm exhausted.'

She withdrew into the cocoon she'd created long ago. Inside, there was no judgment, no rejection, only a sense of refuge. Free from the outside world, she wove her own comforting dreams. After Mala's death, she blamed herself. Perhaps if she'd guarded her baby more closely, kept her room warmer, better ventilated, her clothes tighter, looser. She should have checked the baby monitor more frequently. The self-flagellation was nothing compared to the silent blame that emanated from Alex's eyes. Sometimes she noticed him looking at her as if searching for the answer to his own unbearable questions. Each time he dismissed her, brushed her off or challenged her motives, she experienced guilt tantamount to having been charged. At the time, Sam sealed the guilty plea when he'd asked his first innocent question.

'What have you done with my baby sister? You took her to the hospital, but you didn't bring her home. You lost her.'

By the next morning, Sam was back to his normal happy self, despite the burns on his back. Debra offered prayers of gratitude as this was a celebration of life, not death. She spent most of the day sitting with him as he played quietly with his Lego or reading books. Later in the day, he perked up, looking for Kali who was always capable of entertaining him with some new activity she'd created.

Through the open window, squeals of delight echoed from the lower end of their garden. A small, brown, puppy rushed past, followed by Sam on unsteady legs. A wig of long red hair slid off his blond curls. Kali, dressed as an angel, ran after him, joining in the chase. She adjusted the wig on his head as the puppy circled, nipping at his heels. Sam hid behind the mango tree before Kali found him, giggling, clutching her tummy. Sam shared her infectious chuckle. They held hands, dancing, as a languid sun ended another day and impatient dusk surrounded them in darkness.

Ethereal Dances

And all my days are trances
And all my nightly dreams
Are where thy dark eye glances,
And where they footstep gleams -
In what ethereal dances
By what eternal streams

Edgar Allan Poe

Sam and Debra stepped into the shopping centre elevator followed by a short dark man who squeezed in before the doors slid shut. They'd been up to the first floor to collect a birthday cake for Mike, which Debra carefully carried in a plastic bag. The doors opened at ground level. Before she could exit, the man turned and grabbed at her breasts, clasping one in each hand. She dropped Sam's hand; tried to push the man away. The coward ran, leaving them in shock. Sam wailed loudly. Debra screamed; swore every expletive she knew.

In the struggle, she dropped the cake and cherries with chocolate chunks scattered all over the box. Black Forest, black day! As she bent to retrieve the cake, she cried but the tears failed to wash away the humiliation.

While trying to resurrect the cake and what was left of her dignity, she comforted Sam before dropping him at preschool. When Debra arrived at the college everyone was jubilant, ready to celebrate Mike's special day. As she sat in the staffroom with the other teachers drinking a cup of tea, she tried to release the tension in her jaw, but it remained locked with anger and shock. She fixed a smile to her face, nodding when required as if it was just another school day. She joined Mike who stood in a quieter corner of the kitchen cutting the birthday cake, handing out slices.

'How's the unrequited love?' Mike grinned.

Tea sloshed onto the saucer where she'd just placed her cake. 'What are you talking about?' She grabbed a serviette to mop up the spills.

'The poetry. I thought you were going to recite it to the male students.' He placed another piece of cake in his mouth.

'Oh that. Sorry, I have other things on my mind.' She mopped up the saucer, and threw the sodden cake in the bin.

'Yes, I noticed. I'm not one to give advice, Grainger, but sometimes it helps to get it out of your system. Then you can get back on track with your life.' He finished eating his cake, licking the cream from his lips and fingers.

'What on earth do you mean?' She thumped the cup down on the bench.

'Whatever it is that causes you to walk around with a dreamy expression on your face. You look as if you're on another planet.'

'You've no idea what I've just been through.' She threw her hands to her face.

Lifting the teapot, Mike stopped, his mouth agape. He held it in mid-air while he stared at her. 'Why what happened?'

'I was in the lift when some bloke grabbed hold of my breasts, one in each hand. I was holding Sam's hand while clutching your cake in the other.' She remembered her emotions, the initial fright, her crushed pride. She caught Mike smiling and stopped him before he could turn it into a joke.

'It's not funny, Mike. I feel vulnerable and violated. In fact, I'm so bloody furious I can't stop thinking about it.' Her voice sounded shrill in her ears.

'You should have kicked him in the goolies.'

'Yes, I should've done. I swore at the coward. But I was too stunned. I wasn't expecting it.' She sat down and rubbed her eyes, hoping to erase the shabby images.

'And you made this sacrifice to get me a cake? I really appreciate it.' Mike placed his hand on her shoulder.

'Never again.' She shook her head. 'That's the last time I make sacrifices for any man, even you.' She looked at Mike who appeared lost for words. He turned to Rahim who had just walked in.

'Debra has just been groped.' His tone reflected no sign of surprise.

'Oh no! Are you okay? What happened?' Rahim's face darkened with concern.

'I'm incensed and hurt that someone thought he could treat me that way. Trapped in an elevator, with a child, no hands to defend myself. Sam witnessed it all.' She looked down at her clenched fists.

'I'm really sorry, Debra.' He gently placed his hand on her shoulder.

'It's not your fault.'

'But I feel responsible for you.' He patted her arm, and she felt tears welling.

'Look at me!' She pointed at her flared trousers and long-sleeved T-shirt. 'Fully covered legs, arms, armpits. What more do I have to do? Wear a scarf over my head?' She bit into her lower lip, fighting off tears.

'I can understand why you're upset. You have every right to be,' Rahim said.

'Unfortunately, Grainger, you stand out in a crowd,' Mike said. 'A novelty to be admired from afar, and sometimes touched it seems. I sympathise with you; there are some real weirdos out there. They get their rocks off by this type of behaviour.' He turned to Rahim.

'Harry, I'm not going to be able to go to Singapore with you next month. I think it clashes with my UK annual leave'.

'Oh no! That's a shame. The college has paid for two of us to go to the conference.'

'Perhaps you can ask Grainger if she wants to go,' Mike muttered as he walked out leaving the two of them looking everywhere except at each other.

Debra's mouth gaped before mumbling a reply. 'Uh, it's not a good time right now. I'm sorry. I can't concentrate on conferences or anything else.'

'I understand. But don't let one person's bad behaviour put you off,' said Rahim. 'There are many good people out there who respect you. We care about you.'

'Thanks.' While she accepted what he was saying, she needed to process it in her own time. As she gathered up her papers, he pushed a folded note into her hand.

In class, the students were unusually restless as Debra struggled to inject a level of positivity into the lesson. She tried to appear cheerful yet the menacing face of a stranger with groping hands kept coming into focus. With a look of fear on his face, his movements were childlike as if he had a challenge to carry out before anyone noticed. His cold eyes though were gleeful with no regard for his victim. With his one clumsy attempt, he'd succeeded in reducing her to something that was worthless, to be discarded like the cardboard packaging on the cake. It was one of those days she wished would quickly end.

When she later arrived home, she grabbed some lunch before stretching out on the sofa to read Rahim's latest letter.

Dear D

After reading your mother's reaction to loss, I had a rare memory of my mother. It was my sister Sophie's tenth birthday, and she was counting pearls on a necklace Mum had given her. It was not a full string of pearls but a silver chain with three pearls set in silver. When she asked Mum why there were three, she told her as we become adults, we acquire pearls of wisdom based on our experience in life. She assured Sophie when she became a mother, she would understand. She believed Sophie would end up with a full string of pearls one day. But Sophie persisted, wanting to know why she had already acquired three. 'Because you have three people who love you,' Mum said. 'A mother, a father and a brother'.

That was enough to quieten Sophie at the time. She had no way of knowing soon after that birthday she would lose two of the precious pearls in her life. The next day Dad and I left England, exiting her life forever. A few months later I celebrated my fifteenth birthday on my own in KL. I had no mother, no sister, or pearls to help me commemorate this special occasion.

I wonder if Sophie ever discovered the wisdom our mother promised she would find with maturity. After all this time, does she experience the joy of our mother's love? Sophie may now be a mother herself. We have all been estranged for so long. Once the bonds have been severed, they are difficult to mend. There are so many unanswered questions. But I'm grateful for being able to share this with you. Thanks for your friendship.

    R.

Rahim rarely talked about his sister, but Debra had begun to understand why. To lose a brother or sister through death or separation was a traumatic experience. As children, you shared so many of your dreams with your sibling that they became the guardian or keeper of your secrets. Should you ever forget something, they would always remember it for you. Of course, mothers represented so much more, helping to shape the lives of their children. The more Debra learned of his life, the more she became interested in him.

After making a cup of tea, she picked up a pen and wrote her reply.

Dear R

I can only imagine your loss. Sadly, families are often our greatest source of pain. With no sense of entitlement, my mother expected little from life. I once asked her why she never wore pearls, and I had a strange sense of foreboding when she said she thought pearls were associated with tears and sadness.

After returning from the war, my father drank heavily. Staggering home one night, he crashed into the terracotta pot hanging near the back door, knocking himself unconscious. Had Mum not gone looking for him several hours later, he might still be lying on the concrete path. But he was a survivor, a commando who fought bravely to create a better life for others. My mother was a selfless soul who dedicated her life to looking after him.

Some days he would collapse on the lawn after drinking. While he was too heavy for Mum to lift, she kept constant vigil by positioning a beach umbrella over his prone form. She adjusted it as the sun changed its angle throughout the day.

From my parents I inherited resilience, and a need to fight for peace at any cost. With their love of music, the passionate rhythms that flooded my body may also have come from them. Since I was a child, any catchy tune or lively beat would cause my feet to tap as my body swayed in time. In my dreams I'm forever dancing, filled with ethereal joy.

After my brother died, I lived most of my time in an expansive fantasy world where I could spread my wings, exploring a realm with no limits. That's when I first found comfort in poetry.

I'm glad you too found poetry in your life at the time when you needed it most.

D. XXX

Celebrating Life

Set your life on fire,
Seek those who fan your flames.

Rumi

Grabbing Sam's chubby hand, Debra half dragged him up the two flights of steps to the airport café. Jo had invited them to join them for beef burgers to celebrate Kali's seventh birthday. As they entered the restaurant, a young girl about Sam's age chased a red balloon towards the doorway, the delighted expression on the girl's face as she caught the balloon somehow familiar to Debra. Her gaze flicked from the young girl to her father calling her, then to his wife who also looked to their daughter. *The two older girls sitting at the table must be the twins and the younger one chasing the balloon, Aleesha.* Rahim had talked about them so often it was as if she already knew them.

At that moment, Rahim looked up, and Debra's chest tightened as she struggled to breathe. He hesitated for a second, greeting her awkwardly before moving into introductions and then the words she'd been dreading. 'This is my wife, Mahani.'

Debra nodded, sensing her smile was too wide, her nod too eager. She found it hard to speak, then stammered, 'It's lovely to meet you, Mahani.'

Fortunately, Sam bridged the gap between them as Mahani gazed at her with a small, puzzled frown. 'I've got my bat in the car!' he yelled, tripping over Rahim as he ran forward. The spell was broken. They all looked at Sam, anticipating his next move.

'And this is Sam.'

There was an awkward silence. Then Debra and Rahim laughed nervously while Mahani asked, 'What did he say? He's very cute.'

'He's talking about his cricket bat,' said Debra. 'He takes it everywhere hoping someone will play with him.' Looking down at the luggage, she added, 'Are you flying out somewhere?'

'Yes, I'm taking the girls to KL as I need to visit my specialist again. I have a few health issues.' Mahani wiped a strand of hair back from her perfect heart-shaped face.

'Well, I hope everything goes well over there. It's lovely meeting you. I'm just catching up with a friend here. It's her daughter's birthday.'

Once Debra began talking, she didn't stop lest the silent pause created more embarrassment. *Is my voice too loud? My speech too fast?* Yet Mahani's gentle voice appeared calm, with perfect timbre, her reply affable.

'It's a pleasure to meet you too, Debra. I hope we meet again.'

Guilt and envy coursed through Debra – he belonged to her – and she had no right to think otherwise. They had a strong friendship, which should be enough. How could she compete with this beautiful, loving, young wife, the mother of his children? Filled with these feelings of doubt and sadness, she greeted Jo, seated at a table close to Rahim's family.

Before sitting, she took Sam to the counter and ordered him a burger. While he waited for his food, he ran back to where Aleesha chased the balloon. Kali joined him as Debra sat down at Jo's table, facing away from those at the table behind her.

'So, who's the guy?' Jo tipped her head towards Rahim as she studied the strained expression on Debra's face.

'Oh, that's my boss.'

'Really? Well, he keeps looking at you,' she whispered, leaning across the table.

'Don't be silly.' Debra tried to laugh it off.

'Nonetheless, what I would give to have a man look at me in such a way,' Jo said with a hint of sadness.

'I'm sure Gareth does.' Debra reached out to pat her hand.

'No. Unfortunately, he hasn't so much as looked at me in a long time.'

'Oh Jo, I'm sorry. I know what it's like to feel unwanted. I sometimes think Alex doesn't notice me. He lives in a world of his own.' When Debra looked at Jo, she seemed only a shadow of the woman she thought she knew.

'Really? I had no idea,' said Jo. 'It's sad that we allow ourselves to be defined by our men. Perhaps we need to remind ourselves of our own self-worth. Life goes on, and besides, there's Kali ...'

She looked towards the children playing at a nearby table.

'I agree. We should be giving ourselves the love we need. Is everything okay with Kali? She seems anxious at times.'

'She has witnessed certain things.' Jo returned her attention to the food on her plate.

'You mean Azri?' Debra pushed for more information.

But Jo turned sharply and scanned her face. 'What about Azri?'

'Did Kali mention what he buried in the garden?' Debra quickly backtracked.

Jo looked relieved. 'Oh that. Gareth says it's something from his uncle.'

'Ah, here come the children.' Debra swallowed the last of her drink. She would like to ask Jo more about Azri's uncle. However, she suspected Jo knew little about his affairs. Besides it was Kali's birthday. A time for celebration.

***

For each of Sam's birthday parties Alex had chosen a theme, and enjoyed getting the kids involved in the action. When Sam was younger, Alex had floated inflatable sharks in their swimming pool until one little girl cried for hours and the sharks had to be quickly removed. Another time, Alex placed concrete crocodiles by the fishpond as part of a jungle theme. That year the kids were not convinced they were real. Two unsupervised boys pushed the heavy crocodiles into the pond causing mass carnage of their fish stock.

Six months had now passed since they'd arrived in Brunei, and Sam was about to turn four. Alex stated adamantly that this year it would be a pirate's party, complete with a slippery plank balanced across the swimming pool, but Debra suggested the kids were too young. Instead, she decorated a cake as a pirate's chest, adding gold chocolate coins with liquorice logs. From an old shirt she fashioned a fancy costume complete with eye patch, and placed a toy parrot on Sam's shoulder. Alex organised his own costume. They invited a few of Sam's friends, including Kali, to help him celebrate. Debra buried a small plastic treasure chest of coins in the garden.

After the children helped Sam open his presents, they played 'pass the parcel'; Alex erected a few rope swings in the mango tree and helped each child swing from one branch to another while Debra prepared party food. Eventually, Alex, wearing an eye patch, a pirate's hat trimmed in skull and crossbones, and carrying a shovel, poked his head in the door.

'Where did you bury the treasure?' he asked.

Debra pointed towards the mango tree by the McKenzie's fence, so Alex walked towards what looked like a freshly dug patch along the fence. After preparing the last of the party food Debra went out to help him. As she skipped across the lawn towards the neighbour's fence, Alex wrestled with a large wooden crate that he had levered out of the ground.

'No, that's not it,' she yelled, pointing to the nearer side of the mango tree. 'It's over there.' But Alex was already prising open the lid of the crate he had unearthed. Nothing could stop him.

She tried again. 'No, near the tree ....'

The colour drained from Alex's face as he peered at the contents of the crate. From where Debra stood, rooted to the spot, she glimpsed, not coins, but bank notes, a crate full of them. He looked at her in disbelief, lost for words. Aware of the children eagerly awaiting their treasure, she sprinted over to where she'd buried the small plastic treasure chest in the long grass by the fence; dug it out with her hands as she called the children to gather around. After steering them inside the house, she let each child dive their hands into the small plastic chest. Expressions of delight accompanied each shout of glee as another eager hand pulled out a handful of money or a few chocolate coins.

Alex came back inside the house, sweating profusely. 'I've re-buried it in the same spot. Where do you think it came from?'

As the children ate their party cakes and sandwiches, Debra nodded in the direction of the neighbour's house. 'Azri,' she whispered.

'What are we going to do about it?'

'We'll figure something out later. Let's get these kids fed first.'

Once the children finished their party food and all the party games had been played, Debra sighed with relief as she waved them goodbye.

Hidden Treasures

Hundreds have looked for you,
and died searching in this garden,
where you hide behind the scenes
But this pain is not for those who come as lovers
You are easy to find here
You are in the breeze and in this river of wine

Rumi

The party over, Alex and Debra sat down to relax with a quiet drink, but their thoughts remained on the crate full of money. It was like an elephant in the room, obvious to most yet no one wanting to mention it. They looked out past the rows of pineapples to the mango tree near the neighbour's fence.

'Jo said the crate was something from Azri's uncle,' Debra said, fetching a platter of crackers and dip and placing it on the small table beside Alex.

'Who in the hell is Azri's uncle … and who buries money in the garden?' Alex dipped two crackers into the French onion dip.

'I guess people who have something to hide. According to Lena, Azri was at Labuan with the guys who arranged her husband's visa. Perhaps taking bribes is more lucrative than we think.' She grabbed the bottle of wine from the fridge and refilled their glasses.

'Maybe we are best to keep out of it. Hopefully he'll move the crate somewhere else. If not, I will be having a word to Gareth.' Alex took another sip of wine.

Eager to steer the conversation towards happier times and away from events outside their control, Debra nodded. 'I'm pleased you're taking such an interest in Sam's birthdays, and all his special milestones.'

'I wasn't close to my dad.' Alex's disclosure surprised her as he hadn't done that before. 'I vowed I would be a better dad with my own son, and don't want Sam to suffer the way I did. Despite the many hours I spent helping him in the shed, there were days when we hardly spoke at all. I thought our time spent together would bring us closer, but it didn't. It only created more tension as Dad preferred to be alone.'

'Your mum often said when your dad came back from the war, he was never the same, but she didn't tell me why.'

'Mum made excuses for Dad because of the war but she let him discipline me, and boy was he tough! He wanted to make a man out of me when all I wanted was to be a kid. I dreaded the many times he took out the strap. There were times when I hated him.' Alex ran his forefinger around the base of the stem of his glass.

'You never told me about your childhood.' She looked more closely at this new image of Alex, viewing him in a different light.

'No, I found it hard to talk about. It was shameful. He was a real bully at times. If I didn't eat my vegetables, he would bring me Kip's bowl and tell me to eat the dog's food. I was about Sam's age. Poor old Kip would sit at my feet, looking confused. He didn't care about his food, he just licked my feet, letting me know he was on my side.' Alex took off his glasses, rubbed his eyes.

'How awful for you. It makes you wonder about the depravities men faced during the war. Your mum said that your dad's first letters were eloquent and full of hope. It was the only contact he had with the outside world. But then his letters became dark and depressing, with insufficient words to express the horrors of war.' She walked over behind Alex's chair and placed her hands on his shoulders. 'My father was also affected by the war.'

'I think they all were. Dad told me to appreciate my life.' He rubbed his glasses on his shirt then placed them back on his nose. 'I can't imagine what he experienced but it certainly turned him into an angry old bastard. He took his anger out on me. As a kid, I never understood why. Although I now have a better understanding, it's hard to forgive him.'

'I'm sure they wanted to love us, but their demons got in the way. They were mere pawns in someone else's war, just following orders. Only kids when they were called up to fight, to build airstrips or railways in faraway lands.' She massaged Alex's shoulders; stroked his arms. 'We're fortunate we can choose the life we want. Our fathers didn't have that choice. Their overriding instinct was always survival at any cost.'

'Nevertheless, I was only a kid. When I tried to win Dad's approval, nothing impressed him. That's why I got away as soon as I could.'

'It's not surprising you didn't want to stay at home. I never knew life was so difficult for you. I'm glad you told me.' She moved in closer to kiss the top of his head. 'I'm sure Sam won't suffer the way you did. It's been a tiring day for us all. Let's go to bed.'

Next morning, Alex was woken by a phone call from an engineer telling him an apprentice had left a spanner in the engine casing. The engineer found it before it caused too much harm, but Alex needed to get to work early. Debra offered to make him breakfast, but he didn't want to eat. She cajoled him into sitting down long enough to drink his tea and eat a slice of toast. As she kissed him goodbye and gave him a hug, his shoulders stiffened and he pulled away.

When Debra arrived at work later that morning, she found a note in her pigeonhole. This time, it was in a sealed envelope. Her life of juggling relationships and balancing on the edge was becoming risky; people at the college might notice one tiny mistake, one careless movement. *But I'm not doing anything wrong. I am only sharing letters. But it might be misconstrued. Be careful. Be vigilant.* She popped the envelope into her briefcase; she would have to wait until she was alone before opening it.

> *Dear D*
>
> *I hope you were not embarrassed bumping into my family the other day. Seeing you in a different setting was strange and unexpected but thrilling all the same. I am sure it was an awkward moment for you. Later that day my daughter pointed to a picture of Olivia Newton-John in a magazine. She said, 'Look, Daddy, that's your girlfriend,' I'm sure I blushed even though it may have been a weird coincidence. I wondered if she was reading my thoughts. Mahani said, 'Debra seems like a very nice person' (and she is a good judge of character). She then blew me away when she added, 'Why don't you invite her around? I would like to see more of her.' Now, that is something I do not think I could handle right now.*
>
> *I just wanted to make sure you are okay.*
>
> *R.*

Driving home, Debra pondered over Rahim's words. Even if they hadn't done anything wrong, their relationship was becoming complicated. They were entangled in a net of impossible emotions that were proving too powerful to deny. To deal with her excess energy, she sat on her yoga mat to meditate for ten minutes. Then she lay down performing Yoga Nidra, focusing on each part of her body in rotation. She set herself an intention, a resolve of what she wanted to bring into her life; repeated it three times. For too long she'd been prepared to accept far less, allowing her needs to take second place. With this intention she wanted to acknowledge and bring about some necessary changes in her life. She deserved to be loved, respected, and she wanted so desperately to belong.

Reflecting on her current situation, she realised what they were now facing: despite the strictures that the local society, religion, and law imposed on them, they both had partners, and children they cared about. The thought of being locked up in a local prison without husband or child was too frightening to contemplate.

Trying to block out these terrifying images, she breathed in deeply, invoking guidance while surrounding herself in peace and love. Her peace on this occasion was short-lived as Jo arrived with Sam, having collected him from preschool, and wanted to discuss the latest social activities she was planning for the week. Decisions regarding Debra's future would have to wait.

Behind the Veils

Behind the veils
intoxicated with love,
I too dance the rhythm
of this moving world
I have lost my senses,
in this world of lovers.

Rumi

To celebrate the most auspicious, formal event of the year, the Sultan's Birthday, they were invited to the home of the British High Commissioner. Debra pulled out her best dress, a multi-hued silk that captured the light with flashes of scarlet one minute, burgundy the next; she fretted over the transparency of her bodice so draped a matching silk wrap around her shoulders. Alex swore as he tied his crimson bowtie for the third time and struggled with the upper button on his shirt.

Perched on a hilltop at a convenient bend in the road, the British Residency had extensive views of the river. As they approached, party lights twinkled around the garden where erected marquees were scattered on terraced lawns. Servants ushered them towards the High Commissioner and his wife who had positioned themselves under a large ceiling fan inside the entrance hall. Greeting those in the queue with the familiarity of old friends, they kissed each cheek European style.

As they waited in line, Debra clutched her Glo-mesh purse, agonising over what she should say. 'There are only three standard questions that anyone ever asks at these social functions,' Alex assured her. 'The first is, "What does your husband do?" The second, "Have you been on leave recently?" and the third, "Where are you planning your next leave?"'

'What about the wives?' Debra exclaimed in a hoarse whisper. 'Isn't anybody interested in what *we* do?'

'Shush!' Alex elbowed her, but she understood more clearly Jo's constant frustration. Women's work might be noticed but it wasn't taken seriously.

'It's lovely to meet some newcomers.' The High Commissioner extended his hand while his wife beamed at them and delivered her welcoming banter.

Emerging into the inner sanctum and the vast marble floor, Debra and Alex mingled with the crowd. White-jacketed waiters greeted them with trays of champagne glasses as white-gloved hands served platters of prawns, caviar, and smoked salmon canapés. Alex made a bee line for Jim Lyons to talk aircraft while Debra moved towards Jo, who was talking to a Brigadier with an unmissable walrus moustache.

'Oh yes, Toulouse. The weather will be perfect that time of year. You'll have a wonderful time.'

No doubting which question the Brigadier just asked Jo. From where she stood, Debra glimpsed Mike decked out in a white dinner jacket and black bow tie. If not for his beard, she wouldn't have recognised him. A waiter hovered around Mike, balancing a tray of punch glasses, a starched white napkin draped over the crook of one arm. Mike sculled several glasses in quick succession. A dark man stood facing Mike, similarly dressed in formal attire. Mike looked up and beckoned Debra to join him.

'Look who I've smuggled in.'

As the man turned to face Debra, he smiled, first with his eyes, then with his mouth, and her breath momentarily left her. Like a teenager, risking everything simply to see his face or savour the sound of his voice, she moved in closer and noticed tiny beads of sweat had gathered on Rahim's upper lip. She couldn't believe others did not hear the humming in her ears, the thumping in her chest.

'I … didn't know you were coming. I'm pleased you did.' She fiddled with her wrap, draping it tighter around each shoulder.

'I wasn't going to come but you know how forceful Mike can be. I feel like a fish out of water.'

'You'll be fine but whatever you do, don't let him drive you home.'

She looked to where Mike was taking another drink from the waiter's tray. Standing as close to Rahim as she dared, looking as disinterested as she could, she couldn't help fretting about the white starched collar rubbing against his tanned neck. She longed to take out her handkerchief and wipe the sweat above his lip.

'You look lovely,' he whispered.

'Thank you.' She looked around; noticed Alex glaring at her through the French doors. 'I think I'd better check on Alex. He doesn't look too pleased.'

'I'll see you later.'

As she reached Alex, he pulled at his bow tie and grumbled. A rotund Italian man joined them, and rambled on about the intricacies of the marble he'd supplied to build the Sultan's new palace. With rapid hand gestures, he described every proposed detail for the inlay. When Alex deigned to join in the conversation, he simply scoffed at the amount of money being spent. The Italian took his leave and Alex sought out a waiter for another drink.

Jo shrugged, shook her head and hurried out to the garden. Only a few minutes before she'd been talking to Rosa, Jim Lyon's wife, and was still fuming when Debra joined her.

'That woman assumes all women are stay at home housewives. There is another world out there for women who want to work. Doesn't anyone care about *my* career?' Jo threw her arms in the air.

'I can understand why you're upset. For what it's worth, I care about what you do. I think you're amazing. You're a lot smarter than most of the men here.'

But Jo continued her tirade. 'It's the role of those little women to make their men feel great. If they have careers, it will detract from the importance of their husband's. Anyway, we only came here to make an appearance. Why do we bother, Debra?'

'It's what the Brits like to do when they live overseas. We are the privileged guests. It's better than staying at home and never venturing afar. Speaking of Brits, here comes Mike.'

'Are you two women talking about me?' Mike slurred as he staggered towards them. Rahim, following closely behind, looked nervous. Before they could reply, a tall, elegant British woman approached their group and introduced herself as Jill Hislop, the wife of the Manager of the Hong Kong and Shanghai Bank.

'Wow!' exclaimed Mike, 'That's a long mouthful. I guess you get a lot of practice saying it though. I only need one word to describe myself. Teacher.'

'And what about you? What do you do?' The woman cleared her throat and stared from Mike to Rahim.

Before Rahim could reply, Mike interjected. 'Richard is a Harley Street specialist.' He slurred the last word. Then more discreetly behind his hand, he whispered, 'He's treating the Sultan, you know.'

His hand trembling, Rahim's dropped his canapé onto his shirt front. He coughed, then stammered, '… er have you been on leave recently?' He cringed while Mike tittered into his handkerchief.

'I've just been back to the old country. But it's so cold there. I'm always glad to come back here to the sun.' Jill Hislop's husband came to her rescue, steered her towards another group deep in conversation about houseboats in Kashmir.

Mike joined Jo for a cigarette, leaving Rahim and Debra alone once more. As she stepped back to create a respectable distance between them, her silk wrap snagged on the hedge. Rahim reached out to free it and rearranged it around her shoulders. It was the tiniest movement, the gentlest touch, an innocent gesture, but Debra looked up to see Alex scowling at her from the terrace.

She motioned for him to join them, but he turned towards the drink waiter and grabbed a glass of punch. After he sculled the first, he put the empty glass back on the tray before taking another. When he looked her way, she waved again for him to join them. But he moved in the opposite direction, bumping into the British High Commissioner's wife who tried to engage him in polite conversation. As Debra hurried over to rescue him, she heard her last question.

'Who is the dark-haired gentleman with your wife?'

'I've no idea who he is. Probably another teacher,' Alex slurred, pointing at Debra. 'My wife is a teacher, you know. You can always tell a teacher, but you can't tell them much.'

At that moment, Debra wished the marble flooring would crack open and swallow her and her drunken husband into the bowels of the earth. Smiling sweetly at the High Commissioner's wife, she gently steered Alex towards the nearest exit. It was time to leave.

But suddenly, the clouds opened up and crowds rushed in from outside as heavy rain lashed the windows. As usual with monsoonal storms, there was little warning as large raindrops flooded the potted palms and splashed onto the tiled courtyard.

'I'm sorry.' She mouthed the words, looking back to where Rahim stood alone, following her with his gaze.

By the time they left the party, it was raining incessantly. With this amount of rain, Debra felt wary about driving – it was difficult to tell where the road ended and the monsoon drains began. Rivers of mud gushed down the hill from houses balanced on slopes and puddles deepened in the dips in the road. Sliding on the slippery surface, their car repeatedly swerved from side to side. Even with the wipers on full speed, they couldn't cope with the worsening deluge. Unable to brake adequately, she greatly feared skidding into the gushing drains. Like a boat, their car pushed out a bow wave and Debra prayed continuously for the engine to keep going. Her feet shook on the pedals as Alex slurred and shouted apocalyptic warnings.

'I am trying to steer!' she shouted above the noise of drumming rain on the roof and the whoosh of the wipers. 'But the current is too strong.' The volume of water kept pushing them off course and the level was now up to their doors. It seeped in under her feet, wetting her shoes.

Suddenly the car nosed down into deeper water, submerging the headlamps, plunging them momentarily into darkness. More water seeped into car, and Alec bellowed his displeasure. Accelerating, Debra ploughed on through it, praying, her hands trembling on the steering wheel. Manoeuvring blindly in the treacherous conditions was a living nightmare, her eyes wide open seeing it all. Finally, their house appeared, a beacon at the top of a rise. She breathed again; forced her jaw and shoulders to release their tension. As they glided up their steep driveway, a huge whoosh of water rushed under the back seat of the car and, when she opened the car door and climbed out, coloured plastic pieces of Sam's Lego floated across the floor mats. With her hands still shaking, her legs feeling rubbery and difficult to control, she teetered into the house.

Alex stumbled into the bedroom and fell on the bed fully dressed. Debra poured herself a brandy, wrapped her shaking hands around the glass and waited for the warm liquid to calm her nerves, to relax her trembling body.

***

Next morning, Alex surveyed the damage to the car before dragging his thumping head into work. While some of the water had dried out, a thin coating of mud extended above the car's headlamps. Reluctant to talk about the previous evening, Alex said he didn't remember Debra questioning him about his conversation with the High Commissioner's wife – perhaps he had also forgotten seeing her talking to Rahim.

Later, when she arrived at work, Mike and Rahim were on their third cup of coffee, their bleary eyes a testimony to the night's celebrations.

'Rahim, I'm sorry about last night. It's unlike Alex to get so drunk, especially in front of the High Commissioner's wife. I hope you weren't offended.'

'No, I am fine. I am just not used to drinking alcohol.' He ran his hand through his hair. 'I certainly drank more than I normally would.'

'I think someone may have spiked the punch as everyone was plastered, not just us,' Mike said.

'It was incredibly scary driving home on those flooded roads,' Debra admitted. 'Jo and Gareth had to abandon their car and wade through the water. How did you guys get home?'

'I don't remember. I was so drunk when we got into the car. Harry was helping me when I tripped on the kerb and fell into the flooded drain. He fell in on top of me.'

'Oh my God! You know what people say about those monsoon drains: "if you haven't already fallen in one, you're about to." I bet that sobered you up in a hurry.'

'Actually, I found the entire evening quite sobering.' Rahim handed her a cup of coffee.

'I guess we've been struck off the British high society list,' Debra said, smiling. 'There won't be any more invitations for us.'

Images of people behaving badly flashed before her eyes, like a movie played on fast forward.

'I don't give a toss. All that small talk and snobbery.' Mike lowered his eyes; peered down his nose.

'Well, you have to admit the food was amazing.' She remembered the delicious selection of hors d'oeuvre and appetizers artistically arranged on silver platters.

'It was a great opportunity for a piss-up. But then, life is too short to be serious.' Mike laughed and scratched at his beard. 'Isn't that why we all chose this decadent expat lifestyle? ... so, we could escape from the real world.'

'I guess so.' She recalled Alex's angry expression before they dashed from the party, making their hasty exit. Focusing on what Mike was saying, she pondered: *How does one escape from the real world? Is it possible to slip into a more enticing one? It's very tempting, but first you need to escape!*

A Drop in the Ocean

You are not a drop in the ocean.
You are the entire ocean, in a drop.

Rumi

Immersed in the lifestyle expected of expats, Alex had bought a jet boat to take them to one of the nearby islands, to meet up with Jo and Gareth. Since the Sultan's Birthday party, Alex had been moody, reluctant to talk. At the last minute he decided to launch their boat at the ramp in the centre of town instead of from the yacht club, the easier option. Clad only in brief shorts, T-shirt, and rubber thongs, Debra felt self-conscious of her inappropriate attire. Being Friday, crowds of Muslim men scurried to the nearby mosque.

According to Alex, launching was a simple procedure. He would slide the boat off the trailer from the ramp, then tow the trailer away while Debra held the boat's rope to prevent it crashing against the concrete sea wall.

With Sam reluctant to stay up on the wall, she lifted him onto her hip before descending the slimy green boat ramp. Clasping the rope tightly in one hand, she followed Alex's instructions, pushing the boat away each time it edged in closer to the concrete ramp. As a sudden rogue wave brought the boat in even closer, she stepped out onto the slippery slope to push it away when, without warning, her feet slipped from under her; she landed on her back with Sam sprawled on top of her.

Holding onto Sam and the rope, she tried to crawl up the precarious incline, but each new wave brought the boat perilously closer to them, the ebb dragging them further into the river. Out of nowhere, a hand appeared in front of her as an elderly Malay *haji,* appropriately dressed for the mosque, reached out his arm. He first helped Sam to safety then returned to assist Debra.

By this time, her bare legs and brief white shorts oozed green slime; her rubber thongs floated in the river, and blood poured from grazes on her elbows. Embarrassed by her flagrant state of undress, she thanked the kind man for his assistance. Then Alex returned. He leapt into the boat, turned on the engine and yelled at her to drop Sam into the boat two metres below. But no amount of coaxing would get the hysterical boy down off the sea wall, let alone into the boat. As Sam clung to Debra's legs, she had no choice but to jump from the high wall with him in her arms. Crash-landing into the stern, they hit the esky and crumpled in a bloody, slimy mess.

Attempting to steady the boat from the sudden impact, Alex yelled above the sound of the throbbing engine, 'You're not really a boatie, are you!'

'No, but you can't deny I'm a good sport.'

With her legs and elbows throbbing, her back bruised from the fall, she choked back tears. The throbbing engine drowned her voice but did nothing to quell her hurt or her anger. As she sat nursing her wounds, she questioned why she let herself be treated this way. But her silent tears were swept away, unnoticed in the wind and salty spray.

Jo, Gareth and Kali were waiting for them at the island in their tin boat – not one designed for water-skiing. Watching Gareth astern with the tiller in his hand, Debra imagined he thought he was steering the Titanic. Still licking her wounds, she insisted Jo take the next turn at skiing behind their jet boat. The engine idled while Alex waited for Jo to give the thumbs up. She fastened the skis to her feet, untangled the ski ropes, angled the nose tips up above the surface ready to launch up out of the water once the boat gained enough speed to tighten the rope. Zigzagging her way across the waves, she made it look easy.

Earlier, Gareth had attempted to do the same thing but after failing to lift his rear end out of the frothy swell, when they returned to shore, he'd raced on gangly legs for the privacy of nearby bushes. When he waddled out with water dripping from his clinging lifejacket, he announced he was going home. He'd had enough and there were things he needed to do at work. Jo and Kali stayed, without questioning Gareth's decision to leave.

After he left, Debra asked her, 'Does Gareth often go into work on his days off?'

'Just lately he's doing lots of strange things.' Then she hesitated and shook her head. 'I don't know what's going on.' After grabbing a cold beer from the esky, she sat on a log, pulled the ring tag on the can, and took a long swig then wiped the froth from her mouth. 'I get such a rush from being out there on the water.'

Alex insisted Debra show some interest by having a turn at skiing. But Jo warned her about exposing her open wounds. Debra wasn't sure if Jo was referring to exposure to salt water or more predatory elements lurking in the water. Finally, she succumbed to Alex's pressure and took a turn, but it ended abruptly when Sam tripped on a rock and grazed his knees. His cries carried to her across the water.

Then Jo steered the boat so Alex could have a turn, while Debra sat on a log with Sam. Like Jo, Alex relished every moment spent on the water; he loved to experiment with tricks on a single ski, skiing one-handed, twisting his body from side to side. As Alex helped Jo lift Kali onto the boat, they teased each another, and Jo responded by laughing, and touched his arm.

Debra wondered what Alex really wanted from his life. Was she the ideal wife for him or would he be happier with someone like Jo, who was adventurous and loved the outdoors? *Maybe he wants a fun person who can make him feel better about himself. Can anyone ever be content with someone who doesn't understand who they are? Perhaps I'll never know.*

After revealing their skiing prowess, Jo and Alex stepped out of the beached jetboat, their faces flushed with physical exhilaration. Debra prepared lunch, and lit a fire while Alex fashioned a portable grill from a sheet of wire mesh to barbecue their meat.

The Spit looked like a long sandy island but joined at one narrow end to the mainland. While never refreshing, the warm tropical waters were allegedly safe to swim in. The white, sandy beach surrounded by jungle provided a shady backdrop with mangrove roots creeping down to the water's edge. Ever vigilant of snakes and scorpions, Debra strung a hammock between two trees for Sam to stretch out in the shade, then went back to checking the fire and grilling chicken wings before laying them on a large metal plate balanced on a log.

On hearing a sharp cracking sound, she spun to see the branch above Sam's hammock snap and fall as a monkey leapt from it and swung to the ground. Several others followed until a large troop of monkeys hit the sand and rushed towards her. A ferocious alpha male bared his teeth as he moved in closer.

Glancing around, Debra grabbed the closest thing to her – a can of Pringles – and hurled it at him. Gathering it up, he ripped off the plastic lid, and tipped the tube of potato chips onto the sand. Immediately, hairy hands shoved handfuls of sandy crisps into screeching mouths.

Not content with the crisps, the alpha male leapt towards the chicken wings. Debra picked up the plate and hurled that as far away as she could, backing away as soon as it left her hand. Caught between the relative safety of the water and Sam, who was lying in the hammock, she yelled to Alex, who sprinted up the beach, followed closely by Jo.

Kali screamed, which woke Sam with a start. Debra raced forward and yanked him out of the hammock, and, without waiting for her pulse to stop thumping in her ears, started to run.

In her peripheral vision, she caught sight of something racing out of the mangrove, and stopped, then spun. Staggering back, her jaw dropped open. Darting from the tangled vegetation, a huge monitor lizard threw its head up and rapidly surveyed the scene then, gathering speed like a racehorse, charged towards the monkeys, pounding legs kicking up sand behind it. With a flickering tongue, a threatening hiss, it dashed past Debra and Sam. His mighty tail lashed sideways as it reared on hind legs, razor claws slashing at the snarling face of the largest monkey.

Its mighty tail lashed sideways as it reared on its hind legs, its razor claws slashing at the snarling face of the largest monkey. The alpha male screamed and, with blood gushing from his face, limped away, his clan following him, whimpering.

The victor feasted on the chicken wings, tossing them down like popcorn. All that was left was sandy soy sauce roasted in the embers of the dying fire. His appetite momentarily sated, the monitor sauntered back to the depths of the mangrove.

'I thought I'd seen it all, but that really takes the cake,' Jo said, slowly shaking her head.

'… or the chicken wings,' Alex laughed, enjoying his joke.

The 'Ski Better Juice' – a concoction of rum, lime, and grenadine syrup – helped calm their nerves, but Alex needed another swim. Jo ran in to join him and they frolicked in the waves while Debra cleared away the remains of their food, trying to avoid the animals returning. Numb with shock, she sat on the log cuddling Sam, waiting for her racing heart to slow. Kali sat next to her, gently stretching her arm around Debra's shoulders as she snuggled in closer.

'It's okay,' Debra said, glaring towards Alex and her friend. 'I'll protect you.'

A Tree Called Life

Here is the deepest secret nobody knows
(here is the root of the root and the bud of the bud
And the sky of the sky of a tree called life; which grows
higher than soul can hope, or mind can hide)
and this is the wonder that's keeping the stars apart
I carry your heart (I carry it in my heart)

E E Cummings

Early the next morning, Debra rolled out her yoga mat and slipped into Warrior Pose. She raised her arms above her head, but it seemed the warrior inside had surrendered her courage, exhausted her energy, and lost her resolve. While her grazed elbows stung from her fall the previous day, her aching back had borne the brunt of bruises. Reluctantly, she moved into Warrior Two, performing the routine, experiencing the strength in her arms, bent knee, firm legs; she tried to focus, to push aside thoughts of yesterday, to let go of her ego. She inhaled deeply, let it out slowly, did it again; she turned her head with a forward outstretched hand, and felt some of her inner strength returning as she re-connected with that tiny warrior within. No matter how fragile she felt at present, she worked at gathering her strength, gaining her power and, whatever happened, she wouldn't let anyone take it away from her.

Later that morning, she walked into the staffroom where Mike was once again bragging about the size of his koi. Rahim had introduced Mike to the delicate skill of breeding koi, and shown him how to maintain their ideal environment, yet Mike loved to take the credit. She walked across the kitchen to make a cup of coffee.

'Sam keeps asking where the fish have gone from the pond in our garden.' She pulled a face. 'I think they must have died.'

'Or perhaps they are hiding under the algae,' Mike smirked.

'There is a shop on the outskirts of town that sells accessories for ponds. I can take you there,' Rahim offered.

'That would be wonderful. Mike said I could have some of his fish, but I think he's reluctant to part with them.' She picked up her cup and leant against the bench, as Mike looked up long enough from reading the newspaper to acknowledge her comment.

'My prize koi must be well looked after. Plenty of TLC. Do you think you can handle that, Grainger?'

'Mike, I can handle anything.'

'Rahim is the pond keeper so he can choose one for you.' He hesitated before adding, 'Well maybe a few.' He returned to reading his newspaper.

Choosing a Friday when they were not teaching, Rahim and Debra visited the pond shop, which was more a garden centre that specialised in ponds and equipment, such as pumps, UV filters, skimmers, and lights. Rahim recommended several products that would eliminate all her algae problems.

They wandered around the garden admiring the spectacular displays of waterfalls and ponds, enjoying the tranquility. The sun shone in a brilliant blue sky, and all around the ponds were resplendent with golden fluorescent koi darting among white lotus blossoms. With no one else about, silence surrounded them and dragonflies skimmed across the water in flashes of red and blue.

'You're in the wrong business,' Debra teased Rahim. 'You should have been a salesman.' She looked down at the heavy bag of products she'd just purchased at his suggestion.

'You are very easy to please, Debra.' He smiled and looked upon her face. 'I love the way you tilt your head when I am explaining something to you … and the way your eyebrows hover – you look as if you are really interested.'

'That's because I find your voice soothing, Rahim. Hypnotic. You could probably sell me anything. But I would rather listen to you recite poetry than give instructions on how to eliminate algae.' She laughed lightly.

'Maybe one day I will recite poetry for you. Would you like a cold drink? We can sit at one of those tables over there.' He picked up the bag and pointed at a nearby café.

Debra looked at the cafe where two men sat at one of the outdoor tables. The pale, balding man wore a beige safari suit. The young man had dark hair streaked with blond. He wrapped his long, manicured fingers around the older man's hand. When the older man reached out to ruffle his hair, the youth giggled.

Rahim had started walking towards the table, and she had no choice but to follow him.

Azri was the first to react, smiling sheepishly before nodding at Gareth who followed his line of sight. Composing himself, the consummate actor, Gareth, looked from Debra to Rahim.

'Debra, my dear, how are you? What on earth are you doing here?'

'Buying products for our fish pond. Trying to get rid of the algae.' She pointed at the bag Rahim carried. 'This is my boss, Rahim.' Then, turning her gaze on the odd couple, she said, 'And this is Gareth, my neighbour and Azri, er … his gardener.'

Rahim extended his hand while Azri scanned Rahim's body with an air of familiarity.

'Would anyone like a drink?' Rahim tried to ease the awkward silence. Gareth graciously declined, and said they were leaving. While sitting, sipping their drinks, Rahim looked at the departing car. 'What's going on there?'

Debra shook her head slowly. 'Gareth might be thinking the same thing about us. I hope he doesn't tell Alex he's seen us.' She told Rahim about Lena's sighting of Azri at Labuan the day they were there, and her suspicions regarding his behaviour.

'I hope your neighbour knows what he is involved in. Especially if it is bribing immigration officials. That may have serious consequences for them both.' Rahim looked as if he was about to say more, then as an afterthought he added, 'I am taking Mahani to KL to visit her specialist again. You know she had polio as a child?'

'No, I didn't. I hope she gets good results.' She took a sip from her drink; swallowed too quickly. The icy water caught in her throat. 'Are you concerned?'

'No, not really. She is amazing the way she copes with the girls. I do not know where she gets her energy.' He leant back in his chair and gazed into the distance.

'You obviously care about her a great deal.' Debra scanned his face, looking for clues. *Why this sudden need to promote his wife? Why is he focusing on her positive qualities?*

'She has been like a sister to me. When I first went to live in Malaysia, she was kind to me when I knew no one else.' He fiddled with his straw, didn't look at her, as if this sudden disclosure was a sensitive topic for him. 'It was a lonely life before I met her. I have therefore always been protective of her.'

'Rahim, is there a reason why you're telling me this?' Panic rose in her chest, and she struggled to breathe. 'Is there something else you need to tell me?'

'No, I just wanted to share with you about Mahani. I do not want to keep anything from you.'

The afternoon had drifted away and, as they traced their steps past the pond, Debra mulled over whether she really wanted to know more. At this moment, she didn't want to share him or his thoughts with anyone else.

Large silvery koi darted among the reeds, fanning their translucent tails as a flash of gold followed creamy white. Placing his hands on her shoulders, Rahim turned her around to look at a larger koi.

'This silvery one will soon have offspring. Life goes on.' He made no effort to remove his hands. 'It is a shame this day must end. I have really enjoyed spending it with you.'

'Yes, it's been lovely. Thanks for bringing me here.'

She wanted to say more but the shop owner walked towards them. As they moved apart, the space between them felt heavy with their awkward farewell. *Is Rahim getting cold feet?* She pulled a book from her handbag and handed it to him, her note concealed within its pages. 'You might like to read this. It's a poet whose priority was always love. He had no doubts.'

'Thank you,' he said, gently fingering the cover of the book. 'Yes. One of the best love poets of his time. I shall enjoy re-discovering him.' He opened the book; unfolded the note.

Her latest note was an effort to share everything with him and she hoped he was happy to share his innermost feelings with her. She'd become addicted to reading his notes, absorbing each word, sensing his passion. The thrill of sharing such eloquent prose was something she didn't want to end. As he read her note, she scanned his face for confirmation – a glint in his eye or a sign of impending doom. She dreaded anything threatening the friendship she'd come to depend on. It was something she relished and was not ready to relinquish.

> *Dear R*
>
> *I hope you enjoy Cummings. Throughout my teens, I clung to the unwavering belief in romantic love. I longed to hear the passion of Cummings' words whispered in my ear. I, therefore, hoped that my father would have*

whispered similar terms of endearment to my mother.

When I asked Mum about love, she told me I would know it when I found it. By this, I hoped she meant it was such a momentous occurrence that the earth would move for me. The stars would burn brighter, the moon would shine its silvery beams directly onto me. I wanted to learn the intimate details of how she met my father and how they fell in love. With her dispassionate reply, my dreams of romance, like a shredded silken thread, floated away on the breeze. 'Love isn't everything,' she replied.

It wasn't enough to convince me to give up on love. I was determined to try harder, to seek further afield. When love was in short supply, poetry provided me with what was missing in my life.

From what I've learnt recently, I now understand there are many forms of love. From the Sufi poets, I've discovered divine love survives more than a lifetime and that which we seek will take us on a journey that never ends.

Mum preferred to practise selfless love, but I've learned that unless we love ourselves, it's difficult for us to love anyone else. It's only through love that we find inner peace.

PS   I think we need to find an alternative post box, somewhere away from prying eyes.

Regards

D.

She watched as he folded the note, placed it back in the book then held it up to his heart as he waved her goodbye. The sun chose this moment to peek out from behind the clouds, brightening everything in its path. The sky appeared bluer, the trees greener, her body lighter but a heaviness filled her heart as she dragged herself back to the car.

The Sun's Birthday

(I who have died am alive again today,
and this is the sun's birthday; this is the birth
day of life and of love and wings:
and of the gay great happening illimitably earth)

E E Cummings

Despite participating in many social activities, Debra couldn't shift the restlessness she felt. She turned to yoga to burn off excess energy and release her pent-up passion. She moved into an old faithful – Cobra Pose – which balanced the spinal nerves, and toned the female reproductive organs. As she lay face down on the mat, her bent elbows, her hands placed next to her shoulders, she lifted her head, chest and navel off the floor. She held the pose for as long as she could, slowly released the breath, and lowered her navel, chest and head to the floor.

This was something in her life she could achieve with an easy level of control, and she felt great. Stimulating yet calming, after several rounds she had redirected her energy and lifted her spirit. But it was only a temporary fix. There were deeper concerns outside her control, and she wasn't sure how to handle them.

Today was Sunday, the amah's day of rest. Debra drove Lena to the small catholic church on the hill, one of only two Christian churches in town. Most of the congregation gathered outside the church were young ex-pat Filipinas. Both churches relied on visiting priests from across the border to conduct their services as no priests resided in Brunei.

With Alex in Seattle looking to buy new aircraft from Boeing, Debra offered to take Sam and Kali to the Yacht Club for the afternoon so Jo could sail. She'd arranged to meet up with her after she finished her yacht race. Debra also hoped to pick up some sailing tips from watching Jo and the rest of the sailing crowd.

On the way to the yacht club, she stopped at the museum where she and Rahim had chosen a secret letterbox to hold their private messages. She imagined the several bronze cannons mounted on the museum wall were guarding the area below. But the cannons were now only for decoration. While exploring one day, they had discovered on one of the cannons part of a metal mounting had been worn away, creating a small opening beneath.

This space was now their personal repository. Debra squeezed her fingers into the concealed area, felt a rush of warmth course through her when a note tickled her fingertips. Easing it out, she quickly dropped it into her handbag, to read later in private.

At the yacht club, Debra parked under a shady grove of tall casuarinas; and followed the children as they jumped out of the car. A frenzy of activity awaited them as yachties dragged their brightly coloured dinghies towards the water. Some attached mainsails or jibs that flapped lazily in the gentle breeze; others slapped on sunscreen, or slipped on hats. At least one helmsman shouted instructions at their inexperienced crew.

She spotted Jo crawling around her Laser, making last-minute repairs to her well-worn vessel. Before Debra could wish her good luck, Jo swore and threw a broken cleat on the ground.

'That's it. I'll have to crew for someone else.' She raced towards the clubrooms looking for a suitable helm.

In a shady area under the clubrooms, the children played in the sand for a while before entering the water. Some of the club members had dug a deep narrow channel to make it easier to launch their boats and Debra waded out in it until the warm water reached her waist. She floated beside Kali and Sam as they played in a small canoe, with the gentle waves rocking the canoe and washing over her. When they'd had enough, they showered and moved upstairs to look at the dinner menu.

Crowds had gathered throughout the day and Debra chatted to friends, all the while her gaze casting around the room. There was only one person she hoped to glimpse but he didn't appear to be there. As she finished ordering fried rice for the children, Jo and Mike walked in, Jo laughing at Mike dripping puddles onto the slatted wooden floorboards.

She smiled, and asked the obvious question: 'Did you have a good sail?'

They answered in unison, 'Fantastic.'

Debra wanted to share their exuberance, to experience the same rush they got from being out there on the water. She envied Jo's lean fit body and her confident manner as she took off her wet captain's cap. Her hair was flattened, but she had a strong defiant air about her, a mix of rebellious pirate and competent captain.

'You look like you've been walking underwater, Mike.' Debra's smile widened.

'Well, it's better than walking on clouds. Have you come down to earth yet?' Mike's knee-length shorts were drenched, his rubber sailing boots squelching.

'I'm fine,' Debra quipped back.

'I think she looks great,' Jo said.

'I'm not disputing that,' Mike agreed and gave Debra a second glance before striding to the bar. 'It's the way she floats around in a dream state.'

While the children ate, Debra wandered out onto the balcony and leant on the railings; the last vestiges of sunlight sparkled across the water and the casuarinas near the entrance changed from greenish-grey to black. They reminded her of the large trees surrounding her home in Perth. Memories washed over her as vast as the natural bushland where they used to live.

A year had gone by since she'd left Australia, but the nostalgia resurfaced when she least expected it. Like the ghostly branches silhouetted against the fading light, her feelings of homesickness eventually disappeared. By the time Jo and Mike returned, the river had turned an inky black, and a huge magical moon extended its beams, connecting her to this new land, so full of hope and promise.

Choosing a table on the balcony, they collected their meals from the bar – beef rendang and satay chicken – and listened as the club's commodore announced the race results. Cheers went up all around when Mike and Jo placed first. As Mike attempted a mock bow, he knocked the table, spilling his drink. The crowd cheered more raucously. Then he raised his glass to Jo. 'To my expert crew,' he said.

'You're a real champ, Jo,' Debra shouted.

'And what about the person who steered the bleedin' boat?' Mike's mouth dropped open.

'You're not bad either.' Debra patted him on the back but her thoughts focused on what she wanted to ask. 'I thought Rahim was going to crew for you today.'

'Yes, he was,' Mike said, moving his chair closer, 'but he's still in KL with his family.'

Debra's fingers tightened on the glass at the mention of Rahim's family. She pictured him in his youth, playing sport at his prestigious public school. 'He used to sail in England, I believe.'

'Yeah, that's why he likes the laid-back lifestyle here. And it's better than living in KL.' Mike drank the last of his beer.

'Doesn't his father hold some prominent position in the Malaysian government?' She wanted to know so much more about Rahim's life, but quickly picked up on Mike's quizzical expression, asking, she presumed, 'Why do you want to know?'

'Yeah, he's the education minister …' Mike rose to head back to the bar but leant in closer and whispered, 'Dangerous liaisons, Ms De Bra. Stick with sailing in calm waters, not rough seas.'

Debra's cheeks flushed and she quickly turned her focus on the darkened water. Emerging like a shy lover, the moon, now high in the sky, revealed its full nakedness. She stared in awe but as she turned to share this amazing moment with Jo, she too had gone to join Mike at the bar.

A lover's moon, she muttered under her breath.

One Zen belief is that, when waves no longer rippled the water's surface, it finally reflected the moon. Another is that once lives become calm or unruffled, a similar awesome perspective is said to emerge. Rather than becoming clearer though, Debra's perceptions of life remained cloudy. She found peace with those she hardly knew, yet sometimes felt fractious with those she knew well. She wondered if Rahim experienced the same contradictions in his life. *Is he at peace or is he restless like me?*

In the light of that brilliant moon, she read his latest note.

> *Dear D*
>
> *Thanks for bringing me back to Cummings. I was first introduced to him at Leys College in England*
>
> *"I thank You God for most this amazing day   for the leaping greenly spirits of trees."*
>
> *No doubt it complied with the ethos of my public school which was to encourage its students to be grateful for the beauty of nature and the generosity of God. I then became interested in Cummings when I first went back to Malaysia. My favourite poem was always 'I Carry Your Heart'. I remember it brought me great comfort at a time when I needed it most. Unlike the "deepest secret nobody*

knows", my favourite page was marked with the imprint of a rose. Long after its petals had withered, a trace of its fragrance remained.

I believe some of Cummings' work was quite erotic. He first thrived in the daring world of the 1920s when poets began writing about sex as something enjoyable and beautiful. With his honest portrayal of physical love, he described in detail the feverish excitement of sensuous experience. Later, he also wrote on spiritual aspects of love. But it was his ability to touch people directly that I admired the most. So, thank you Cummings and thank you, Debra for sharing him with me.

It's only now that I appreciate the simple joys of life, the beauty of nature. I too believe that love is the secret to life. I hope you continue to follow the path of love the way a sunflower follows the sun.

PS   Let's keep using this post box. There are too many prying eyes at work.

Much Love

R.

She wiped away a tear, thinking of her mother who never knew the love of a man who could set her heart on fire with a few written words. Love isn't everything, she'd said. *Oh, Mum. Love is so much more. A certain look, the gentlest touch, a shared thought, a moment in time. The hope and longing of what is to come. The thought that you never knew love makes me sad.* As Debra read the poetry of Cummings, she could feel that love. When she read Rahim's words, she could imagine him there with her, soothing her with his voice.

Come to Me in Dreams

Yet come to me in dreams, that I may live
My very life again tho' cold in death:
Come back to me in dreams that I may give,
Pulse for pulse breath for breath:
Speak low, lean low,
As long ago, my love how long ago.

Christina Rossetti

Driving beside the high stone wall that separated the museum car park from the jungle below, Debra scanned the area, looking warily for anything suspicious. She parked a reasonable distance from a black car where a middle-aged Malay man sat reading a newspaper, and she picked up a pen to write her latest note, her fingers and heart excited to be sharing her thoughts with him. Her words flowed unhindered in an outflow of wild expression and vivid dreams.

Dearest R

Last night I dreamed I was swimming. Huge waves crashed over me but as I stroked towards the shore, I was dragged further out in the ocean. Sam, distressed, open-mouthed and speechless, stood on the shore before slowly disappearing into the distance. Behind me, your ghostly face and outstretched arms beckoned me into the sea. Mists of spuming sea spray frothed until I could see nothing more. Only blackness as a rogue wave caught me in its

*wake, sucked me into its eddy, and spun me faster until I
hit the ocean floor. I awoke coughing, spluttering, tasting
the saltwater in my mouth.*

*I feel as if I'm losing my mind. What's happening to
me?*

As always

D.

The words written, she climbed from the car as the Malay man looked up from his paper and turned his head towards her. Since the groping incident in the lift, she felt nervous about men who lurked or stared. She glanced further around … a stooped gardener in a large straw hat pulled weeds from a garden bed near the front entrance and a mother in a batik sarong ushered her two small sons out through the glass doors, neither probably much help to her if she needed it.

Their secret meeting place behind the museum sat close to the tombs of some of Brunei's oldest sultans, where well-maintained lawns sloped down to the banks of the Brunei River. Steep stone steps led to a solitary wooden bench concealed from the road by encroaching jungle that created a natural secluded shelter.

Rahim had told her the history of Brunei's famous ornate fifteenth-century bronze cannons – *Bedil,* he called them – which now concealed their billets-doux, penned in moments of longing and loss.

As she posted her letter into the depths of the cannon, her fingers touched what felt like paper. She pulled out several large brittle leaves before again contacting a carefully folded note. Prising it out quickly, she replaced it with her own note; cast a glance around to be sure no one lurked nearby and rushed to the car, eager to enjoy his latest letter. As she walked past the man in the parked black car, he gave her a slight nod before returning to his paper. *Has he been watching me? I'm sure I've seen him somewhere before.* Nevertheless, she stopped long enough to read Rahim's note.

My Dear Debra

Lately I've been having strange dreams. I dreamed of a woman with delicate fingers and long flowing hair who prised open my heart like a large flower, peeling it back petal by petal. Pain was shooting down my chest into my abdomen and groin. I was growing increasingly larger until finally my chest exploded. As each of the tiny petals floated on the breeze, they came together and created a man far greater than I could ever be. I could look over the clouds, catch the sun, hold it in my hands, feel its golden rays showering over me. Long delicate fingers were stroking my warm body as soft hair brushed over my skin. I grew at least ten feet tall. When I told my daughter, she said I would be too big to fit into this world. Her words seemed somehow prophetic. They unnerved me. Perhaps I'm going crazy. What do you think? Is it madness or is it simply love?

Love R.

Driving home, Debra reflected on the coincidence of their dreams. *Are we so enmeshed in each other's thoughts we are now sharing fantasies? More likely the stressors of our complicated lives are taking the same toll on us. Not unusual outcomes, I guess, for two people facing a world that has fought to keep us apart. Not surprising either that we have sought solace in the comfort of poets who understand such adversity.*

Debra called in at the Post Office, eager to check if any overseas parcels had arrived. She'd been awaiting some new poetry books she had recently ordered through a mail order catalogue service in Singapore. One was a book of poems, penned by a poet she was keen for Rahim to read – a Chilean poet and politician who'd recently won the Nobel Prize for literature. In his acceptance speech, he'd stated: *A poet is at the same time a force for solidarity and for solitude.* Described by another great Latin American writer, Federico Garcia Lorca, as *an authentic poet, of the kind whose bodily senses were shaped in a world that is not our own and that few people are able to perceive,* Debra simply had to read him; she couldn't wait to experience the longing and warm connection of this poet and read the love poems for which he was renowned.

She'd also ordered another book of Sufi poetry, and a video of the latest popular film, *Grease* for some lighter entertainment. Alex had become fed up with the restricted selection of programs and had one night roared, 'If I have to listen to another Quran reading, I'll scream!'

Deprived of the latest news and trends, she also felt cut off from the outside world; it was like being trapped in a bubble where time stood still, the real world outside nothing but a dream as she lived a fairy tale existence in this faraway Shangri-la.

When she handed over her card to collect the parcel from the post office, the young man serving her disappeared into a back room. When he returned with her parcel, two other men were with him. Jo had warned her that any books or videos brought into the country were subjected to strict censorship laws by the Religious Affairs Department. As the first young man ripped open her parcel with a knife, he handed the books and video to the other two men who took turns scrutinising them.

Debra cringed when she read Pablo Neruda's profile on the back of his book of poetry. As a member of the Communist Party in Chile, would they view his book as an example of Communist propaganda? The three men mumbled to each other as they passed the books from one to the other, and she began to fret about the book on Sufism. Would the Religious Affairs Department interpret this as deviationist Islam?

After much deliberation, they told her they needed more time to examine them. Her hands shook as she took back the card; felt scared by their threatening tone and worried what they might do. When Jo's friend sent her a novel for her birthday, the censors wasted no time in defacing the book, ripping the cover and several pages. It was only later when Jo discovered the remains of a nude woman on the cover, that she understood why they were angry. She said she was so embarrassed she didn't know where to look. Debra hoped they would not subject her to the same ordeal when she returned in two weeks' time.

Several weeks later, she collected the books and video. Despite being considered controversial topics in Brunei, the two books with references to Communism and Sufism remained unscathed. There were no obvious curled pages or blackened thumb prints. But the video cover of Grease was defaced by the tell-tale imprint of the censorship stamp. As the two younger censors handed it over the counter, they exchanged sly smirks. One of them looked Debra up and down before averting his eyes. Suppressing the urge to slap his face, she hurried outside, slid into her car and slammed the door, then exhaled slowly.

That evening as she watched the end of Grease, the music swelled to an anticipated crescendo and the graduating students at Rydell High launched into their lively dance routine. Sandy and Danny joined them, clad in their sexy black leather gear. Just as they were about to begin their raunchy dance, the film flickered, there was a deafening cut, and the dancers disappeared from the screen. Gone were the shared looks, the subtle gestures of love. Gone were the joyous moments of carefree youth. Gone was the shiny red sportscar taking Danny and Sandy to an exciting destination somewhere into the future.

A Love I Seemed to Lose

I love thee with the passion put to use
in my old griefs, and with my childhood's faith
I love thee with a love I seemed to lose

Elizabeth Barrett Browning

'So, who's won the Lottery?' Debra asked Jo as she pulled into her driveway in a shiny red BMW.

'Oh, Gareth thought it was about time we replaced the old Toyota. Azri's uncle knows someone who gave him a good deal.'

'Do you know much about this beneficent uncle? Have you met him?' Debra tried to stop her eyebrow from rising.

Jo shook her head. 'No.'

It was Tuesday night and Jo's turn to drive to the Hash, a special time to commiserate with each other, an opportunity to offload or offer support when needed.

'It might be slippery scrambling up those hills today,' Jo said, looking at the dark grey rain clouds gathering.

It wouldn't deter them though, as coming home covered in mud, and scratches from razor grass, was all par for the course. Debra admired the shiny new vehicle before stepping into the car. 'Are you sure you want to get it dirty?'

'We'll have to take off our muddy boots before driving home. And we can put towels on the seats. Hopefully, there won't be too many paddy fields. I don't relish sinking knee-deep in that mud. All those leeches, yuk!'

'Where's your sense of adventure? There's nothing that's

stumped us so far. I'm sure we can do it again,' Debra laughed, but she lingered over Jo's pale, tired expression.

'I'm looking forward to getting rid of some of my pent-up frustration. It's been a terrible week.'

'It's not like you to complain, Jo. Is it the pressure of work?'

Jo remained silent and when she spoke, her words were barely audible. 'No, it's Gareth. I've been going through all the possibilities … I think he might have another woman.'

'Oh, Jo.' When Debra looked closer at her friend, Jo's face appeared thinner, and dark circles marred the skin under her eyes.

Jo adjusted the seat position and the rear-view mirror, all the while Debra waiting for her to continue. Eventually Jo shrugged and took a deep breath. 'Recently Gareth's behaviour has changed, and he's been staying out late at night.' Jo's jaw tightened.

'Gareth's no longer interested in me. I feel as worthless as a discarded pet. While there hasn't been much intimacy between us since Kali was born, we've always been good friends. Now I feel invisible. Gareth spends a lot of time at Jim and Rosa Lyons' house, so I assume Rosa is his new interest.'

'That must be upsetting for you.' Debra reached out to pat Jo's shoulder. 'I, too, worry about Alex's behaviour at times.'

Despite having personally witnessed some of Gareth's odd behaviour, Debra had dared not mention it to Jo. 'I can tell you are worried, Jo. Sometimes when we're under stress, these things appear bigger than they really are. Can you talk to Gareth? Are you sure you're up to this run?'

'Yes, you're probably right. I might be overreacting. Let's enjoy our run.'

Jo cleared her throat, and they made their way into the jungle.

After clambering up the first hill, Jo ran on ahead with the front runners. A river crossing via a slippery log challenged many of the women. One woman in an oversized T-shirt adamantly refused to cross the log, which held up the line of runners. Debra offered to squeeze in front to help pull her across. Finally, she agreed, and Debra leapt across the remaining gap to the riverbank on the other side. As she reached out for the woman's hand, she looked in the murky depths below, searching for water snakes. She stretched as far as she could and, as the woman's hash boots touched the far side of the bank, the women cheered.

As Jo had predicted, the run consisted of wet ground, with slippery climbs up steep hills and, on the far side of a hill, a clump of thorn trees. The front runners had the foresight to attach coloured paper to the sharp protruding thorns. But they failed to alert the back runners of leeches, which sucked onto their legs as they waded through a disused paddy field. As they plunged up to their thighs in oozing mud, the women ahead shrieked as they whacked at their legs.

Debra expected to find Jo waiting for her but when she arrived at the drink bin, she couldn't find her. Standing in shorts covered in mud and a drenched T-shirt, she sculled a can of 7Up.

'Has anyone seen Jo?' she called out.

'She stormed off after a heated conversation with another woman,' one of the women replied.

'What? What happened?' Debra became worried.

'Jo overheard someone saying they saw Gareth embracing a young Malay man. I thought everyone knew,' the woman replied defensively.

Yes, everyone except Jo.

Stranded by Jo's sudden leaving, Debra begged a lift home with a woman who was ready to leave. When she arrived home, she raced over to Jo's house but found it in darkness. The door, however, was unlocked, and Debra walked into the large living area.

'Jo?' she called out, but her voice bounced off the walls.

Then came the tiniest sound, like an animal whimpering. She found Jo sitting on the floor with her arms crossed, clutching her bent knees, rocking back and forth. Strong, confident Jo who could tackle anything, her comforter, her rock, had disappeared into a dark, deserted corner. Debra sat down and hugged her, and they remained that way, entangled in her pain, still wearing their muddy hash clothes. Finally, Debra helped her to shower and change into dry, clean clothes. She made her a cup of tea and several slices of toast.

Next day, she made a prawn curry and took it across to Jo.

As she opened the side gate, Jo stood by the front door, electric drill in hand. She had lengths of timber, which she had measured and pre-cut, and was now inserting screws into what appeared would be a set of shelves. *Hard to believe this is the same woman from last night,* although her puffy eyes suggested she'd not slept well.

After deftly attaching the shelves to the wall, Jo arranged the diving equipment into each customised shelf, trying to find order in the unexpected chaos of her life. There was a compartment for the fins, masks, and a larger area for oxygen tanks. She had considered every tiny detail. As Jo turned to pick up another tank, Debra could see her pyjama shirt buttons didn't line up with their holes and her pants were inside out.

'I was sick of all this mess.' Jo swept her arm in an arc. 'I had to do something to sort it out. Nobody else was going to do it.'

Debra placed the curry on the kitchen bench. 'The shelves are now looking great. It's probably a good time to have a rest.'

'I keep asking myself, apart from the sex, what does he have in common with that gardener?' She placed the drill on the ground.

'Perhaps it's the freedom – to be accepted for who he is. Not all relationships provide us with everything we need.' Debra sat next to her friend on the front step.

'But he never told me about his special needs.'

'He may have feared rejection. If he's kept his secret all these years, I guess it's harder to disclose now. Some people like to conceal their real identity. They feel safer that way. But we don't ever get to know who they really are.'

Debra passed Jo the bag of nails, and she took out two to hammer into the shelf. 'We came to Brunei because Gareth wanted to get away from my ex-husband, and my child from a previous marriage. He wanted to make a clean break from past relationships … found them too complicated to handle.'

'My God! What about this mess? Too hard to handle? It couldn't get any more complicated than this! How am I supposed to cope with everything now?'

'It's not going to be easy. But you weren't to know. Don't be too tough on yourself.'

'You know I liked that Gareth always bought me sexy underwear. I now wonder who's been wearing them. I feel as if he has disassembled that which I gave freely and discarded it as worthless.'

'You're still the same woman, Jo, worthy of love and respect. Remember what you told me? We can't let the men in our lives define who we are. We deserve the best in life, the same opportunities as them.' Debra rested her hand on Jo's shoulder. 'Let's go and have some lunch.'

'I just don't want to be alone again. I've been through it all before.' Jo threw down the hammer and stood gazing into the distance.

'I can understand that. It can't be easy for you, Jo.'

While Debra had never feared being totally alone, she had often experienced overwhelming loneliness.

The Edge of the World

Today our bodies became vast
they grew to the edge of the world
and rolled melting into a single drop
of wax or meteor.

Pablo Neruda

As Alex was in Munich negotiating a deal with Lufthansa, Debra asked Jo to help with preparations for Mike's party. While Jo hung the last of the paper lanterns around the garden, Debra busied herself blowing up balloons, attaching them to the latticed pergola. With Sam's help, every second balloon escaped onto the unforgiving thorns of the bougainvillea. Mike had insisted on hosting the party at his house before he left to spend several months in the UK with his wife and family.

While Debra shelled the prawns, Sam amused himself with one of the discarded tails; he didn't like to think the prawn was dead, so treated it with the respect he gave to most small creatures. Since he'd been old enough to explore, Sam had been fascinated with lizards, spiders, and beetles. Debra feared he would pick up scorpions from underneath potted plants or the venomous green snakes that sometimes slithered into the house unnoticed. He now stroked the hard shell of the discarded prawn tail, his large blue eyes totally focused.

Next, Jo prepared vol au vents in Mike's kitchen, while Debra arranged prawns on a slice of cucumber before placing them on a platter. Mike stood next to her mixing his "innocuous punch".

Judging by the many bottles of spirits he poured into the bowl Debra warned herself to avoid it at all costs. It looked and tasted potent.

'How many people are you expecting tonight?' she asked. 'Have you invited everyone from the college?' She chopped a pineapple in half; scooped out the flesh from one of the halves.

'I think most people from our department will come. Harry wasn't going to come but he changed his mind when he knew you were coming.'

He paused from mixing the punch to search her face for any sign of reaction.

'We are only good friends you know.' She laughed. 'We have a lot in common, our love of poetry. We exchange ideas through our writing. We're just good mates.'

As she cubed the pineapple and threw the pieces into a bowl ready to place onto cocktail sticks, she checked her tumbling emotions, unsure if she was ready to disclose them yet. Nor had she sorted them into any logical order.

'Well, I don't want my two good mates to get hurt. You be careful, Debra. It's a perilous path you're treading. You don't want to step on anyone's toes.' His eyes fixed on her and his brows knitted in a frown. 'I know you think I'm a hypocrite, having fun while my wife is away, but it's different for me. Mine are only one-night stands.'

'Our connection is purely platonic. It's spiritual, of the mind. Besides, I'm a big girl. I can look after myself.'

While she listened to the conviction of her words, her stomach tightened with indecision.

'I think what you have is different. Something deeper, more dangerous. I've noticed the way he looks at you. The chemistry between you is palpable.'

'I can handle myself.' As she mixed a curry dip to place inside the scooped-out pineapple, she shrugged to shake off the guilt.

'Are you really aware of the possible danger?' he muttered to himself as he emptied bags of ice into the esky.

Somehow the last of the cocktail onions found their way onto toothpicks with the pineapple. She hid her fluster, grabbed Sam's hand, and exited via the kitchen.

Later as she washed Sam's hands, one tightly clasped fist still held the prawn tail. She gently pried away his clenched fingers.

'It'll be okay, Sam. You can wrap it in a tissue if you like.' Only a few weeks earlier he'd walked around holding onto a dead cicak, so upset the gecko had lost its tail, squashed in the glass sliding door. Despite its bloodied missing tail, he'd carried it around all day.

After reading him a bedtime story, she showered, pulled on a comfortable jumpsuit but then spied the lime green dress. Failing to impress Alex on her first attempt at a romantic reunion, it was a shame to waste such a lovely outfit. She brushed her curls, traced her lips with a lipstick, and looked at her reflection in the mirror. If Alex was there, she'd ask him how she looked. He would answer predictably and automatically. 'You look fine.'

Grabbing her purse and car keys, she drove back to Mike's house. From the many cars parked along the street, it looked like being a large party. A familiar white Fiat parked under a tree sent her heart racing. As she entered through the garden gate, Mike who stood nearby, gave her a hug.

'My God, Ms De Bra, you look stunning. I thought you were bringing Jo along.' He thrust a glass in her hand.

'She's coming later.' She tested the drink, swilling it in her mouth. 'Is this your innocuous punch? It's rather strong.'

'Oh, go on. One won't hurt you.' He ladled a few extra pieces of fruit into her glass.

'Easy now, I'm pacing myself so I can drive home.'

'Your good mate is over there. Some of the paper lanterns have fallen so he's stringing them around the frangipani tree.' He pointed to the far corner of the garden to where lanterns dimly lit the pond. The heavy scent of frangipani and sandalwood mosquito coils drifted on the sultry night air as she moved towards the pond, Rahim watching her as she ducked under the bougainvillea. She bent to push a white balloon out of the way, conscious of her short skirt and revealing neckline. A strange shyness crept over her as she brushed down her skirt like a nervous teenager.

He remained by the fishpond. 'Mike is right. You do look stunning,' he said as she drew near.

Debra laughed, embarrassed by his compliment, then demurred. 'We make a good match.' She pointed to his lime green body shirt.

'I do not normally wear this shirt.'

'Mike mentioned one of your girls is sick. Is she all right?' She reached out to balance her glass on the edge of the fishpond.

'Yes, Aleesha has been throwing up all day. Mahani has stayed home with her, so I will not stay long. I just wanted to make an appearance for Mike's sake. It is certainly going to be quieter at work without him. He has asked me to house-sit while he is on leave. He wants to ensure his koi get plenty of attention. Mahani is going back to KL for a couple of weeks, so I will stay at Mike's place then.'

Rahim leant one hand against the tree; the other contained an identical punch glass of the same potent mix.

'He's always bragging about those fish. What would he do without your help?' Debra leaned in, peering at the koi in the pond.

Rahim also moved in closer. She turned, and her balanced glass tipped over the edge. He reached out to grab it and his arm moved around her waist. They hadn't been this close in a while, yet she remembered the warm tingling sensation as he touched her skin. Up close, she could smell his aftershave, a hint of citrus and musk. Not overpowering but evocative. Like her pent-up emotions. It lingered in the tropical night air.

'That was lucky,' she gasped as he caught her glass.

'It is the koi,' he said. 'They are said to bring good fortune to those who witness their gentle nature. You will have to come round here when Mike is away. I will choose some young ones for you to put in your pond.'

'Thanks, I'd like that.' She peered into the splashing water, at the flash of gold and silver. 'I believe the Japanese view them as a symbol of friendship and love.'

'You are right. There are many cultural beliefs associated with koi. As they swim upstream, their perseverance is likened to that of brave Samurai. If they are caught, it is said to be like facing the sword of the warrior. By lying still, they can accept death with courage.'

'Such sad options for those who bring joy to others. It sounds like they are doomed whatever option they choose.' Debra wished there were more positive alternatives for those who chose to swim against the current. She looked over to where Mike was stringing up a disco ball. Prisms of light flashed across the dance floor. 'I think we'd better join the party or Mike will come looking for us.'

When they entered the house, the party was in full swing, everyone dancing to Dire Straits' *Sultans of Swing*, the beat bouncing off the walls. Jo made her entrance, clapping, her arms thrust upwards, her head thrown back, totally at ease; she revelled in her own rhythm, gyrating as she thrust her elbows out to the sides. Gareth was nowhere to be seen.

'Let's get this party moving!' Mike cranked up the speakers as *Saturday Night Fever* blasted across the floor. He called everyone to line up for the Brooklyn shuffle. A poor imitation of John Travolta, he thrust one arm in the air, pointing, duplicating the star's moves. Jo rubbed up against him, bumped each hip against his. As they shimmied across the dance floor, Jo whispered something in his ear, and they laughed.

Grabbing Rahim's hand, Debra pulled him onto the dance floor, and they also laughed as they fumbled their way through the provocative disco moves. The energy between them became electric as they attempted pelvic thrusts and elbow rolls, both caught up in the rhythm of the music which flowed through their bodies. For a moment, Debra forgot where she was. Then slowly she became aware of her work colleagues watching her. Sweat dripped down her spine, gathered under her breasts. With her energy spent, she longed for fresh air, and moved towards the garden.

Someone had started a Conga line which snaked its way around the garden beds. Mike reached out and pulled Debra in front of him as they kicked and twisted down the line. Being at the front, Debra veered towards Rahim, standing alone, and pulled him in front of her; she wrapped her arms around his waist, sensing every move he made. They made a figure eight around the fishpond, inviting those at the back to follow. She leaned in closer, hoping Rahim could feel her breath on the back of his neck. She revelled in the silky texture of his shirt under her fingers as she snuggled around the curve of his back.

By the time they'd snaked around the room, out the door, across the courtyard and past the fishpond again, the line collapsed in a heap. Reluctantly, she let go of him but not before breathing in the musky warm saltiness of his skin. As they ducked under the large frangipani, Rahim plucked a fragrant blossom, placed the frangipani in her palm and closed her fingers around it.

'Thanks, it's my favourite.' She lifted it to inhale the heady scent.

'I remember.'

According to Rahim, while westerners tended to admire the

fragrant tree and planted it in their gardens, many Asians viewed it as unlucky. The Chinese cemetery in town was full of frangipanis, planted there in the hope the fragrant blossoms would appease the spirits. Debra walked over to where Jo leant against the bar. Jo stared at her, silently questioning.

'It's only a flower.' Debra opened her palm.

'No, it's a token of love.' Sad lines transformed Jo's once happy face.

Like all their precious moments together, time became the enemy: Rahim needed to go home to his family. He'd already stayed much longer than he'd planned and headed towards the gate.

Moving into the shadows, Debra pulled a book from her handbag, and handed him the promised poetry, along with her concealed note written in green ink.

Dearest Rahim

Thanks for sharing your dream. Perhaps you're afraid that if you dare to dream too much, you will get more than you bargained for, that you would no longer fit into your own skin, let alone your existing world. Your daughter senses your fear.

Maybe it's a positive sign. You have been chasing the sun for so long. Now you're about to look over the clouds to catch it, hold it in your hands, feel its golden rays showering over you. I hope so. You deserve happiness.

I recently discovered this poem of Pablo Neruda, 'The Eighth of September'. I hope you enjoy his poetry. A Chilean politician, he wrote under this pseudonym to avoid his father's disapproval. While known for his erotic love poems, he is also known for his love of humanity. It is said he often wrote his poems in green ink, to symbolize that hope was often present even in his darkest moments.

As I read this poem, it reminded me of the dream I told you about where a rogue wave caught me in its wake, sucking me into its eddy, churning, pulling me down deeper and deeper. It was uncanny.

As you dream of growing larger, perhaps you too are subconsciously channelling Pablo! Maybe our bodies are becoming so vast they will grow to the edge of the world. If you think you are going mad, then I'm going mad with you.

Much Love

D. XX

As he walked through the gate, lit by the overhead lantern, he held the book close to his heart, then turned and waved.

Sniffing the Twilight

And I pace around hungry, sniffing the twilight,
hunting for you, for your hot heart,
Like a puma in the barrens of Quitratue.

Pablo Neruda

When Debra arrived at the college on Monday morning and pulled into a parking bay, she looked up to see Rahim parking his car next to hers. Rain bucketed down, and he offered her his umbrella and his endearing smile as he climbed from the car, which set her pulse racing. As she squeezed in closer, she sensed the familiarity of his body as she stumbled on the wet surface. He took the note she slipped into his hand without reacting and they made small talk about Mike's party. It felt strange – after such an enjoyable evening, how could she simply return to the strictures of everyday life. She'd been consoling herself with the words of an erudite poet who inspired her to write her latest note since that evening.

> *Dearest M-H*
>
> *It was great talking to you last night. I like the nickname you said your mother gave you. "Matahari", her sun. I'm sure she worshipped you too. I also like the nickname you gave me, "Mimpi". I hope I'm the realisation of the "dream" you've been waiting for all your life.*
>
> *I've just finished reading the evocative words of Pablo Neruda and I'm filled with longing. I can't wait for you*

to read his 'Sonnet XI' and tell me what you think. I don't believe I should be prowling the streets like a puma in this state of mind. I feel so restless yet so alive, aware of everything around me. The colours are brighter somehow, the smells stronger, sounds are clearer. Perhaps I really am losing my mind or just simply hunting "for your hot heart".

Much Love

Mimpi

Debra tried to focus on the day's lessons and her students' upcoming exams; she wanted to ensure the students were well-equipped with plenty of work for revision. As she walked past Rahim's office, she glanced in through his partly opened door. He stood, leaning against his desk, in deep conversation with Mike. She could only surmise Mike was giving Rahim similar warnings to those he'd offered her the night before. She lingered, listening, hoping to learn more of Rahim's feelings for her.

'Think about what you would have to give up ... your job, your family. I know she's a great woman, but she's strictly off-limits, mate. She's like a rare gem, to be admired but not touched.' A slight pause followed.

Then Rahim replied, 'But she is the most precious gem. I do not want to lose her. She brightens my life in a way that makes me feel whole again.'

A shiver ran up her spine. *We feel the same way.* Feeling jittery inside, she walked silently to her desk and tried to concentrate on marking student papers. She shuffled through assessments without reading them, flicked through them again, and tried to make sense of her pile but found it difficult to settle. Mike finally greeted her as he sat at his desk then he buried his head in a newspaper. She thanked him for a fabulous party, surprised he'd come into work when he was flying to the UK that evening.

'I wasn't going to come in, but I have some paperwork to

finish off. You might want to read this Aussie newspaper when I've finished.' He smoothed out the page before folding it back. 'It looks as though Imran Khan is doing well in the Sydney test. He led his side to an easy eight-wicket third test win.'

'Life's not just about cricket, Mike. I have more important things on my mind. Like getting this marking finished.' She watched Mike reading his newspaper, his feet resting on a pile of books under his desk.

'Maybe this article might interest you.' He pointed to another page. 'It's a book review about feminism. *The Female Eunuch*. Apparently, it's a bestseller.'

'Now, that's something I would like to read. Women deserve the same conditions and respect as you guys. Yet we need to work harder to get them. Why is that, Mike?'

'I love it when you get riled. Shall we start calling you Germaine? It has a nice ring to it. Germaine Grainger.'

'I'm happy to follow someone like Germaine Greer who's fighting for women's voices to be heard. I'm glad there's someone out there who cares about our freedom, our choices in life. If we try to show any leadership, there's usually a man who wants to crush us, and take away our power … … sorry, I'm not really in the mood for humour today.' She rubbed her forehead, pressing away the tension.

'Wow, what's got you fired up? You're normally so passive. Life is too short to be serious, Grainger.' He laughed as he stood, stretched out his long arms, barely inches from touching the ceiling fan.

'Sorry. I have one helluva headache. I'm blaming your potent punch from the party last night. I just want all my students to pass with good grades.'

'Believe me, there is no doubt about that. They will all pass. That is outside your control.'

She grabbed her papers and headed for class, pondering over

what Mike had just said. The greyness of the day added to the heaviness of her mood. Her head throbbed and Zaharia, one of her brightest students, complained of dizziness, so she accompanied her to the sick room. As Debra turned into the corridor, she almost collided with a dark thickset man who she'd noticed previously walking around the college. With an air of officialdom, he glared down his nose at her, his expression far from friendly.

'What are you doing here?' He flashed his gold-filled teeth in a sardonic grin. His hands shimmered with gold rings and a sparkling wristwatch graced his arm, but his eyes lacked lustre.

'I'm a teacher here. Debra Grainger.' She extended her hand, but he declined to accept it; averted his gaze in a dismissive gesture. She withdrew her hand and pointed to the sick room where she'd just left Zaharia. 'One of my students is not feeling well.'

'You should not be here.' He strode off without introducing himself. The insult hit her like a slap on the face. She wanted to cry but wouldn't give him the satisfaction of seeing her crumble.

If only Rahim was here. I could ask who this strange man is. Have I accidentally encroached on his private office space? Or does he consider I am taking a job that could be filled by a local?

Zaharia told her later he was Muhammad Osman, the director of the college.

By the end of the last lesson, Debra looked forward to going home. Rain still pelted down, and dark ominous clouds filled the sky. Bright forks of lightning chased thunderclaps, almost catching their resounding booms across the sky. She followed the last of the students out through the decorative iron gates and rushed to the carpark. A group of male students huddled together; one pointed at her car as they whispered amongst each other. She assumed her new Subaru wagon with its shiny silver paintwork impressed them.

Torrential rain had already flooded the monsoon drains by the time she drove out onto the road. A crack of thunder split the sky, and a metallic knocking echoed from the wheels. Up ahead, the flooded road set the car sliding, more, wobbling from side to side. The steering wheel dragged through her hand as the tyres aquaplaned, ripping away her control. She tried to negotiate the bend, but the car's rear end spun around, the spinning wheels catapulting her nose-first into the overflowing drain. Partway down, the front wheels hit a large log half-buried below the water. Frantically, she flung open the door, fell out into the tumbling water, desperate to cling onto anything that prevented her being swept away. Determinedly, she clawed her way out of the drain and, drenched and covered in mud, dragged herself up onto the flooded road, where she steadied herself on shaking legs. She looked across the road where two cars had pulled over. One was a four-wheel drive, the other a white Fiat.

Rahim ran towards her, fear marring his face; he held her arms, his eyes sweeping over her assessing her for injuries. The driver of the four-wheel drive checked out the car and offered to winch it out of the drain. When it was back on the road, he said: 'Have you recently had work done on this car? Your wheel nuts are horribly loose. Some have already fallen out, and it wouldn't be from this.'

Rahmin frowned. 'A random attack,' he suggested. 'It is not that uncommon around here. One of those things that happens.'

'So, they find a shiny new car and take pleasure in defacing it?' Debra's jaw dropped open. "I can't believe people would act in such a way.'

He shook his head. 'I do not know why they do it, but they do.'

Debra sighed and shook her head, feeling comforted as he draped his jacket around her shoulders. He reassured her, brushed stray sodden curls from her face; insisted he take her to the hospital.

After driving her home, he parked his car down the road from her house but, as he reached out to hold her hand, she hesitated, thoughts running through her head. *Has someone been spying on us? Maybe they're watching us now. As a European woman, who seems to know more than the locals, have I unknowingly upset someone at the college?*

Rahim appeared to be reading her thoughts. 'I can't imagine why anyone would want to hurt you. Try not to take it personally.' He placed his arm around her shoulder then kissed her gently on the top of her head, like a father kissing a child.

She wanted to stay this way forever with Rahim holding her, soothing her with his gentle voice. But she had started to shiver, her muddied clothes clinging to her damp skin. Besides, Alex would be waiting for her at home. When she walked into the house looking drenched, covered in mud, Alex immediately suspected someone had sabotaged their car.

'I bet it's to do with the hangar contract. I should have given it to that local company. But the Japanese quote was cheaper.' Caught up in a barrage of possible scenarios, he rambled on, listing many suspects.

'Alex, you did what you thought was right with the contract. It isn't as if you are cheating anyone. But this is not about you. It's about me.' She plopped down onto a chair but immediately saw the wet patches on the brown corduroy fabric and stood again. Alex now ranted about the red BMW and how they should target that if they wanted revenge. He inclined his head towards the neighbour's house.

'For God's sake, Alex. They are not targeting you. I think it's someone at the college who tampered with my car.'

'Why do you say that? They have no right to attack my wife!' He started to rant again.

'My wife! My life!' Debra screamed at him. 'Everything does

not always revolve around you, Alex. This is about me. It's about being a European woman in an Asian country, a woman trying to compete in a man's world. They want to put me back in my place where they think I belong. I wasn't hurt, but it could have been worse. I'm sick of men bullying me, telling me what I should do.'

When he replied, Debra noted an unfamiliar consoling tone in his voice. 'You could have been killed,' he said. 'What if Sam was with you? I care about you both. I want to keep you safe.'

'Thank you for caring about us.'

She handed him the mechanic's card with the address where he could collect the car. But when she thought he had exhausted the subject, he asked again about Gareth's new car.

'I don't want to know, Alex. Let's hope they used the money in the crate … that it's now gone from our garden.' Debra climbed the stairs to escape his diatribe.

'I thought she had more sense, mixed up with that gardener. And what about Gareth?' he raved.

More than anything else, she wanted a hot shower. After turning on the tap, she stood, letting the hot water soothe her nerves. But her hands trembled as she massaged shampoo into her dirty hair. Trails of mud ran off her arms and legs, swirling into the drain as she kept replaying the scene of the accident. For a moment she had truly thought she was going to die. She shivered again at the realisation as she stepped out of the shower, and wrapped herself in a large fluffy towel.

Though Alex was still convinced it was someone at the airport seeking revenge, she asked herself again if it might have been those students at the college. *But they would have needed tools, and someone would have witnessed them doing it. Overall, they're a great bunch of kids.* As far as she knew, she had no enemies.

Lena had a hot cup of tea ready for her when she entered the kitchen. She looked as if she'd been crying.

'What's the matter, Lena? You seem upset.'

'Mam, I'm worried about my sister. Viola is unhappy working for her boss. She has been crying over the phone.' Lena wiped her eyes with the back of her hand.

'Perhaps you can ring her tomorrow. Find out if we can visit her. He can't treat her like that. She's entitled to a day off each week. Men can't treat women like slaves. Doesn't he work for the government?'

'Yes. Mam. I appreciate your concern.'

By the time she had tucked Sam into his bed, she gladly dragged herself into hers. After such a stressful day, she succumbed to a restless exhausting sleep.

Sometime later, she awoke to noises – cupboard doors banging – and although darkness prevailed outside, Alex was already turning on taps, slamming drawers. The clock clicked over five am.

Her eyes felt dry, and her body felt drained from having tossed and turned all night. While her mind cried out for sleep, her body wanted to relive every intimacy of the last few days. Aroused by his gentle touch, her body was wide awake, and her nostrils held his familiar scent. When she finally fell asleep, she dreamed of being chased into a formidable wasteland. When she cried out for Rahim, it was Alex who answered her call. However, it was not the strong, confident husband she knew. Instead, the haunted face of a wild animal with disjointed bony arms reached out for her hands.

Alex walked into the bedroom and grabbed his car keys, and she sat up in bed, trying to think. Something inside her had changed. Despite being sleep-deprived, her mind was completely focused.

'I've been thinking that maybe we should leave Brunei,' Alex said. He appeared agitated, twisting the car keys in his hand.

'What are you saying? We haven't finished our three-year

contract.' Her stomach lurched at the idea of leaving but she felt greater concern at his change of heart.

'I'm just worried about everything that's going on. I think we might be better off at home.' He continued to click the keys, pressing them between thumb and forefinger.

'That doesn't sound like you. I thought you liked a challenge. You're good at your job. You enjoy the lifestyle. Why would you want to go home?' She looked at him more closely, trying to pick up any clues in his face.

'I'm fearful of what might happen to you. Some things are outside my control. I want to be able to protect you and I can't. Perhaps that's what worries me. Other people are calling the shots. No one seems to listen to me anymore.' His shoulders slumped as he stared into space.

'I can take care of myself. Despite the car accident, I'm much stronger now.'

She climbed out of bed and stood beside him. 'I'm not going to let these things get me down. Nor am I going to let anyone bully or threaten me. Why don't you take a few days off? Have you been to the doctor yet? You promised that you would try to relax.' She reached for his hand as he shoved his wallet into his back pocket. 'Please hold me, just for a moment.' She wrapped her arms around him. 'I care about you. I want you to be happy.'

'You will have to drop me off at work, but first we'll call in at the mechanic … find out what's happening with your car. I've got heaps to do. You'll have to hurry.' He kissed her briefly, but his mind was obviously elsewhere. His smile and hug lacked warmth, and his eyes already focused on the door.

As he hurried from the room, large silent tears rolled down her face. An old spectre of insecurity hovered and threatened to unnerve her but she determinedly fought it back. She wasn't going to let any man, whoever he might be, undermine her confidence. Quickly throwing on some clothes, she followed

Alex out to his car. Unlike her car careening out of control, she now had a firm grip on life and new energy surged through her. Something had changed in her.

After dropping Alex at work, she followed the line of traffic exiting the airport. Not used to driving Alex's Range Rover, the the seats being so much higher than hers, she realised she should have adjusted the seat as her legs had to stretch to reach the pedals. Approaching the roundabout, she nervously anticipated the gaps in the traffic when a sleek silver sports car shot past in front of her. Then, with only a very small gap available, a shiny black sedan with tinted windows approached; she seized her chance and accelerated in front of it. As she negotiated the turns of the roundabout, a second and a third identical black sedan followed, one behind the other. Too late to do anything else, she remained stuck in the middle of a motorcade.

She concentrated on the silver sports car in front, which zipped along at an alarming speed. The black car behind her had also gained on her and hugged her rear bumper. Then it tried to overtake her, but the narrow road with cars approaching on the other side prevented it. Her hands sweating on the steering wheel, she accelerated to widen the gap between her and the tailgater. She couldn't keep up this life-threatening speed. Her heart raced and thumped in her chest as the car behind flashed his headlights.

The palace was still a fair distance ahead, and there was no way she could drive through the palace gates. Up ahead near a small bridge, roadworks blocked part of the road, bollards spreading out in line. Several workmen rushed to move the bollards out of the way to let His Highness pass through.

A patch of unsealed road ahead led off from the main road and Debra took a chance. Her legs trembled as she quickly indicated to turn right, then accelerated and skidded onto the dirt road. She waited as the three black sedans raced past trying to keep up with the Sultan as he sped across the rickety narrow bridge. Staring after them, too shocked to breathe, she panicked. *What if the driver following me took down my number plate. Alex's numberplate. There's no way I can tell Alex about this.*

Searching for You

The minute I heard my first love story,
I started looking for you,
not knowing how blind that is.
Lovers don't finally meet somewhere.
They're in each other all along.

Rumi

Debra parked Alex's car at the back of their carport, hoping to keep it well concealed, and hoping to keep a low profile. At the college, she would make herself scarce for fear of bumping into Muhammad again. Thoughts of possible sabotage or retribution frightened her but were not half as scary as her feelings for Rahim. It was only yesterday yet it seemed like a year. Images of him constantly whizzed round in her head, and living without him was proving unbearable. At the trill ring of the telephone, she hustled down the stairs, grabbing it on its fifth ring.

'Debra, are you able to talk?'

'Yes, but I wasn't expecting you to ring. Is everything all right?' she whispered. The urgency in his voice made her nervous, tongue-tied. She worried about her neighbours listening in on the party line they shared.

'Yes, I am fine. But I must talk to you. Are you able to meet me at our special place?'

'I can be there in fifteen minutes.' She hung up, struggling to conceal her excitement.

Remembering to keep Alex's car out of sight, she parked

178

behind the museum in a spot not visible from the road, immediately noticing the identifiable white Fiat parked amongst the few other cars there. Nervously scanning the parking lot, she climbed from the car: a well-dressed Malay couple with a young child were preparing to leave; at the end of the car park, two young men leant against their car smoking. They watched her closely as she walked towards them. Behind them, Rahim walked sedately down the terraced lawns towards the river.

She quickened her pace towards the museum, which was soon due to close, then veered off to follow Rahim at a respectable distance. As she descended the long flight of steep stone steps to their secluded garden seat, her legs trembled. But her heart beat rapidly at this unexpected opportunity.

He greeted her with a hug. 'I am so glad you came. I left in such a hurry I forgot to bring the letter I wrote. But I can tell you that I too have been pacing like a puma. The difference is I am pacing up and down in a cage, feeling trapped, like I need to escape.'

'It's great you're here.' She broke his hug so she could see his face. 'I panicked when you rang. I thought there might be a problem.'

'Debra, I simply had to see you, to hear your voice.' He wrung his hands, emphasising the words, his urgency contagious.

'I know what you mean.' Her voice sounded husky, breathless at his admission. 'It's only when I'm with you that I feel like a whole person.'

'I have really missed you. I know it was only yesterday. But you are the best thing that has happened to me in years.' He reached for her hand. 'I cannot sleep. All I think about is you. I fear people might be reading my thoughts.'

She noted the circles under his eyes, the deeper lines of his brow. 'I know. I miss you too. I've been wandering around in a daze most of the time. I don't know what I'm doing. I can't concentrate on anything.'

He wrapped his arms around her; kissed her. Not a strong passionate kiss but a gentle kiss that tingled all the way down her spine. She rested her head on his shoulder as he gently stroked her arm.

'I have wanted to do that for so long,' he said.

She looked at the sensitive, handsome face, his eyes full of sorrow and love. When most of her life had felt strange and uncertain, he had been the one constant in her life, and she had no doubts. She needed no convincing. As the sun broke through the clouds, releasing its brilliant beams, the birds sang louder.

She took a deep breath. 'Do you have the spare ticket for the Singapore conference? I'd like to come with you'. She felt shocked yet exhilarated at her own boldness. *Perhaps it's the effects of too much sun living in the tropics. But I'm affected as much by the moon. Am I going crazy?*

'Are you sure?' Rahim's face immediately brightened. 'It is only a couple of weeks away. That would be amazing.' He pulled her closer and they stayed like that until their breathing synchronised, their energy merged.

'I need to get away for a few days. There's so much going on around me. Alex is really stressed with his job. He's talking about leaving Brunei. I'm ready to explode. I need a break.'

'I have been worrying about you too. Since your accident, I keep hoping you are safe.' He kissed the top of her head.

'Alex is convinced it was someone at the airport seeking revenge on him. But I can't help thinking it was directed at me. Perhaps it was someone at our college. Do you think someone's been watching us?'

'I hope not. You asked me who owned the black Mercedes. Muhammad is a friend of my father. That's how I got this job. My father too works for the Ministry of Education. In Malaysia. I contacted Muhammad about the job as I did not want my father wielding his power like he usually does.'

A numbness spread through Debra, like the sensation in those split seconds after an accident before the wounds are discovered. 'Do you think your father could be using Muhammad to spy on you?'

'I would not be surprised. He is capable of anything … after what he did to Sophie.' He pulled out an old photo from his wallet of a young woman with sad brown eyes. She had Rahim's fine features but a lighter complexion – the sister he left behind in England.

'When she was eighteen, Sophie flew to Malaysia to reconnect with our father. Unfortunately, she had a drug problem. When my father found out, he used his contacts in immigration and had her deported back to the UK.'

'Oh, poor Sophie! Debra linked her arm through his.

'By this time, my father had another wife and three young children. He said he did not want Sophie bringing disrepute to his family. I was also going to meet up with her but when he heard about the drugs, I was powerless to help her.'

'Sometimes these things are outside our control. I lost a baby after Sam. Her name was Mala.' She took a deep breath before continuing. 'No matter what I did to protect her, it was obviously not enough. Although I loved her and kept her safe, I guess I have always felt responsible for her death, that it was something I did or failed to do. I'm sure Alex thought it was my fault. Why do we end up harming the ones we love the most?' Her lip trembled, and she buried her face in Rahim's chest.

'That you loved her was enough. There is nothing greater than that.' He nuzzled his face in her hair then took out his handkerchief and offered it to her. 'I often question why my mother did not contact me …' A plaintive sound squeezed from his throat and he was unable to continue.

'Perhaps she did. Your father may have destroyed her letters.'

Debra took his hand in hers; gently stroked it.

'I always feared her rejection but dreaded my father's control. I could never ask him about the letters. It would give him a sense of power to know that.' He sighed deeply; shook his head.

'Mothers never stop loving their children, Rahim. But sometimes they get caught up in their own pain. The expectations of the role are too overwhelming. Perhaps you should contact her. It might help you to heal.'

'You are helping me to heal. You are the best friend I have ever had.'

'Two weeks seems like a lifetime. How will we survive?'

A loud crash drowned out Debra's next words and she looked towards the high stone wall separating the car park from the lawns and the jungle below.

'That sounds like two cars colliding ... it's time to leave.' She grabbed her handbag from the seat and kissed him gently, a kiss he returned more intently as he folded his arms around her.

'You go on ahead. I will wait and follow you in a few minutes.'

As she climbed the steps to the carpark, two drivers argued about the state of their cars; one had appeared to have reversed into the other. One man spat out a cigarette butt, squashed it with his foot. *Thank God they didn't crash into Alex's car.*

She quickened her pace, and climbed into the Range Rover; drove away as quickly as she could. Stealing another glance at the two men in the rearview mirror she knew she couldn't afford to get involved in other people's problems. Right now, she had enough of her own.

***

Alex walked in through the front door; placed his squash racquet on the sideboard. Her heart raced, scared that he might be reading her mind or notice the glow in her cheeks. He peeled off his black velour tracksuit, and placed it with the dirty clothes in the laundry. Debra screwed up her nose as the sweaty odour wafted past her. Lena brought Alex a glass of cold orange juice, and offered one to Debra, but she declined. Alex had picked up her car from the mechanic and parked it next to his in the carport. She thanked him for collecting it, and asked if it had been repaired as he'd requested.

'Yes, your car's fine now. I needed that game of squash though. It's been a busy couple of days as we flew in a new car for the Sultan. We had to take all the seats out of the aircraft. There's always a lot of pressure every time we handle one of his new cars.'

Alex rested his head in his hands as if the weight on his shoulders was too heavy to bear. 'Everyone gets nervous, making sure there are no scratches or bumps.' As he lifted his head, his eyes lit up. 'You should see the car though. It's truly amazing – pure speed and luxury.'

'What type of car is it?' She already had a clear image in her mind.

'A sleek silver sports Maserati Ghibli. Of course, he always insists he's the first person to drive it. Can you imagine how fast that car would go?'

'Yes, I can imagine.' She looked at Alex, careful to conceal her smug expression. She also knew how difficult it would be for his security men to keep up with him if he insisted on driving at those breakneck speeds.

If You Forget Me

Everything carries me to you,
as if everything that exists, aromas, light, metal
were little boats that sail toward those isles
of yours that wait for me.

Pablo Neruda

With Mike on leave in the UK for four weeks, Debra agreed to meet Rahim the following week at Mike's house. While eager to meet up with Rahim again, she had that lurching feeling in her gut, like she'd swung too high on the swings. She felt exhilarated yet scared at the same time. She showered quickly, sprayed on her favourite Charlie perfume, and looked for Sam to say goodbye. Recovering from a cold, he still continued to wheeze, and had a deep rasping cough that worried her. He was reluctant to settle down for an afternoon nap. *Perhaps I shouldn't go.*

But Rahim is waiting for me.

Her head spun with the dilemma, the choices she needed to make. Lena offered to find Sam and make sure he had a nap.

As she drove her station wagon into Mike's driveway, she noticed Rahim standing by the pond feeding the hungry koi. Wearing a pale lemon polo shirt tucked into his jeans, he blended in well with the yellow hibiscus hedge. She waved as he wandered over to greet her.

'Mike's amah is ironing downstairs, but we can read upstairs if you like.' He held the book of Neruda's poetry that she'd given him.

They walked upstairs, stepped into the living room and closed the door, their time together precious; they didn't want to share it with anyone. Debra lowered herself onto the leopard print upholstered sofa, almost squashing the tabby cat curled amongst the cushions. She gasped as he meowed and ran away, then smiled.

'What are we going to read today?'

'This is what I wrote after reading Pablo's poetry. But what I want to say about love comes from my heart.' He unfolded a note from his pocket.

Darling Debra

Thank you for introducing me to Pablo. He has my ear, he has my heart. I wish I could create magic from words the way he does. While caressing the lyrics he breathes new life into them. When Pablo writes of the boundless desire, the infinite ache, I think he is reading my mind, channelling my thoughts.

Lately, it does not matter what I am doing, everything reminds me of you. As I carry out mundane tasks, I picture you doing the same. I long to know what you are thinking. Every time I see someone in a crowd wearing a favourite colour of yours, I get excited thinking it is you. I smell your fragrance on everything around me and I hear your voice on the wind.

My love forever

Rahim

'Can you sense it? It is what I feel for you.' Gently, he took her hand and placed it on his heart. 'When Pablo writes about the infinite ache, I understand what he means. It is like a huge weight crushing down on me.'

She felt the vibration spread along her arm, into her chest, frightening yet exciting her. Reaching over, he cupped her face in his hands. She breathed in his scent of sun-blessed saltiness. He kissed her gently, and she sighed. Tracing every detail on her face, his fingers moved across the curve of her nose, the shape of her lips. He slowly wound one of her curls around his finger. All the while, she explored each of his fingers in turn, the size of his hands, the muscles of his forearm. She captured every detail to memory, treasuring it away. As an artist shapes an image, it was as though her body existed only after he touched it, bringing it to life. As their bodies awakened, he slipped his hand under her shirt. When he tried to lift off her blouse, she resisted, pulling away his hand, shyness engulfing her, like a child about to have its blanket pulled away.

'It's a while since I've revealed my body to anyone. I fear you won't like what you see.' She grabbed his hands in hers.

'You are beautiful,' he whispered, nuzzling his nose in her neck. 'I know that without looking.'

Cautiously, then more urgently, she awakened to his gentle touch. As their passion rose, their bodies relaxed. They leant back in silence, her blonde curls buried in the dark hairs of his chest, his arms encircling her.

Slowly, the ceiling fan clicked and whirled once more. Outside, the cicadas returned to their rhythmical buzzing. Someone coughed and Rahim looked towards the door.

'Did you hear that?'

She listened. Once again came the sound of wheezing, rasping coughs. The sound was recognisable, but she couldn't comprehend – it didn't belong. *How could he have found his way here?* Then the amah downstairs spoke, as if talking to a child. Rahim threw on his shirt, and opened the door while she struggled with her blouse.

He turned to her, looking puzzled. 'It is Sam.'

Her face froze as adrenaline pumped through her body. She

hurried down the stairs, hugged Sam, soothing him with calming words, kissing him, stroking his hair over and over. Finally, her mouth started to move, and she was able to speak.

'Darling, how on earth did you get here?'

'He was sleeping in the back of your car, Mam,' Mike's amah replied, hovering in the background.

Choking back tears of panic, she turned to Rahim. 'I shouldn't have come.'

Awash with shock and guilt, Debra let the tears flow. No amount of retribution would make up for the shame. *I'm a terrible mother.* She turned to Rahim who'd been observing this sorry sight of a woman, a lover, a mother. His eyes filled with sadness as he stood stark still.

'I can't do this,' she said, slowly shaking her head.

'Debra, I am sorry. You go now. I will talk to you later.' He gently touched her shoulder.

Debra rang Lena on Mike's house phone to let her know Sam was with her; she sounded relieved that Sam was safe. All the way home, she silently chastised herself for the flagrant neglect of her child. *I'm a dreadful mother. A dreadful mother!*

Later, when she sat down to dinner with Alex and Sam, she feared what Sam might say about the incident, but Alex was preoccupied with what was happening at work. On several occasions recently, he'd been called out late at night to prepare for unscheduled flights involving top security. Each time, he expected to receive a briefing from Gareth, but when he searched the airport, Gareth couldn't be found.

'It's not good enough. He calls himself Security Chief but when he's needed, no one can find him.'

Then he talked about another manager who'd recently flown to London on annual leave, but whose baggage had mysteriously ended up in Manila. 'Revenge. They don't like us,' he muttered, seemingly unaware of anyone else at the dinner table. Debra looked at the worry lines on his brow. He picked at his thumbnails, a stress habit she'd seen before, but it worried her more to see it now.

At the end of the meal, she escaped to the kitchen to make a pot of tea. Her hands shook, and the lid flew off the kettle, crashing to the floor. Water spilled everywhere. When she looked inside the kettle, she reeled back and called to Alex.

'I've discovered why the tea has been tasting strange.'

The bleached skeletal remains of a cicak stared back at them – it had been trapped in the spout until recently dislodged by Debra's shaking hands. *How long has this alchemy been taking place?*

'Don't show Sam. He loves those things.'

'What is it?' Sam followed them into the kitchen.

'The lid flew off the kettle.' She grabbed a cloth and mopped up the water. Sam looked at his mother then turned to his father.

'Guess what, Daddy? I saw Mummy …'

She froze, and the blood drained from her face. Fear leapt from every pore. The cold deathly silence was palpable. This was her retribution. She was about to be exposed.

'What do you mean, Sam?' Alex asked.

'In that mirror.' Sam pointed to the wall behind Debra's shoulder. 'I saw her.'

Her pulse thumped loudly in her ears. She barely grasped what Sam was saying next. She hugged him tight, smothering him in kisses. When he asked for more stories as they later cuddled on his bed, she gladly read him all the stories on his bookshelf. She wanted him to know how much she loved him. She held him close, squeezing her eyes shut to contain tears of love and joy. Her darling boy, the channel for her pent-up love, was worth all the frustration she'd endured, the sorrow of the baby she'd lost. She felt truly blessed as she stroked his soft hair, and breathed in the warm, earthy smell of his body.

Debra knew she'd been given a second chance with Sam. She

also knew she must reconsider her relationship with Rahim. As it had intensified, so too had the risk of being discovered. She'd been foolish to think people wouldn't find out. All night she fought restless sleep mingled with tortuous dreams. An odd dream had tricked her into thinking they could be together as she relived their brief precious moments. But on waking, she remembered it had only been a dream.

I'm selfish to think I deserve a special friend who loves me as I am, someone whose presence transforms me into a far greater being than I could ever hope to be. Maybe it's just this strange, exotic country, the loneliness with Alex often working away, the grieving, the loss. As she continued to chastise herself, she vowed she would not let anything else ruin her family's security. She would end her relationship with Rahim immediately.

***

Next morning, Debra sat on the floor, building Lego with Sam as he'd requested a garage to house his Matchbox toys. As she engaged in the activity, Rahim never far from her mind, her breath caught at the sight of a small Fiat car Sam was pushing into his new garage. The toy was red rather than white, but it was enough to remind her of him.

The ultimate challenge was to build a castle, but as she built Lego walls ten blocks high to keep out Sam's dragons, her mind continued to wander. While he enjoyed his imaginary castle, living within the safety of a fortress which kept danger at bay, other dangers lurked, tempted and threatened to destroy a family's security. As she created this idyllic inner sanctum, she bonded with Sam who was happy to keep the structure intact for several days, adding Lego people and horses.

He grabbed a white horse and handed it to her. 'Can you ride this?'

'If only,' she said. 'If my world was a fairy tale, I'd gladly ride away with my prince.'

'What does a prince look like?

'Dark and handsome,' she said, without hesitating.

'How about this one?' Diving into the bag of Lego, he pulled out a few squat Lego men.

But none of them could match her prince. It needed to be him. In the flesh. As tears gathered in her eyes, Sam wrapped his arms around her neck.

'Mummy, what's the matter?' He snuggled in closer.

'It's okay, darling. I just need to get a tissue.' She rushed from the room, bumping into Kali as she slipped through the door.

At the sight of Kali, Sam's face brightened and in no time, they were both absorbed in another imaginary game. For the first time in several days, Sam happily crashed down the castle walls. With the children engrossed in their game, and nothing to distract her from her endless longing, the emptiness inside that no one else could fill overwhelmed her.

She gazed at the phone on the sideboard. *Should I call him? Just to hear his voice.* Mindlessly tapping her fingers on the edge of the chair, she felt pleased when the children suggested they get beef burgers for lunch.

'Can we go to the airport café?' they both yelled.

'Where else! Only place in town for burgers.' She grabbed her purse and car keys, and they jumped in the car.

After parking at the airport, they ran up the front steps to the café inside the terminal. The airport was quiet in the middle of the day with only a few flights departing, but the café was full of people hungry for comfort food. The children ordered spearmint milkshakes to wash down the beef burgers and chips. Debra settled for an iced lemon tea, and they finished off with ice cream cones and took them upstairs in search of a departing aircraft.

The viewing balconies were open to the elements but with

little breeze the area felt hot and humid. They spied one solitary aircraft about to take off. As the ground crew removed the stairs from the aircraft doors, they didn't have long to wait before it taxied down the runway and lifted into the clouds. Sam rammed his fingers in his ears at the loudly revving engines.

'Where is this plane going?' Kali asked.

'Ah, Singapore, I think.' Debra turned around to look at the flight information board where green lights blinked in the departure box, confirming the destination. She thought of the airline tickets in her briefcase, the work conference in Singapore.

'Yes, that flight is going to Singapore.'

Different Directions

A strange passion is moving in my head
My heart has become a bird
Which searches in the sky.
Every part of me goes in different directions
Is it really so that the one I love is everywhere?

Rumi

Gazing at the messy pile of clothes strewn across her bed, Debra chose a green print dress and folded it neatly into the suitcase. She then spied a blue silk dress hanging in her wardrobe and pulled the green one out and replaced it with the blue. She also removed her comfortable walking shoes from the case. Frantically searching the bottom of the wardrobe, she found a pair of chic silver sandals. They would be ideal for day or night wear.

She sifted through her underwear drawer, choosing the black lacy knickers with matching bra and added them to her pile. She held up a red satin nightie, questioning if she would get to wear it. She threw it in anyway. Her crochet bikini went in before she changed her mind. Then she focused on choosing practical everyday clothes. As she grabbed a skirt, a long-sleeved shirt, and a pair of trousers, she reminded herself it was only for a few days.

Her head whizzed with difficult decisions, and she found it impossible to focus on any one thing. Finishing her packing, she turned to find Alex standing behind her. She halted, fearing he may have been reading her thoughts.

'This is for you.' He handed her a small gift box wrapped in silver paper, with matching ribbon. 'It's from Mala.'

A sob rose in her chest, and her bottom lip trembled. Once she started, she couldn't stop. He placed his hand on her shoulder as she untied the bow and peeled away the tissue paper as carefully as she could.

'She knows how much you loved her.'

As she opened the black velvet box, she wiped her tears away on the back of her hand. The freshwater pearls slithered through her fingers, and she looked stunned. *Could her affirmations be working?* Alex hugged her, and she sobbed a lifetime of tears, for Mala, and the inexplicable loss in the world.

'I know it wasn't your fault.' He paused for a moment, looking into her eyes.

She gazed at his face, hearing the voice she knew so well but couldn't believe what she now heard. 'You have no idea how much that means to me … that you don't blame me for her death.'

'I've been doing a lot of thinking lately.' Alex sat down on the edge of the bed and, pushing the clothes to one side, patted the bed for her to sit down next to him. 'When I told you about my dad, the way he criticised me, I realised I'd been treating you the same way. I'm sorry.'

'Thanks. It means a lot to hear you say that. I appreciate your honesty.'

For so long she'd waited to for him to say those words, to receive his love. As she looked at the lines softening around his mouth, she remembered his expression but it had been long ago.

'I know it doesn't pay to dwell on the past. We have so much to live for in the future. You reminded me that we have the freedom to choose.'

'Yes, unlike our fathers. We have so much to be grateful for.' This dramatic change in Alex's behaviour stunned her. But she also felt cautious. *Will it last or will he revert to his old former self?*

'That close shave with death you had in the car …' He adjusted his spectacles, thinking.

She too remembered the loosened wheel nuts, her car skidding out of control; recalled the panic as it crashed into the drain, relived the terror she'd felt.

'I've been thinking about how hazardous life can be, and how much I would miss you if anything happened to you.' He took the pearls and placed them on top of the blue silk dress in the case.

Like a roller coaster, her head spun, and her emotions spilled upside down. *Oh! Alex. If only you knew how dangerous life could be. You probably imagined me dying a respectable death with my reputation intact, a traumatic but not totally unexpected event where mourners would gather around giving you the support you needed. If you only knew the risks that I've taken. Could you envisage the disastrous scenario of a wife in prison, a child without a mother, your loss of job, being deported or a reputation left in tatters? Somehow, I don't think you possibly could.*

'You might want to wear the pearls at the conference,' he said, taking her hand and pulling her onto the bed. He pushed the pile of clothes onto the floor. She felt like an automaton about to be switched on. 'Happy Anniversary.' He kissed her lips, ears, and neck.

Debra gulped, trying to squash her look of surprise. With so many thoughts whizzing around in her head, for the first time in seven years, she'd forgotten their wedding anniversary. Her mind was a mess, full of doubt and indecision. Should she go to Singapore? Or should she stay with Alex?

Having waited so long to receive the love Alex showered on her now, she felt reluctant to leave.

When she finally fell asleep, Alex's arm draped around her waist, she dreamed of Mala: she was alive; Debra could smell her sweet warm skin, her milky breath, hear her cry, feel her chubby hand wrapped around her finger. Mala looked at her with her baby eyes wide open to her world, trusting her; she lay poised with her rosebud mouth as if wanting to say something but not knowing how. Suddenly her baby face morphed into Sam's. He giggled his childish laugh as he cuddled into her. An intense moment of love washed over her before the faces disappeared leaving her with nothing but a feeling of guilt. Then an image of shimmering midnight blue silk, a string of pearls and the sharp sound of snapping as they scattered all over the floor. Her body began to whirl.

'What's the matter? Alex grabbed her arm. 'You were calling out, making strange noises.'

'I think I'm unravelling.' She blinked quickly, waking, and propped herself up on the pillow.

'Debra, I know I've been letting things get on top of me. I need to chill out. I want to make the most of our life here. What we have is too good to give up. But you too need to get a grip. You sound as if you're losing it.'

'Yes, Alex, you're right.' She searched for his hand and shut her eyes, snuggled back into the pillow. But when she closed her eyes, her mind still whirled. It felt as if the more she whirled, the lighter she became. After three turns, each of her layers was spinning, unravelling until she was stripped bare, revealing herself to the world. In the ecstasy of the moment, she was freer, lighter than ever before. *Where am I? Who am I?* she wondered into the dark beyond, to a place where she knew another person spun in unison. And she needed to be with that person.

Love is Endless

I said to the night,
If you are in love with the moon,
It is because you never stay for long.
The night turned to me and said,
It is not my fault. I never see the sun,
How can I know that love is endless?

Rumi

On the plane to Singapore, Debra spent most of the two-hour flight thinking about Rahim, about the time they would spend together. The book she'd brought with her remained unread. Each time she tried to read a few pages, memories of him distracted her. When she thought of him, a familiar tingling sensation spread down her spine. She couldn't wait to join him.

When she'd left home that morning, she'd felt anxious, fearing the whole world had guessed her guilty secret, as if it were etched in her face. Alex showed little concern as he drove her to the airport. He thought an English Teachers' Conference was an acceptable reason to go to Singapore. Besides, he didn't have to organise the trip. As he kissed her goodbye with a brief peck on the cheek, there was no repeat of his tender words from the night before. His former declarations of love were a million miles away as he prattled on about the tasks awaiting him at work.

Her vow to end the relationship with Rahim proved only to show her how challenging life would be without him yet she felt frightened and excited. No longer could she pretend their behaviour was innocent, or totally acceptable. What began as a companionable andante had accelerated into an uncontrollable agitato. Their slow waltz had become a frenzied tango and there was no turning back.

While most attendees were staying at the hotel where the conference was being held, Rahim had booked them into a quieter hotel not far from the Raffles and Singapore Cricket Club. She'd had plenty of time to fret waiting for his noon flight to arrive, but it was now 2.45 and she paced up and down. Should she ask at reception if he'd left a message?

Her initial excitement had eventually turned to doubt. She bit her lower lip, imagining various calamitous scenarios, the worst being that someone had found out and prevented him from leaving. Her stomach grumbled with the need for food so she moved towards the downstairs café facing the lobby where she could wait for him. Descending in the elevator to the ground floor, she breathed in deeply to calm her nerves. The elevator doors jerked open … And there he stood.

His whole face broke into a smile. She had an urge to throw her arms around him, but they came together with outstretched arms, bumping into a harmless handshake.

'I thought you weren't coming. I imagined all sorts of disasters,' she whispered, leading him towards the reception desk.

'I am sorry. My flight was delayed. It was so frustrating. I could not wait to see you.' He rested his bag on the floor. 'But I am here now.' He grinned again.

They dropped his bags off before going to the café, and after lunch, they returned to his room. Like two teenagers unable to control their rampant lust, they knew the first spark lit would ignite fires they couldn't extinguish. Exploring each other cautiously only made it worse and heightened their desire. They fondled, discovering each touch a more exciting sensation than the first.

Hastening to the bed, his dark body covered her light, his brown hardness probing pink softness. With her breasts nestled against the dark hair of his chest, she pressed her nose against his neck, inhaling his warm, salty skin. She licked his neck; rolled her tongue around his earlobe and he kissed her mouth, gently at first as if moulding her shape. Then another more forceful kiss that served as a promise demanding a response. He caressed her as if handling something precious and rare, yet his movements were determined and demanding. She cradled him gently as she would a child, then pulled his hips against hers, responding as a lover.

Their bodies locked together in a rhythm of pleasure and pain. He cried out and she answered with a plaintive sigh. Showered in love, as the last of the shudders left her body, she sobbed. Not a gut-wrenching cry but a quiet, creeping-out-before-you-know-it type of sob. They lay there entwined long after the peak of passion subsided. She wanted this ephemeral moment to last forever yet felt filled with an inexorable sense of doom.

'I wish it could be like this forever.' He buried his face in her hair, tightened his arms around her. 'In our own little world. I want you to know how much I love you, whatever happens.' He cupped her face with both hands. 'But I dread having to leave my girls. I vowed I would never do what my father did to us.'

'I know.' She wriggled out of his arms to look at his face. Leaning closer, she whispered in his ear, for fear the gods might hear her declaration and take it away. Not having experienced this intensity of love before, she feared losing it − it was too precious to lose, but too perfect to last. 'Let's not think about it now. It's way too painful.'

'You are right. Let us make the most of our few days together. Tonight, we will dine at the Raffles.' He kissed her gently then pulled back the sheet. As he walked towards the bathroom, she admired his naked form.

After he left the bed, she could smell his scent on the pillow and inhaled deeply. A smell of love, acceptance, sharing and trust. She joined him in the bathroom, and he opened the shower door. After he finished lathering her with foam, he washed it off, rubbing lightly, stroking her skin. It was the gentlest touch, but enough to ignite their passion once more. He insisted on wrapping her in a large towel, drying every part of her body. She reciprocated rubbing, massaging his smooth olive skin.

When it was time to dress, she chose a simple silk creation with many hues of blue that reflected midnight one moment, indigo the next. She attached the strand of pearls to her throat, added matching studs to her ears, each tiny pearl a replica of an immortal image of beauty. Like the pearls, she hoped their love would last a lifetime.

***

They dined at Raffles, a hotel built for sweethearts, with an ambience of sensual desire. In this place where paramours had been wooed since time immemorial, she floated in a euphoric haze. A romantic setting mingled with old worldly charm, as they strolled under rustic archways near sparkling fountains, Debra imagined Somerset Maugham writing at one of the side tables. They requested a table in a private corner of the garden, partly concealed by bright flowering pot plants. As they sat, a lover's moon shone through the travellers' palms creating striped patterns of light and dark. The cloying fragrance of frangipani hung over the courtyard on this balmy tropical evening, and poignant love songs from a string quartet lingered in the languorous air as elderly waiters slowly shook out starched white napkins.

Debra watched as Rahim plucked an oyster from one of the open shells nestled on a bed of ice, shivering with delight as it slid down his throat. She copied him, savouring the briny tang, but as she licked her lip, juice dribbled down her chin. He laughed, then devoured each of his six oysters while she struggled to finish two. They followed with an icy lime sorbet to cleanse the palate then, by silent deliberation, the waiters simultaneously lifted heavy silver food covers. At Rahim's request, they were served a traditional English fare of roast beef, with Yorkshire pudding. As he lifted a Brussels sprout onto his fork, he muttered, 'My favourite.' And as a waiter ladled gravy onto his plate, Debra grinned at the large pile drowning his meat. Lost in this timeless setting, they felt totally at ease. If it wasn't for the antique silver anchoring her to the table, she could have floated away.

Later, the waiter pushed a chrome dessert trolley to them, poured rum over a Bombe Alaska and lit it. Through the bluish flickering flame, Rahim's eyes widened, his expression childlike as he savoured the dessert. 'Mmm, it is as I remember.'

As they sat sipping Singapore Slings, a photographer asked if they would like a photo, but they declined – there was no need when this memory would be imprinted on their hearts forever. In their quiet corner of the garden, they danced the forbidden steps of love to a secret rhythm only they could hear. They twirled, moving as one, and, long after the music had stopped, their bodies swayed, connected to the vibrations.

'Mimpi,' he whispered, 'You are the dream I have been dreaming all my life.'

'But I'm real.' She pressed down on his arm. 'And I want to stay that way.'

Later that night, back in their room, they lay as restless as a ship on a tumultuous sea of endless dreams, staying awake to capture each sensual movement, each cherished whisper. If one of them drifted to sleep, they were jolted awake, touching the other, arousing desire. Words were not needed as Rahim guided her once more. The somnolent moon shone through the window, lighting the way. When an impatient sun stretched its long fingers of light across the bed, they greeted the golden dawn drenched in love.

The next day, the conference challenged them as they sat listening to endless lectures, all the while propping up sleepy heads and heavy eyelids. Yet nothing could wipe the look of elation from Rahim's face. Each time she stole a glimpse, he looked tired yet contented. Like restless children, they couldn't sit still. Each time she moved her leg, she could feel the warmth of his leg touching hers.

'According to the program, our college director will be presenting after this speaker,' Debra whispered, moving in, and absently resting her hand on his knee, then she realised, quickly removing it.

'Yes, I noticed Muhammad earlier when we were checking in,' he murmured, his face so close to hers she could smell the evocative salty scent, and felt his faint breath on her cheek. She blushed as it aroused memories of the night before. As she tried to focus on the speaker, her thoughts dwelt on Rahim's father and his connections to Muhammad. She scanned the front row of seats set aside for guest presenters and glimpsed Muhammad's large shoulders, his thickset frame. As he scratched his head, his rings and wristwatch sparkled in the dim light. She watched Rahim fidgeting with his pen. His chin flopped onto his chest and the pen clattered on the floor. His eyes flew open, and he turned to her, mouthing the words, 'I'm so tired.'

***

The next day they visited Sentosa Island on the cable car. From the top of the World Trade Centre, they looked out over spectacular views of tree-lined streets, lush botanical gardens, and Singapore skyscrapers. Encapsulated in glass, they were cocooned from the heat and noise, alone in their capsule safe, and invisible to the outside world. *How easy it would be to pretend it was perfectly natural being here together like this without a care,* she sighed.

With a gentle jerk and thud, the cable car stopped where jungle paths wound their way up the hill from enticing sandy beaches below. They walked across red wooden bridges, past high feeding platforms of a butterfly house, where mating butterflies posed in their entanglement. As they stood beside the waterfall, Rahim lifted her hand, stretching it up as high as he could. Silently, they looked up, witnessing a flutter of brilliance and colour as a large turquoise butterfly landed on their hands. Its mate soon joined her in a show of spectacular poise. Too scared to move, they remained like statues, not wanting to disturb this precious connection with nature.

The glimpse of ocean welcomed them and rocky sea walls created intimate lagoons of crystal-clear water surrounded by palm trees and white sand. Debra's face felt hot, and her clothes clung to her in the humidity as she stripped down to her yellow bikini. They found a deserted spot where they could enjoy the lagoon exclusively. Slowly she swam towards the middle, Rahim following close behind, his strong brown muscles gliding through the water. And there, where he caught up to her, he wrapped his arms around her waist, and pressed her to his chest. Her breasts spilled out of the crochet bra and his lips found hers with a new familiarity as they frolicked in the water like a pair of carefree dolphins, losing all sense of time.

Then the sun disappeared for a moment as a grey cloud passed overhead, obliterating the blue sky. Everything fell silent. Suddenly, Debra sensed eyes peering into her back and shivered, at the same moment Rahim looked over her shoulder. She followed his gaze – it was definitely time to leave. She gathered her clothes, wrapped herself in a towel and headed for the change rooms nearby.

As she rushed into the toilet block, a door slammed in the cubicle next to hers. Quietly, she pulled on her clothes and listened for common sounds of bodily functions next door. Silence. Then the faintest noise as something metallic hit the wall. She waited for the sound of a zipper, a rustle of clothing or the flush of water. Nothing. She contemplated looking under the adjoining wall but imagined eyes peering back at her. The image made her pulse race.

After an interminable wait, she made a move – it was now or never. She rushed out, pushing the door in the adjoining cubicle as she went. It was locked. She ran towards the exit and kept running. Small birds flew under the eaves of the iron roof as wind buffeted the branches, shaking leaves to the ground. She looked around for Rahim, but he was not there. She ran towards the cable car, her sandals slipping on the wet sandy path. As she rounded the ticket office, she crashed into him.

'I was worried about you.' He placed an arm around her shoulder.

'I just thought I saw someone. It's nothing.' She looked back over her shoulder.

'You are shivering. Let us get a move on.'

The sun had come out but grey clouds hung over the horizon. On the cable car, they were once again alone, but an uncomfortable heaviness hung over them. Aware of a sad, inevitable ending to their long-awaited sojourn, Rahim suggested they walk around Chinatown before returning to the hotel.

They meandered through the many shops and food stalls, gazed at fake designer handbags and Rolex watches. A small food stall with large striped canvas awnings provided some temporary shade while the smell of sweaty socks lingered in the air from the vendor selling durians. On cue, they both grimaced and ran to the next stall where a toothless Chinese woman tempted them with bamboo fans and gold painted cats, while a stooped man selling battery-operated toys tried to lure them to his stall. Beneath red paper lanterns, he sold monkeys drumming drums and remote-controlled cars. To demonstrate, he steered a small black car along the dirt floor, whizzing through and around their feet. He laughed as they both jumped and leapt through a side opening in the awning. On the other side of the street, the owner of an outdoor food stall had spread out a few tables and chairs. Dried cuttlefish and Peking duck dangled on large hooks above the counter. The small tables covered in red plastic cloths were weighted down with insulated buckets of rice.

Two men sat at the nearest table eating from rice bowls, but facing Debra and Rahim was an older man with a wispy beard. A large thickset man sat with his back to them. As he turned, raising his hand to summon a waiter, a flash of gold came from his fingers and wrist. He seemed to be staring directly through them. They ducked into another stall where a man stacking sugar cane inserted a few sticks into an ancient juicing machine. Amidst the din of grinding and clanging, Rahim ordered two glasses and they sculled the sickly, sweet juice.

'Do you think he recognised us?' Debra wiped the sticky stream that dribbled from the corner of her mouth away with the heel of her hand.

'If he did, we are together because we are attending the same conference.' Rahim's brows arched together as he placed the glasses on the counter.

Debra wished she shared the same certainty. She worried someone might have discovered their secret, especially Rahim's father. As they wandered around the stalls, the Chinese woman greeted them with the same toothless grin, convinced they were now definite buyers. She waved her exotic curios once more, pulled out a carved wooden Buddha, a small porcelain elephant. She tried to tempt Debra with a painted fan; thrust a red and yellow elephant into Rahim's hand. He passed it back to her, but she gesticulated, insisting he buy it. To placate her, he finally agreed on the price.

'An elephant never forgets!' he said, placing the small ornament in Debra's hand.

How could I possibly forget? There is nothing or no one who fills my every thought, my waking day, my dreams at night. Like many lovers, she'd learned how to thrive on the faintest memory; she'd memorised the rhythm of his voice, the smell of his body, every line on his face. The taste of his lips she would take to her grave.

On the walk back to their hotel, they passed the Singapore Cricket Club with its green bamboo blinds and iconic brown sloping roofline, Rahim reminiscing about his first trip to Singapore as a teenager. Debra tried to imagine him as a seventeen-year-old sneaking off when his father was away, to watch India play cricket in their one-day fixture against Singapore.

'It was my first taste of freedom. I caught the bus from KL. It was bucketing down, and you could hardly see the clubhouse.' He circled his arm to indicate the surrounding *padang*. 'This oval was all flooded like a lake. They called off the game. It was a long, dreary bus ride back to KL.'

She pictured the disheartened young man, his despondency compounded by the disappointment of that young boy years earlier in England whose dreams of cricket had been wrenched away by his father when he took him to Malaysia. When she looked at him now, she saw a trace of his vulnerability in his smile, and the way he laughed nervously.

On their last night together they stayed indoors, making the most of their precious time together, a candid desperation in their lovemaking lest it be their last. In the morning, Debra flew out on the early flight; Rahim scheduled to leave at noon. During the flight home, she spent every moment reliving each tiny detail of their weekend together, locking it away in her memory.

After their return from Singapore, they agreed on a trial separation – for one month – as it had become increasingly risky for them to be seen together. Since their weekend in Singapore, they could no longer trust themselves to practise proper restraint. If they found themselves in the staffroom together, they deliberately steered away to opposite sides of the room. She didn't need his proximity to excite her; simply being in the same room with him she felt charged enough to turn on a light bulb. They promised each other they would be more discreet, fearful that their disclosure would lead to their demise. Although it was probably too late for caution, there was no turning back.

In the Hand of Love

Sometimes love hoists me into the air,
Sometimes love flings me into the air,
Love swings me round and round His head;
I have no peace, in this world or any other.

Rumi

Alex's face looked drawn as he strode into the living room. His trousers now hung lower on his hips, his belt needing taking in a notch. Despite having been in the sun, his face looked pale.

'I'm not feeling at all well, Debra,' he said, 'and when I went to the bathroom, there was blood in my urine.' He shook his head. 'I hate the medical system here, but I don't have a choice – I have to go to the hospital and see a doctor.'

Since his earlier efforts to convince her that the hospital was great, they'd discovered there were only a few GPs. For those patients with chronic or acute conditions, there was a distinct lack of specialist care. Debra doubted he'd trade his productive work time to sit for hours in a crowded hospital waiting area. She poured him a glass of water, prompting him to keep up his fluids and gently reminded him of his promise to take time out and relax.

'I've been too busy. We've had more engine problems.'

'Well come sit down. Dinner is ready. We're having apricot chicken, your favourite.'

'I'm not hungry. I didn't eat lunch until three o'clock. My apprentices keep bringing me food. I'm sure they do it so I'll give them good assessments.' He took another sip of the water before pushing it aside.

'Surely that's not the only reason. What sort of food do they bring you?'

She spooned apricot chicken onto her plate while he listed rambutans, mooncakes, sometimes chicken curry. He looked at her plate and decided he'd have a small portion.

'It sounds like they care about you. You never told me that.' She ladled apricot sauce over the chicken on his plate.

'I'm sure there are some things you don't tell me.' He peered at her over his glasses.

Her pulse quickened. She tried to relax the muscles around her mouth. 'Well, what do you want to know?' she asked, choking on a mouthful of chicken.

'Nothing really. I know I can always trust you.'

As he cut his chicken, she focused on the napkin on her lap, fiddled with the edges, folded it in half, then placed it on the table. The ceiling fan clicked and whirled. She drew a deep breath. 'Yes,' she nodded, hoping he didn't notice the muscle twitching below her eye.

With a forced joviality, she changed the subject. 'One of my students told me today I have lovely eyes.'

'She's probably buttering you up … wanting to make sure you give her good grades.' He ate slowly, taking tiny mouthfuls.

'Do you really think so?' Her jaw clenched and her lips thinned at his comment and she resisted shaking her head. Instead, she focused on his appearance, on his skin, which had taken on a grey pallor that matched his greying sideburns – she hadn't noticed this until now. She could make excuses for it – yes, she'd been distracted, but he hadn't always been around either, spending long hours at the airport or travelling overseas for work. A twinge of guilt rose in her throat, and she was sure it was visible on her face.

Sam, who'd been eagerly awaiting his father's return, hopped down the stairs, carrying his latest Lego creation. He'd eaten earlier with Lena. Alex made room for him, patting a space on the chair next to him. He admired the spaceship, but his voice lacked conviction. With downcast eyes, Sam discarded the toy on the table and turned to his mother. 'Can I please have ice cream.'

She took his hand, and they walked out to the kitchen in search of dessert. When she opened the freezer door, a few frozen blocks that looked like beef sausages or mince lay beside a packet of frozen peas. She slammed the freezer door before Sam could ask the question she was asking herself. 'Where did I put the ice cream?'

'We could go to the shops tomorrow and buy some more,' Sam suggested, but Debra was already retracing her steps in her mind. She remembered putting the ice cream into the shopping bag; she remembered taking it out of the car, so at least it found its way home. Lately though, she'd been wandering around in a daze, staring at the shelves in the grocer's shop without knowing what she wanted. On many occasions, she arrived home without the essential items, resulting in another trip back there the next day. Luckily Sam often reminded her of what they needed to buy, as she sometimes lost any shopping list she wrote. It was as if her body was present but her mind lived in a parallel universe, spinning round and round in its own little orbit. Sometimes it returned long enough to remember the person she was trying to forget, then she was flung into space once more.

Later that evening, when Alex readied himself for bed, he called out from the upstairs bathroom: 'Debra, is there some reason why a tub of ice cream is sitting in the hand basin?'

She remembered the toothpaste she'd bought at Chop Hua Ho – the latest brand from America, he'd told her. Would she like to try? Admiring his persistence, she added it to her shopping basket, along with the ice cream.

In the bathroom, Alex stood like a ghost as he stared into the mirror. He looked like he was waiting for someone on the other side of the mirror to tell him what to do next. Slowly he turned, picked up the tube of Stripe toothpaste lying beside the ice cream. Like a robot, he discarded the cardboard packet, then squeezed the tube onto his brush. As he lifted the toothbrush towards his mouth, he blinked at the red and white stripes appearing on his brush.

'What the hell is this?' He tried to laugh it off. But they were like a couple of confused actors forgetting their lines in a jumbled performance of comedy and pathos. She grabbed the ice cream from the basin and put it back in its rightful place lest it wander off to some other bizarre destination.

**

At the college, Debra redirected her pent-up energy into various projects for the students. They cut out newspaper articles to write summaries of what they'd read. She left a pile of newspapers with scissors and glue on her desk but in the morning when she walked into class, they were strewn across the room. Her desk drawers had been wrenched open and their contents emptied onto the floor. She stood at the doorway, unable to comprehend the scene in front of her as she stared in disbelief at the state of her classroom. Apart from stationery and some of her books, she kept nothing of value there. *Why would anyone be interested in my stuff?* With so much mess, she couldn't tell if anything was missing but, as she gazed around at the blackboard, someone had written a sentence, *'We are waching.'*

She dropped her briefcase on the floor, trying to make sense of this violation of her teaching space. Her jaw tightening, her lower lip trembling, the first angry tear reached her lip before she wiped it away. At this moment, more than ever, she needed

Rahim, but he was busy with director's meetings. Besides, they'd agreed to keep their distance.

As the students entered the classroom, she observed their reactions. Some looked embarrassed, others giggled nervously while some stared guiltily at their desks. After an uncomfortable silence, she asked if anyone knew who was responsible for the mess, but she didn't really expect a reply.

Fatimah and Zaharia sidled up to her offering to help tidy the disarray. Together they picked up papers and replaced the contents of her drawers. As Fatimah shimmied closer, she said, 'Thank you for teaching us. You are a good teacher.'

Zaharia moved in to join her, adding, 'Yes. We are very lucky to have you.' Their kind words unleashed the frustration trapped in her throat. She wiped away another tear but thanked them for their help and kind words.

With everyone in the classroom now seated, Debra did what most teachers would do … she circled and underlined each word of the message, creating a lesson out of an unexpected opportunity. First, they examined the sentence structure. Did it need an object or was the verb, 'waching' enough in its entirety. Was the word meant to be 'washing' or 'watching'? Then she noticed another smudged word she hadn't seen earlier. As she looked at the word *'you',* the innocuous sentence now sounded threatening. *We are watching you.* For the remainder of the lesson, that message distracted her, and she felt her anger rising. *Is this an assault on me personally or is it just a student prank?*

At the end of the lesson, all the students except Fatimah and Zahariah filed out of the classroom. Sensing her unease, they hovered, checking to see if she was okay. She thanked them again for their help and their thoughtfulness.

'There's only so much I can teach you. After that, it's up to you what you do with your lives, or how you use your knowledge. If you work hard, you will reap the rewards. Girls can achieve anything. Don't let anyone tell you otherwise.'

They both thanked her before waving goodbye.

As Debra hurried down the now deserted walkway, unlike the constrained life of her mother, she felt grateful for the career opportunities she'd had. She wondered, *Will these young women find a place in a world that offers them the respect they deserve, one that recognises their intelligence, their skills?* Living in a patriarchal society such as this, the cultural expectation was they would marry young, have children, and become housewives. But times were changing. The fact they were receiving an education at all would give them opportunities unavailable to their mothers. With loosening social constraints on women and work, Debra hoped they would have a chance to excel, to be treated equally along with their male counterparts. But there was a long way to go before all women had equal opportunities to men.

As she hurried out of the college, she glanced behind her in case someone was following her, her heart thumping in her ears drowning out all other sounds. Her steps quickened as she strode towards the car park where Rahim's Fiat was parked in a corner. She wanted to wait for him; wanted to tell him about her day and dispense with all the rules of their agreed separation. They needed each other. How else could they survive?

She scoured the college grounds, peered into the surrounding jungle imagining someone hiding in wait. Before she climbed into her car, she checked the wheels, quickly scanning the paintwork. *Has anyone tampered with my car? Who is watching me?*

The Secret Jewel

There is a life in you, search that life,
Search the secret jewel,
in the mountain of your body

Rumi

'I'm climbing Mount Kinabalu.' Jo plopped herself down on the sofa. 'A group of women from the Hash are organising the trip. I think it will do me good to get away from Gareth for a while. Why don't you join us? It's one of those things you'll regret if you don't give it a go.'

This was their first opportunity to chat as Jo had been busy with charter flights for the past few weeks. Before Debra had a chance to consider her proposition, Jo gave her a list of what she'd need to take on the two-day climb.

'Bring plenty of water and a few snacks to eat while climbing. Instant noodles for the one night we will be sleeping on the mountain. You will need something warm. Temperatures at the first hut are around 6°C but can drop to minus 3 at the summit. Lighter comfortable clothes will be better for climbing,' she added. 'As we're surrounded by tropical rainforest, you'll need a showerproof jacket. The Malay bearers will carry our packs so don't take too much. It will take us about six hours to climb to the first hut. The second morning, we'll begin climbing at 2 am to reach the summit for sunrise at 5.30.'

'I don't know how I will cope with the climb, but I guess there's only one way to find out.' Debra thought of similar concerns she'd had before trying out the Hash for the first time. Now she didn't hesitate, running every week. 'I'll talk it over with Alex, see what he thinks.'

Alex had climbed the mountain several months earlier with the men's Hash. Apparently, it only took him four hours. He'd reached the summit in record time and said it was a great opportunity while living in this part of the world.

'I'm thinking of climbing the mountain,' she told him later that night.

'Debra, do you know how high it is?' He laughed. 'You will have to prepare yourself. It's 13,435 feet above sea-level – the tallest peak in Malaysia. They recommend you stay an extra night to adjust to the altitude. You don't want to get Acute Mountain Sickness.'

'Prepare myself?' she blurted out. 'Do you mean for climbing the mountain or for failure?' She now felt more determined than ever to climb and would do whatever it took. *And what's more, I'll succeed.*

When Debra told Rahim she planned to climb Mt Kinabalu, he immediately dispensed with the restrictions they'd set themselves. Instead, he suggested they meet in Sandakan once she'd finished climbing.

'We could stay a couple of nights, visit the orangutang sanctuary in Sepilok,' he said.

She quivered with excitement at the prospect. So long had passed since their few days together in Singapore. Despite their agreement to have little contact, she found it a challenge not to phone him or talk to him at the college other than for teaching matters. This month of trial separation had only intensified her desire and made her realise how much she missed him when they were apart.

When she told Jo she'd be joining her in Kota Kinabalu, Jo cheered. Everyone encouraged her, including Alex when he came home a few days later.

'I've decided to fly up to KK to meet you after your climb. I'll take Sam to visit the orangutans in Sepilok. I was going to surprise you, but …' He shrugged.

Heat rushed to her cheeks, but she managed a complicit 'Okay' before breathing out a sigh of relief. *Thank goodness he chose not to surprise me.*

'You don't sound too excited. We've always talked about going there. This is our big chance. Sam will love it.'

'I might be too exhausted after climbing the mountain.' She fiddled with the rings on her finger, stalling for time. 'I'll think about it.'

'You'll be fine. You can rest the first day. It will do us good to have a few days together.' Then his mind quickly switched to more pressing problems. 'I just need to go into work … check if those birds are still crapping on the aircraft.' Alex resented the tiny swifts choosing his aircraft hangar for somewhere safe to roost.

'Your cute little birds won't like all that netting, but I guess it's not as scary as the sounds of gunshot.'

'Either method is better than constant cleaning of the aircraft. It's costing us a fortune.'

Returning from work that night, he sank onto the sofa before taking off his glasses and rubbing his eyes.

'I'm afraid I have some bad news. I won't be able to meet you in KK after all. I need to fly back to Nepal. I know I said I would spend more time with you but there's been some problems with their aircraft. I'm flying over there to check out the defects.'

'That's a shame, Alex. Maybe some other time.' She hesitated. 'I will go onto Sandakan after climbing the mountain. I'd like to rest for a few days before I fly back.' She felt a twinge of guilt at Alex missing out on a trip that was indeed starting to sound exciting.

The following week when Jo and Debra flew into Kota Kinabalu, they arrived at the mountain early and walked around the base camp looking at the display of ferns and orchids. Debra was most fascinated by the strange phallic prey-trapping pitcher plants. With their visual bribe of sweet nectar, they had no trouble luring unsuspecting victims. *Like life itself, full of temptation.* Everywhere she looked, she thought of Rahim. Every sight or smell reminded her of him.

Jo and Debra met the rest of the climbing group at park headquarters where they collected their permits to climb the mountain. The younger, fitter women were keen to get going but a couple of the older ones hesitated. At fifty-five, Wendy hadn't told her husband she was climbing the mountain. Instead, she'd told him she was going on a shopping trip as she didn't want to hear his ridicule when he laughed at her. Mandy, the youngest in the group at twenty-five, while fitter than most, had just found out she was pregnant and was ecstatic. As she told her news, Wendy and Meg exchanged concerned glances. As older, experienced women, they knew the possible dangers of the climb from lack of oxygen.

Debra also remembered the joys of pregnancy and how quickly life could change and take away the joy. While many of the women were afraid of climbing, they were willing to give it a try. United in their endeavour, they wanted to prove to themselves and their husbands what they could achieve. More than anything, Debra had to prove it to Alex.

'Well, I can't be tempted if I don't have them with me,' said Jo taking one last puff of her cigarette before throwing the packet in the bin.

On commencing their climb, the breathtaking scenery changed from damp earth and rocky outcrops to huge trees and lush jungle vines. Debra slowed on the ascent, stopping every thirty minutes to regain her breath. Each time she stopped, the cold seeped through her sweaty T-shirt. She wanted to climb faster but her head throbbed and nausea rose in her chest. Meg asked if she was okay.

'You look pale. It's probably altitude sickness,' she said. 'You need to rest, take a few deep breaths.'

Aware of the huge shadow looming above, Debra rested, admiring the spectacular views but the cold wind pierced through her, forcing her to move on. Their group split naturally into three smaller groups. The fastest climbers streaked away leaving her in the middle while some of the slower climbers tended to struggle, preferring to climb at their own pace.

She looked down to where the steep path disappeared around the bend. Nothing moved. And a heavy silence hung over everything, no birds, no breeze making a sound. She absorbed the meditative stillness; reminded herself there were many ways up the mountain and took smaller steps, aware of each tiny movement. For a moment she shifted into another world, into her solitude. This was her journey, and she had to climb it her way, in her own time.

Her belief that she could do it spurred her on to show Alex she could achieve this as well as any man. She pushed on through the headaches and nausea. *I am emotionally stronger, and I'm willing to fight* became her mantra. Searching deep within herself, she'd found a woman she didn't know existed. The small, frightened girl who once lived there had gone. Never far from her thoughts even in this natural wilderness she could hear Rahim's voice urging her on.

Tripping on a tree root, she reminded herself to concentrate, to take it slowly. Up ahead loomed the first hut and she looked forward to resting. But Meg arrived to tell her Jo had twisted her ankle and was sitting further down the path.

Debra grabbed extra water to take back to Jo and found her resting on a rock. She had fashioned a walking stick for support but grimaced as she stood.

'I know you're hurting, Jo, but we're not too far from the first hut.' Debra checked Jo's ankle for swelling. 'Can you push on a little further? We can strap this up once we get there.'

'I will have to dig deep. My last reserves were used up long ago,' Jo panted and, resting her arm on Debra's shoulder, staggered up the steep path beside her.

That night the temperature fell to freezing in the Spartan accommodation erected below the peak, so they stacked on piles of sleeping bags to block out the cold. Beneath the looming shadow, an impatient night plunged them prematurely into darkness. Without electricity, they amused themselves playing "Botticelli". Creating images in the dark of handsome movie stars, they tried to identify celebrities with sexy eyes or unforgettable hairstyles. Regardless of which famous person they were trying to guess, Meg asked the same question: 'Is it Sean Connery?' Eventually, someone threw a pillow at her and they rolled around laughing, their tired aching bodies momentarily forgotten as they relished in the playful company of supportive women.

With her head still throbbing from lack of oxygen, Debra found it hard to sleep, and needed to use the outdoor toilet. To reach it, she had to wade through puddles with plastic bags fastened around her socks. Silence prevailed when she returned to her bunk, each exhausted woman falling asleep, like dominoes dropping one by one.

All except Jo, who, in her small private corner of the hut, continued to whisper. She told Debra how her parents were impressed with her first husband who used to ring her several times a day. Later, they learned it was to make sure she was at home so she wouldn't bump into him with his other woman. Jo had no idea and nor did her parents. Lying in the dark, Jo let out her secrets.

'I was so naïve. I can't believe I trusted him. But he always seemed such a considerate man.'

'By the sound of things, you're well rid of him, Jo. I'm sure your decisions were determined by the limited resources you had at the time. Don't be tough on yourself. We don't always have the answers we need to deal with what life throws at us.'

'But have I learned anything from my previous experience? That's the important thing, isn't it? The choices we make in life should be determined by the wisdom we've gained. I've now been deceived a second time when I was least expecting it.'

As Debra lay shivering in her bunk, she thought about what Jo had been through. *Would she judge me as "the other woman" if she knew about my secret life? Would she view me as the terrible person responsible for breaking up another man's family?* Despite her fear of being judged, Debra wanted to share with Jo an important part of her life.

'There's something I need to tell you, Jo. I know you may not understand the reasons for my actions, but I'd like to explain to you how I feel. There's someone I care about deeply, apart from Alex. It wasn't meant to happen, and I hope you aren't shocked by this as your friendship means a lot to me.' Despite disclosing in a whisper, the gravity of her words bounced off the darkened walls and the silence strained to conceal her secret.

'Nothing shocks me anymore, Debra. Anyway, it's more than obvious. You've been acting like a lovesick teenager for some time now. It must be gratifying to be loved so deeply by a man.'

'I could try justifying it by saying it began as a friendship, an amazing relationship of the mind and spirit. That we had no intention of becoming involved physically, but I guess you don't really want to hear that.'

'Your friendship is important to me, Debra. I would never judge you.' Jo's words drifted off into the darkness, mingled with the sounds of gentle snoring that echoed around the room.

'Thanks, Jo. You've no idea how much that means to me.' Debra breathed deeply as her aching body finally relaxed for the first time that day, and exhaustion forced her into restless sleep.

Next morning, they reached the summit as the first golden rays greeted the dark sky. Even the altitude sickness couldn't dampen the elation Debra felt when she reached the top. Cold seeped in through her jacket, but her lack of sleep and throbbing head were forgotten as she took in the amazing view and enjoyed this rewarding sense of achievement. As she gazed at the ethereal vistas, she thought, *this must be the closest thing to heaven*. The sun spread out its beams, regenerating life as a new day was born.

Having fully absorbed the marvel of it all, they staggered down the mountain, their knees trembling, their backs aching. The ascent had taken six hours, the descent slightly longer as they assisted Jo down the wooden steps. The steep drop jarred their knees and strained their calves, but they remained jovial. On reaching park headquarters, they lowered their stiff bodies into the nearby Poring Hot Springs, and while wallowing in the hot water, followed by icy cold pools, amid shrieks of laughter, the women conspired.

'When I get home,' Meg said, 'I don't care how much I ache, I'm not going to let Don know. I am going to keep a spring in my step and say it was an easy climb.'

'Here, here!' a few others agreed

Debra happily ignored her aches and pains as she thought of what lay ahead. Nothing would stop her enjoying the next few precious days. Thinking of Rahim, her fingers and toes tingled in nervous anticipation, soon followed by an inexorable tide of elation.

After waving Jo goodbye, Debra took a bus to the Kota Kinabalu airport where she wiled away the time looking at the local crafts on display in the gift shop. She admired the woven baskets but chose a colourful necklace of threaded beads with matching bracelet, created by local Kadazan women. Consisting of fifteen strings of tiny beads, traditional motifs had been woven into the jewellery. They depicted cultural legends of a hero, his weapon, a venomous mystical snake, and a flower bud to act as an antidote from the snake's bite. The last motif she considered would be most useful should she run into such danger on the next stage of her journey.

The Shadow and the Soul

I do not love you as if you were salt-rose, or topaz
Or the arrow of carnations the fire shoots off.
I love you as certain dark things are to be loved,
In secret between the shadow and the soul.

Pablo Neruda

Fewer people boarded the small aircraft for the short flight to Sandakan and Debra had barely relaxed before they prepared for landing. Unlike the airport at Kota Kinabalu, Sandakan had a relaxed atmosphere, where people moved at a slower pace. Debra flagged a taxi and within twenty minutes had arrived at the Sabah Hotel.

Time stood still in this place, where steep nature trails led down from the hotel into the depths of dense, surrounding jungle - a private tranquil setting compared to modern resorts with expansive golf courses and million-dollar views. Entering the lobby felt like stepping back into the world of Joseph Conrad. Debra could imagine his characters sipping a gin setengah, as they relaxed in rattan armchairs, reading *The Straits Times* clamped into wooden newspaper frames and she instantly felt at ease.

The cool, wooden floorboards and ancient ceiling fans gave some respite from the oppressive humidity, but a constant stream of sweat trickled between her breasts and moistened her back. She lifted the damp, tangled mess of hair at the nape of her neck, and finger-brushed back her fringe as she gazed around the lobby. An elderly Sikh porter trudged in carrying her bag. While waiting for the desk clerk, she noted the warning signs against bringing durian into the hotel. She recalled the smell of damp rotting socks from the Singapore market stall and immediately her thoughts were back with Rahim.

The same porter slowly dragged her bags down a hallway that smelled of history rather than fruit. Her room looked comfortable, yet the décor, like the porter, showed signs of aging. A faded Indian wall hanging embroidered with tiny mirrors faced the windows. Admiring the intricate detail of each tiny motif, she ran her fingers along the perfect stitching of the matching cotton bedspread, now a muted shade of its original vibrant indigo. At one time this had been a splendid hotel, but it had witnessed the passage of time.

Keen to explore her surroundings, she hurriedly unpacked a few items of clothing, changed into a lighter full-length sundress, and added a long-sleeved cotton cardigan. Her unruly hair wrapped into a top-knot, she fastened it there with a couple of tortoiseshell combs. After taking the stairs down to the spacious lounge adjoining the lobby, she sank into an ancient leather chair, her fingers running along the studded leather armrests as she waited for the waiter. She ordered gin and tonic with *Angostura Bitters*; looked at the latest *Straits Times* fastened to the old-fashioned wooden frame. Flicking through the pages, she discovered a small headline in the middle of the paper.

Nobel Laureate dies at the age of 69. No! not Pablo! He can't be dead. She scanned the news item, aghast at the passing of such an accomplished poet who had so much to offer the world. She thought of his poems and the moments she'd shared discussing his words with Rahim. When the waiter clanked her drink on the table, so lost in another world of treasured prose, she flinched.

'I'm sorry, Madam.' He mopped at the spills on the small table with a paper napkin, placed a dry coaster under the glass before making a hasty retreat.

His distraction brought her back to the present and she stirred slices of lemon with the small plastic cocktail stirrer, ice blocks clinking against the glass as she created a whirlpool. Her thoughts switched to Alex and how he liked to collect these swizzle sticks whenever he travelled to different places. *Perhaps he's collecting one from his hotel in Nepal.* A pang of guilt hit her as she swallowed the icy drink, the cool liquid spreading through her body as she stared at the front door hoping for signs of Rahim.

She heard his soft soothing voice before she saw him, just the sound enough to make her heart race. As he walked across the lobby, she stood to greet him. He put his bag down before giving her a brief peck on the cheek.

'I was so worried you wouldn't come.'

'There was no chance of that. You have no idea how much I have been looking forward to seeing you. Did you enjoy the mountain?'

'I absolutely loved it. At dawn when we climbed to the summit, I'd never been closer to the sun. I felt like I could reach out and touch it.'

'That will always be an amazing memory for you.'

She nodded. 'I'll remember it many years from now – an achievement no one can take away from me. What about you? How have you been?'

'I am fine. Not scaling mountains obviously, but I have been doing a lot of thinking. Mainly about us. You are the incredible memory I will always have.'

'And you've been in my thoughts wherever I've been, whatever I'm doing.'

After Rahim dropped off his bag, they wandered around the expansive gardens, and Debra breathed in the fragrant jasmine ensnaring most of the garden, including a tall frangipani. How easily this landscape had crept into her heart, connecting her to nature. A lazy lizard, sunning itself by a sun-bleached pool, took fright and ran into the dense leafy jungle. She too imagined disappearing into another world. *What would it be like staying here, far away from the pressures of everyday life?*

'I can imagine how beautiful this was in its glory days,' she said, looking around at the overgrown garden. 'It's a shame that things can't stay the same forever.'

'Beauty may be transient, but love is everlasting.' He picked a frangipani blossom and, as he placed it behind her ear, knocked one of the tortoiseshell combs from her hair. It landed on a pile of dried leaves lying next to the pool. Picking up the comb, he took a tangle of curls, skilfully balled it around his finger before fastening it with the comb. He did it as if he'd done it many times before. She had an image of little girls lined up while their father tidied their hair and was touched and saddened at the thought. He kissed her bare neck; whispered in her ear. 'I remember this neck, these shoulders, these ears.' He nuzzled against her skin.

'And I remember how much I miss you. I think we should go to our room,' she said, stepping back.

Their bodies, like their minds, had become familiar. Tuned into the smells and tastes of each other, they explored with fervour. There was always something new, an added delight, an exciting discovery to enjoy. With their desires sated, the inexplicable comfort of lying entwined in each other conjured the belief that this was how it would always be.

Conscious of their limited time in Sandakan, they hired a car to take in the sights, including the orangutans at Sepilok. Her first glimpse of the rehabilitation centre almost brought her to tears as she learnt of the loss of the animal's habitat, their need to be rescued from manmade dangers, their vulnerability, and how the young ones were taken from their mothers.

Seeing the babies brought back thoughts of Mala and how she couldn't bear to part with her tiny clothes or blankets after she'd died. She'd lifted them to her nose, wanting to remember her unique essence.

'Of all the senses, I think smell must be the most evocative. I found sniffing her clothes a comfort when it was all that remained of my precious baby.' She spoke her thoughts aloud, but he listened without questioning.

'Yes, often the least expected scent brings back the strongest memories. A comfort, but I guess it also heightened your pain.' He stepped across loose slatted planks on the elevated walkway. 'Many smells bring back happy memories too.' He pointed to an overhead tree with low-lying branches. 'This smell reminds me of the writing desk in Mike's living room.'

'Camphorwood.' She plucked a leaf, crushed it then sniffed it before handing it to him. 'It has a distinctive smell, doesn't it – rather pungent and spicy.' She too had memories of Mike's house; the brief moments she'd spent there with Rahim. She recalled passing the camphorwood desk outside Mike's bedroom. Creaking wooden floorboards, clickety whirring blades fanned air over bodies that were sweaty yet sated.

Further along the walkway, the jungle was alive with colour, and a cacophony of sounds. A small noisy monkey swung from an overhead vine, crashing clumsily into a clump of bamboo and Debra angled the camera.

'I wrote you a letter from that writing desk of Mike's,' Rahim said. 'On his Chinese rice paper stationery.'

'I never received it.' She turned to him, wracking her brain to remember a rice paper letter. 'I would have recognised that delicate translucent paper.'

'The letter never reached you. I was distracted by an unexpected breeze and frangipani blossoms parachuting to the ground. I was mesmerised when a similar gust lifted the fragile parchment. I could do nothing but watch from the courtyard as it floated away on the breeze.'

'And you never found it? Perhaps I wasn't meant to receive

it.' She pictured his eloquent prose being read by a stranger elsewhere.

'Don't worry. I will write you another. I remember every word.'

'And I look forward to receiving it.'

After waiting with a crowd of other tourists, they glimpsed a reddish-brown hairy form followed by several more orangutans, swinging towards the feeding platform. A smaller one, not quite a baby, performed somersaults on a rope swing. Rahim placed his hand on her shoulder. She edged in closer.

Feeding time was the only chance to view them, and if keeping a distance from them helped protect their survival, Debra happily obeyed the limited contact rule, letting them roam undisturbed in their natural habitat. She admired the mothers cuddling their young with an instinctive sense of familial love, and was about to comment on it, but stopped.

'I have been thinking about family a lot lately,' Rahim said as if reading her thoughts. 'One sleepless night I lay there wretched at the thought of leaving my girls. After what happened to me, I vowed I would never abandon my daughters. The way my father treated Sophie was abominable. I want my girls to grow into happy successful women.'

'I wouldn't expect you to abandon them.' She reached for his hand.

'But that is nothing compared to my utter despair at the thought of losing you.'

'I hope you never will. I want to be here with you forever.' They stayed holding hands until they became aware of people gathering around them.

Another group of tourists arrived as they made their way to the car. They found a small café in town where they sat drinking iced tea, listening to a local Kadazan woman telling her tour group about a man who made his money collecting birds' nests from caves. Describing vividly how the birds constructed their nests using their own mucous, she explained how local men shimmied up bamboo poles to collect nests from the cave roof. The group responded with sounds of disbelief.

'It's true,' she impressed. 'People eat the soup made from the bird's saliva.' She continued to share stories about local customs and beliefs, her eyes widening at times with emphasis; at other times she scowled.

'If you hear, see, or smell anything unusual, never look behind. It might be the spirits of the jungle. They live in the rocks, mountains, trees, and rivers.'

Later, Rahim and Debra kept their eyes fixed firmly on the path ahead as they explored the site where many Australian soldiers lost their lives in World War II. Debra keenly checked out the camp where her Uncle Bert lost his life. He was only nineteen when he, and others like him, were sent to Sandakan to build an airstrip for the Japanese to protect the oilfields they had captured in Borneo. When the camp closed, the evacuation of prisoners to Ranau became known as the Sandakan death march.

Grey spindly rubber trees stood guard around the skeletons of rusting tools and machinery bearing witness to the evil that occurred there. On one side of the path, stagnant water in a neglected pond reflected its forlorn surroundings.

'I feel as if we are surrounded by death,' Rahim said, his face pale, his eyes questioning.

'Are you okay?' she asked as a large black bird flew down onto the wrought iron railing and fixed its steely eyes on them.

'It might be the drinks we purchased from that stall.' He rushed to the drain at the side of the path and vomited.

Indeed, there seemed to be an eeriness to this place.

Debra waited, her concern for Rahim obvious, but in a short while he assured her he'd be fine. They moved slowly on, and, as he gazed into a pond of dirty water, a brief flash of gold suggested a movement of fish, but the reeds were too dense, the water too muddy to know what lay below.

'It's not a patch on Mike's fishpond and his healthy koi, thanks to your golden touch. You are the guardian of ponds, the defender of fish. I'm sure Mike will be pleased when he gets back next week.'

'Yes, I miss his cheery banter in the staffroom.'

As they wandered up the path, she imagined the weak, sick prisoners who staggered more than two hundred kilometres along inhospitable jungle tracks. Rahim mopped his brow with a handkerchief then peered at the small writing on yellowed parchment inside the glass display case.

'More than a thousand prisoners and only six survived,' he read from the small print. 'What a tragedy!'

Looking around, Debra could only imagine the horror of those who didn't survive and the pain of those who did. 'It was an incredible sacrifice they made for peace. But we haven't learned from the horrors of war, have we? There is so much emphasis on that which divides us. Perhaps we need to focus on our similarities, rather than our differences. Only then can we hope for some semblance of peace in the world.'

Rahim took a moment and sat on the grass to rest. 'The problem is everyone is waiting for someone else to offer peace. They expect it to happen out there. We need to look within. Peace begins with us.'

He spoke so passionately, Debra read the concern on his face, in his eyes. 'If only we were part of an ideal world.' She sat next to him on the grass and took his hand; tried to recall the warning the guide gave to the group of tourists. She told them never to look back. Debra would continue to keep looking forward. Whatever it took, she would make peace with all the spirits, whether they guarded the mountain, rocks, rivers, or trees. 'Just let me keep my own small piece of this perfect world and let it last forever,' she prayed.

***

That night they dined at the Sabah Hotel in the old garden restaurant looking out over the pool. Since visiting the site of the war prisoners, Rahim had been subdued. She covered his hand with hers.

'Are you okay, Rahim? I am worried about you.'

He lowered his head. 'Yes. I am just affected by those around me.'

'You mean the deaths that occurred in Sandakan?'

He mildly shook his head. 'My father has been ringing me more than usual. He half smiled. 'When he speaks to me in Malay, I always answer him in English; it annoys him so much.'

'You surprise me. I never thought you'd be one to play power games.'

'When I was a child, he used to demand that I speak in Malay. Now he knows it does not work to bully me. He cannot force me to do anything. So he uses my family to get at me. He reminds me constantly about Mahani's health … how she would get better care in KL. He says I am selfish wanting to live in Brunei.' Rahim's voice grew louder as his anger rose.

'It sounds as though he tries to make you feel guilty?'

'Yes. He uses my daughters to remind me how much they miss their grandparents in Malaysia. I suspect my stepmother has some part in all of this. She likes to interfere.'

'Perhaps your father misses you; wants to be closer to you.'

'No way,' he scoffed. 'I am sure that is not the reason. It is more about wielding power. He surprised me the other day though. When he rang, he was speaking English. He asked if I'd had a good time in Singapore. I assumed he was referring to the conference, so I told him it was informative with interesting topics. He then switched to Malay and said, '*dia cantik,*' meaning

230

she is pretty. He was talking about you, Debra.'

'How does he know about me?' The knot in her stomach tightened as she feared she already knew the answer. She pictured a formidable man, wielding his power over others, a man using others to find out what he needed to know.

'My father reminded me what I am doing will not help my career or my marriage. I am sure his parents too warned him against running off with my English mother. It did not stop him though. He then told me about a great job in KL hoping to tempt me.'

'Would you consider taking the job?' Her breath locked mid-sentence, and she forced herself to breathe.

'No, I am happy here with you. I do not want to leave. But my father's final words hurt most. He asked, 'Is she worth it?''

'Oh, my God! So he knows about us? What do you think he'll do next?' Her pulse now thumped in her ears.

'Who knows what he is capable of doing!' Rahim shrugged, shaking his head. 'Who knows?'

Debra gazed out through the open doors where large black and white moths gathered under the light. Some of them had flopped onto the mat, discarded their wings, looking spent. Lena had once told her these moths were considered unlucky. When Debra told Rahim, she regretted it. According to Lena, if they appeared on your doorstep, someone you knew was about to die.

'We are awfully preoccupied with death tonight.'

'It's my fault. I shouldn't have mentioned it.' But as the words left her mouth, she questioned Lena's omens. *Are these moths a warning to us?* Her mother, with her extraordinary prescience, would certainly have thought so. The moths in their house had no such sense of foreboding. They would meet their last tragic dance unceremoniously with one sweep of Lena's broom.

'While we are on this morbid topic of death, I was sorry to read that Pablo Neruda died.'

'Yes, I read the *Straits Times* in the lobby. He was only sixty-nine. Too young to die. But what an impressive legacy he left behind. I guess that's what we should aim for in life: something to leave behind. He wrote about three thousand poems in a range of genres. That's quite an accomplishment.'

'Yes. It was not just his erotic poetry that we have come to love. He wrote surrealist poems, historical epics, and of course communist manifestos. So, it is not so much about the dying, is it? It is about living on forever in other people's memories.' He stared at her with warm searching eyes. 'Will you remember me long after I have gone?'

'I'll never forget you. There's a part of you embedded here.' She took his hand, placed it on her heart. 'Right here'.

He held her hands in his, and said, 'And you in mine and I shall keep it there forever, like Pablo, *In secret, between the shadow and the soul.'*

Their last night together, they made love again and again bathed in the moonlight from the window above.

'I'll always love you and I love the person I become in your presence.' Into the vastness of the night, she whispered her declaration. He took her hand and recited Neruda's lines in his unique soothing tone. *I love you without knowing how, or when, or from where. I love you straightforwardly, without complexities or pride. Therefore, I love you because I know no other way than this.*

When sleep eluded her, Pablo's words comforted her throughout the night. They awoke with the sun, the room full of twinkling rainbows that reflected from the mirrored Indian embroidery hanging on the wall. Sparkles of light danced across the bedding, ceilings, and walls, declaring the promise of a new day. Debra looked at the tiny rainbows around the room, and thought of joy, and new beginnings. The despondency that had plagued her the day before had now been replaced with a refreshing new sense of hope.

Risen from the Earth

Thanks to your love a certain solid fragrance,
Risen from the earth lives darkly in my body.

Pablo Neruda

As the aircraft flew into Bandar Seri Begawan, Debra peered out of the plane window, wondering how she could return to the stark world of reality. She'd already visited the toilet, sprayed herself with cologne, tried to escape from the dream state she'd been in these last few days. Flicking through an in-flight magazine, she stared at it without absorbing the contents of the page; she readjusted her seat position and restlessly shifted her legs. Not only had she rehearsed the story she would tell Alex, but she'd agonised over several possible scenarios. She repeated them over and over in her head.

Alex had insisted on picking her up from the airport, and she took a few deep breaths before the wheels thumped down on the tarmac. But none of the rehearsed lies or fabricated alibis were needed and remained hidden behind her tongue. He asked only a few questions about her time away, but his unexpected attention blew her away as he rushed in to hug her as soon as she alighted from the aircraft. Buoyed with love from the previous evening, she stood momentarily stunned. Instead, she looked around for Sam.

'Sam's already in bed … too tired to stay up and wait for your homecoming,' he told her. Her shoulders slumped, registering her disappointment. 'You can see him in the morning. How was the climb? Did you get to the summit?' He strode ahead to the car park, swinging her suitcase with ease.

'I sure did. I climbed it in record time. It was amazing!' She struggled with her carry-on bag, trying to match his pace.

'That's great. I was one of the first runners in my group to reach the summit. Anyway, let's get you home. Lena's made us a chicken curry for dinner.' He opened the car door then placed her case in the boot.

When they arrived home, the dining area looked different. Someone had set the table; a vase in the centre overflowed with magenta blossoms. Candles burned at each end of the table. Grabbing a package from the sideboard, Alex handed it to her. 'Here, it's a gift.'

Gazing briefly around the room, she admired his attempts at creating a romantic setting then examined the strange cylindrical brown paper package; squeezed it; fingered its shape, curious to know what it was.

'Open it,' he said. 'I know you sometimes worry about being on your own. It's something you can keep by your bedside or in your car when you go out on your own.'

'Where on earth did you get it?'

'In Singapore. There's nothing you can't buy in Bugis Street!'

She opened the box; read the instructions on the outside. COMPACT, EASY TO USE WITH AN ADDITIONAL ALARM. If spraying capsicum into the eyes of an attacker failed to disarm them, the shrill siren would probably frighten them off. She nodded.

'Wow! I'll always feel safe now. I can fight off anyone who gets in my way.' Placing the pepper spray on the sideboard, she reminded herself to put it in her car. She sensed Alex hovering, following her with his eyes.

'The other day my young apprentice Ismail said, "your wife is very beautiful".' He laughed.

'And you thought he was buttering you up to get a good assessment?'

'No! I thought what the hell is he doing looking at my wife! But I must say, you're looking rather sexy these days. I don't know what it is but you're looking great. You have a certain glow.' Alex looked at her wide-eyed, an unfamiliar expression forming around his mouth.

Lena brought in the curry and Debra served the tender chicken, savouring the first tasty mouthful. 'Thanks, I will take that as a compliment.'

After finishing the meal, she felt hot and moist, and needed to take a shower. She stood and pushed in her chair but Alex offered to make her a gin and tonic. From behind, he placed his hands on her shoulders, and gently kissed her neck.

'I really need to change into some cooler clothes,' she said, gently easing away from him.

But he quickly poured her a drink. Thoughts of a refreshing shower were forgotten as he handed her a glass, wrapped his hand around hers and held it longer than it felt comfortable.

'I've really missed you,' he said. 'While you were away, I thought about us a lot. I know it hasn't been the same since Mala died. I know I haven't always been supportive.'

'It wasn't easy for you either, Alex.' She recalled the desolation they both experienced following the baby's death.

'But I should have been more attentive. I haven't always been there for you when you needed me.' This sudden, unexpected effort and attention unnerved her. She patted his hand; told him she understood, it was okay. But there was more he wanted to say.

'I'd like to fix things between us. I've been thinking that we should try for another baby. You can start by going off the pill. I know it's not good for your health. You said so yourself.'

Her jaw dropped and drink dribbled from her mouth. She

placed the glass on the table more heavily than she intended. 'I don't know if I'm ready yet.' She noted his puzzled expression, his brow creasing. 'Alex, I'm not sure I'm ready emotionally. It's a big step to take. I still have that fear of loss. It's devastating when someone you love is wrenched away from you.'

Staring at the table, she picked up her glass and gulped another mouthful of gin, then muttered, 'I'll give it some thought. Maybe next year. I'm just not ready right now.'

'Well, we can take it one step at a time.'

Alex encouraged her up from the chair, placed her drink on the table, and wrapped his arms around her. As he stroked her back and neck, fondled her hair, she added, 'While I grieve her, I can sense her essence as if she's here. I fear her presence will be erased completely if I replace her with another baby.'

She edged away from him. 'I just need to take a shower.'

'Don't be that way, Debra.' He moved closer, tucked a stray curl behind her ear. 'You're always complaining I'm not attentive. Don't you want us to be more intimate, to be closer? I think a baby would be good for us.' Taking her hand, he led her towards the stairs.

'But you're not listening to me, Alex.' She tried again, but by the time they reached the top step, he'd unzipped her dress. As they entered the bedroom, he lifted it over her head.

'You care about me, don't you?' he pleaded and before they reached the bed, he had slipped off her underwear, letting it fall to the floor.

'Yes, but I'm trying to …' Her requests fell on deaf ears, and she closed her eyes as the overhead fan continued to clank and whirl. Only the two cicaks witnessed the pitiful performance from their vantage point on the ceiling.

***

After the rain, an unbearably humid day followed where numerous cold showers failed to cool her down. No sooner had she towelled herself dry than her skin and hair were moist again. Sam also suffered from the oppressive heat, so she turned on the air conditioner in his bedroom and they sat on the floor building Lego towers but after a while, he grew tired of the Lego world. She encouraged him with crayons and paper. Engrossed in his works of art, Sam showed her his drawing of a man and a girl. They were both wearing fairy wings.

'That's lovely, darling. Is that Kali?'

He nodded.

'Ah, I thought it might be. And the man, who is that?'

'It's her dad.'

'And why is he wearing wings?'

Sam thought for a moment. 'Because he's flying.'

Debra nodded, smiling once again at the lovely drawing. Apart from the vibrating hum of the air conditioner, all was quiet in the room. Then Sam looked up from his drawing and stared at her with large questioning eyes.

'Lena is crying downstairs,' he said.

Debra listened but heard nothing.

'She is! She's crying,' he yelled. Leaping up, he ran down the stairs to Lena's room.

Debra put down the paper, followed him into Lena's room and found her sitting on the floor folding the clothes she'd brought in off the line. Sam sat on the floor between her and the large wicker laundry basket. Copying Lena, he picked up one of his T-shirts and attempted to fold it in half.

'It is okay, Sam. I can do it.' She took the T-shirt from him, and he climbed onto her lap.

'Are you sad, Lena?' he asked, watching tears trickle down her smooth brown face.

'Lena, what is it?' Debra asked softly, placing her hand on

Lena's shoulder.

'It's Viola, Mam. She wasn't at Mass on Sunday. I can't contact her.' Her voice cracked as she folded a towel.

'Have you tried ringing her?'

'Viola's employer won't let her come to the phone. He said she is too busy. Several weeks ago, she appeared at Mass with bruises on her arm. Viola said her employer locked her in the bedroom to prevent her having a day off.'

'What is her employer's name?' Debra asked, shaking her head.

'I do not know, Mam. Viola only addresses him as *Tuan* or Sir. I know he works for the government and lives in a large house in town.' Lena shook her head. 'My mother in the Philippines hasn't heard from Viola for some time.'

Debra's jaw tightened. 'Let's go visit her employer. He has no right to treat her like that. Do you know the house where he lives?' She started moving towards the door.

'Yes, but I don't want to get you into trouble, Mam.' Lena's voice trembled as she choked back tears.

'We must help her. She's a single woman living away from home. He's exploiting her.' Debra grabbed the car keys from the sideboard, and took Sam by the hand. 'Come on, Lena. Let's go.'

From Lena's directions, Debra found the house and, as they pulled up the sloping driveway, she realised it was no humble dwelling. On the top of a hill stood a palatial two-storey home with large marble pillars framing black double doors. Wrought iron grilles screened the doors and windows where large palm trees cast long shadows across the front of the house. Soon it would be dark. From the garden, dogs ran along the perimeter, leaping and barking as they ran.

Debra climbed out of the car and walked up the driveway, Lena following. Sam's grip tightened on her hand. She pressed the doorbell at the same moment she read the owner's name printed under the button.

Muhammad Osman flung open the door. His huge frame filled the doorway. He stared at her before demanding in English, 'What do you want?'

Too late to back off, Debra realised, her skin chilling. And they were now blinded as outdoor security spotlights flooded them in a circle of light. The guard dogs leapt at the wire fence, snarling and baring their teeth.

'Lena is hoping to talk to her sister … just for a moment?' Debra's trembling hands and voice betrayed her composure. At the sight of his glaring face, any former trace of courage disappeared.

'She is busy. You have no right to be on my property,' he growled. He stood taller, more menacing. Then he switched to Malay and threatened her with words she didn't understand.

Before she could reply, two large men overloaded with muscle appeared from behind the house. Lena tugged on Debra's shirt, trying to pull her away, to no avail, so she took Sam's hand and walked towards the car. But Debra's concerns for Viola had risen.

'Can we please talk to Viola, just for a minute? Her mother is ill. She's keen to contact her daughter,' Debra said, trying to keep her voice calm.

'It is no business of yours. Get off my property or my men will show you where you belong.' At the threatening tone of his voice, the two men moved ominously closer.

Debra had no choice. She backed off and walked towards the car. 'How dare he threaten us like that!' she fumed as she slid back into the driver's seat.

On the long solemn drive back to their house, her anger outweighed the disappointment. 'What makes him think he has the right to treat women in such a manner?' Debra glanced in the rear-view mirror at Lena who now sat quietly cuddling Sam in the back seat and gently stroking his arm.

'I'm sorry, Mam. I shouldn't have let you come. I didn't want to get you into trouble. You are very brave. Thank you for your help. He is not a nice man.'

'No, he is not! Well, we've done nothing wrong, Lena. But we need to defend Viola. She's entitled to the same rights afforded any employee regardless of her sex or position.'

***

The next day at work Rahim called her into his office and shut the door. It had been days since Debra had stood this close to him. Acrobats somersaulted in her chest as she recalled his touch, his smell, his taste. Her initial excitement turned to dread at the sight of his knitted brow as she sat down gripping the armrest on the chair. His eyes showed obvious concern for her as he reached out for her hand across the desk.

'I am afraid I have some bad news for you. I had a visit from Muhammad,' he said solemnly. At the mention of that name, Debra froze. 'Debra, why did you go to his house? You were jeopardising your own safety. He has been looking for the slightest excuse to get rid of you from the college.'

'Well, despite what he thinks of me, someone needs to help Viola. Besides, I had no idea it was the Director's house.' Her fingers turned the rings around on her finger more frantically than ever, first one way then the other.

'He wants you gone by the end of this week. He has threatened to have you deported. Because your contract is not permanent, I cannot fight to keep you here. I am so sorry.'

'But what about the way he treated Viola? We can report him.' Pressing the thumb pad of her right hand against her ring, she pressed against the sharp diamonds momentarily numbing her pain.

'They would never believe you. They would make life unbearable for you. How would you explain it to Alex?' Though reasoning with her, he kept his voice calm, his eyes pleading.

'But he can't prove anything.'

With his bully tactics and threats, Muhammad had finally weakened her resolve. Tears of injustice slowly trickled down her cheeks and she dabbed at them with a tissue.

'Debra, he does not have to.'

Debra knew she could never win, and felt powerless in this battle. It would take more than this incident for anyone to believe her word against his. As she pondered her shattered career, she looked for a sign of hope but there was none. Most of her life she'd prayed to love unconditionally and to have that love returned. Having finally found love, it was about to be wrenched away.

Rahim came round to her side of the desk and wrapped his arm around her. She cried a mountain of tears, wetting his shirt and hers. Hurt and angry for all the injustices that women like Viola were forced to endure, she also cried for the job she loved and the students she was abandoning. But mostly, she cried for having to leave the workplace where she'd spent most of her days working with him.

'I am so sorry. I will arrange a morning tea before you leave. I know the staff and students will want an opportunity to say goodbye.' As he put on his jacket, his shoulders slumped with the weight of the more serious issues awaiting him.

The staff room was deserted as she collected a few personal belongings from her desk – her book of Sufi poetry – the red and yellow porcelain elephant. She was glad Mike was not there to lecture her. Rahim waited while she made a quick search of the classroom, ensuring she hadn't left anything behind in a desk drawer. She would hate to leave something that could be used to further incriminate her. With a heavy heart, she took one last look around the room, remembering each of her students, noting the desks where they usually sat. For the last time, she walked the length of the corridor; passed through the decorative wrought iron gates, sad that her happy time at the college had ended.

The Ends of Being

How do I love thee? Let me count the ways.
I love thee to the depth and breadth and height
My soul can reach, when feeling out of sight
For the ends of being and ideal grace.

Elizabeth Barrett Browning

Debra drove home past roadworks that had become a regular fixture these days, every jarring jolt in the road a reminder of the bumps in her own journey. It set her to wondering: *How am I going to explain all this to Alex?*

Fortunately, when she arrived home, he wasn't there, but rang later to say he might be home late – mechanical problems on the aircraft were taking longer to fix than expected. She tried to meditate but her racing mind couldn't be stilled, and her tears flowed, wetting her shirt. She had no desire to wipe them away – they were a reminder of what she had lost.

Instead, she knelt on the thin rubber yoga mat, placed her forehead on the floor, rested her arms alongside her legs, and curled up into the pose of the child. And like a small child, she tried to block out the real world, to disappear within her own little cocoon of safety. As she breathed in deeply, her body started to relax, and she imagined herself sinking through the floorboards, down into another safer dimension, away from people such as Muhammad and a world that wasn't fair.

Later that evening, during a sundowner with Jo, she stood on the balcony watching black storm clouds gather. As she related the events of the day and her subsequent dismissal, a sudden flash of lightning, followed by a loud peal of thunder shook the balcony. The heavens opened and soon torrential rain briefly obscured everything around them.

'At least you tried, Debra. For Lena's sake and for Viola. That takes a lot of courage. Muhammad sounds like someone you don't want to cross. A bully and a thug. I admire you for what you did. It's not easy for a woman to defend herself, let alone defend other women.' Leaning over the balcony, Jo looked down the road.

'Unfortunately, he is allowed to be a bully as no one challenges him. He can treat women however he likes. His privileges in life are taken for granted, so his behaviour is not accountable.' She followed Jo's gaze.

Down the road, a man sheltered under a large bamboo umbrella, bare-chested and with rolled-up trouser legs; water lapped around his knees. He started moving, and one minute, he was there, walking on the road, the next, he'd disappeared.

'He must have fallen into the drain!' Jo gasped.

They waited expectantly for sight of him or for his umbrella to reappear, but nothing showed. Another fork of lightning illuminated the sky and the dark treacherous road, but there was no visible sign of life, only flooded roads.

'Oh, I hope he is going to be alright, Jo. I hope he gets out somewhere. And now I am really worried about Alex driving home in this,' Debra said, shaking her head. She picked up the phone to report the man's disappearance, then to ring Alex's work, to see if he had even left yet. But the telephone line was dead, a regular occurrence during heavy rain.

Jo shook her head. There was indeed nothing they could do. Finally, Jo spoke. 'I'm so sorry for your sacking, Debra, but things are afoot at the airport as well. Lately, several managers have found their cars with deep scratches gouged into the paintwork. They thought it was an act of retribution as some managers had been mistreating their workers. I feared for Alex's safety over that, more than this weather, and you need to warn him about it. According to Gareth, Alex isn't popular with the locals.'

'Why would Gareth say that?' Debra defended, surprised at Jo's statement. 'Alex gets on well with his staff. With all due respect, Jo, I think Gareth is wrong. Alex has a strong sense of decency and fairness. He wouldn't mistreat his employees.'

'There have been other incidents,' Jo said. 'When I was on a recent flight to Manila, I was devastated to find my antique jewellery had been stolen from my suitcase. It turns out the baggage handlers at the airport while x-raying the bags pass on information to their colleagues as to which bags have valuable contents. My suitcase was slit only in the corner where I had positioned the jewellery case. The only item of jewellery not stolen was a strand of pearls that got caught in the zip of my suitcase. It's also possible the baggage handlers had read Gareth's name on the labels.'

Debra frowned, unwilling to believe anyone would want to hurt Alex. While these incidents were disquieting, she felt more perturbed by Gareth's opinion of Alex. *What an unfair assessment of a hard-working, caring man,* she thought. *While he might be a hard taskmaster, he is consistent, and shows no favouritism. It's more likely a projection of Gareth who is not at all popular with the locals.*

Right then, thunder boomed overhead, shaking the house and plunging them into darkness. Debra raced into Sam's bedroom where the little boy sat up in bed. She carried him out into the living room, while Jo lit a candle.

The vibration of the thunder shook the keys from the filing cabinet and the small porcelain elephant "who never forgets" crashed from the top of the filing cabinet to the floor. Small pieces of porcelain, including the high, curved trunk, scattered across the floor like red and yellow dice. A strange eerie silence surrounded them. Without the hum of the air conditioner, only the steady drumming of rain on the iron roof and the gushing of water through the downpipes could be heard.

'And, Debra, you must be more careful. People are talking about you,' Jo continued in her premonitory tone.

'What do you mean?'

'It's written all over your face. You've been looking so radiant. I envy you but I fear for you. You're taking risks in a small place like this where everybody knows you. You're putting yourself in danger.'

Debra sighed. Jo was right. For the past few months, she'd been walking on air, elevated by her senses, caressed and heightened by love. Initially, her greatest fear had been the risk of being found out. But the thought of getting caught had been overshadowed by the overriding fear of not being able to meet up with Rahim. She looked at Jo's face where stress lines had formed on her brow, tightening around her eyes. Debra felt sure they were not from Jo's concern for her, but from the nightmare she was living with Gareth, lying awake at night, worrying where he was. And she was not surprised Jo was releasing her pent-up angst on her.

The candle in Jo's hand burned down to a mere stub as wax dripped onto her fingers. Staring into the dying flame, she seemed unaware of the hot burning wax. Debra reached across and took the candle from her hand, blew out the dwindling flame. She lit a fresh candle, and placed it in front of them on the coffee table, the candlelight casting strange shadows across Jo's ashen face.

'I'm sorry things have turned out the way they have, Jo. It hasn't been easy for you. You don't deserve it.'

Leaning over, Debra took Jo's hand which was covered in dollops of solid candle wax and gently peeled off the wax. Jo jumped at the sound of a bang as the creaking air-conditioner rumbled into life. The table lamp flickered several times before filling the room with muted light.

***

Late in the evening, Alex walked in, his clothes drenched, his hair dripping from the rain.

Debra handed him a towel. 'I've been so worried about you,' she said. 'We saw a man washed away in the flood drain tonight. I had visions of you …'

'I've had a shocking night,' Alex interrupted her. 'The bad news is I think Jo and Gareth are mixed up in something illegal.'

'What? It couldn't have been Jo. She's been here with me all evening.'

As he scuffed his hair dry with the towel, he looked puzzled. 'Well, the red BMW was parked next to the hangar. Someone took the Cessna out in this bad weather.' He tossed the towel on the back of a chair and rubbed his face. 'It must have been Gareth and his pretty boy. They were standing by the car just before the Cessna taxied out from the hangar. We had to cancel one of our flights as we couldn't get the parts in time, so it was rather late when we finished working on the 737. That's when I saw the Cessna with its landing lights, touch down on the eastern runway.'

'It was too late for anyone to be giving flying lessons and we know it couldn't have been Jo,' said Debra. 'No one goes sightseeing at night, especially not in this awful weather.' *And not only does Gareth know how to fly, but he also knows the airport would be deserted late at night,* she reasoned.

'He couldn't have flown far though,' Alex said. 'He wasn't gone long.'

'Long enough to cross the border?' Debra remembered what Lena had said about Azri issuing illegal visas.

'I'll have to report him. At the least, it's very suspicious behaviour. At worst, it's endangering lives, *and* unlawful possession of the aircraft. He'll be in a whole heap of trouble.'

'Oh, Alex, please don't get involved. Did they see you? It could be dangerous for you. I don't want anything to happen to you.'

He heaved a deep sigh and rubbed his eyes. 'Let's talk about it in the morning,' he said, heading to the stairs. 'I'm beat.'

Debra switched off the light and followed. She would also talk to Jo about it in the morning.

Where Sunbeams Fall

Love's fingers tear up root and stem,
Every house where sunbeams fall from love.

Rumi

After the previous night's deluge, steam rose from the damp grass in the garden. The stifling, still morning air imbued a sense of lethargy that hovered around the fruit trees ravaged by the storm. As Debra looked at the mangoes and hog plums strewn across the lawn, Jo appeared on her doorstep, her arms full of mangoes.

'I've brought a peace offering. I'm sorry for what I said about Alex.' She headed across the lawn. 'Gareth panicked after he saw Alex last night. He thought he'd better confess before Alex told me what really happened. He was pretty shaken up.'

'What was Gareth doing with your Cessna? Alex thought it was you out there in that weather. I told him you were here with me.' She steered Jo towards the kitchen where she lowered the mangoes onto the table.

'I swear, I knew nothing about it. There's no way I would let him take the aircraft. And I still can't believe he did that.' Jo buried her face in her hands, and shook her head.

'Why did he take it?'

'It's Azri. If he wants Gareth to do something, Gareth jumps to it. Anything to impress his pretty boy and that uncle of his.' She heaved a deep sigh. 'They are involved with a group of political activists from Sabah,' she added. 'They've been hiding

249

out here in Brunei. That's a serious offence, Debra. I hate to think of the repercussions. Gareth is too embarrassed to face Alex right now.' She sank into the sofa, dropped her head back and closed her eyes. 'Oh my God. What a mess!'

Debra sank down on the sofa next to her. 'You weren't to know. People often disappoint us when we expect so much more from them. Even when we think we know them well, they let us down.'

'I thought I'd take the Cessna up this morning. It's probably the last time I'll fly. When they find out what Gareth's done, I'll lose my job, my licence. God knows what will happen to Gareth. Do you fancy a flight?'

'Are you sure you're up to flying?' Debra imagined the many painful thoughts whizzing around in Jo's head, and shrugged. *One thing's for sure, she shouldn't be flying on her own right now.*

'It's just what I need. We must get a move on though. I'll go check the weather forecast.' She stood to leave. 'I keep thinking about the humiliation I'll experience when everyone finds out. You know what this place is like. People thrive on gossip.'

'Yeah,' Debra sighed, 'I know what you mean: there's a lot of people who have nothing better to do. They are out of touch with the real world and anything that spices up their lives I guess gives them a thrill. I'm so sorry, Jo. This is the last thing you need.'

While Jo prayed to the sky for fine weather, Debra grabbed a drink bottle and met her at the car. With no other planes on the tarmac, Jo took off without incident. Up in the air, silence reigned except for the gentle vibration and quiet drone of the Cessna's engines.

'This is my kind of heaven,' Jo murmured.

Secretly, Debra felt nervous and her fingers locked onto the edge of the seat as she hoped Jo was up to the task. For the moment though, she tried to enjoy the relative calm, and admired the scenery below.

Jo followed the coastline south towards offshore gas fields, past the rows of animated 'nodding donkeys' pumping oil out of the ground. Out to sea, a crude oil tanker docked at the moorings beside the LNG tanks and semi-submersible drilling rigs, ready to be loaded. Down below, silica sands appeared as sparkling white snowfields, and beyond plastic-bag scarecrows in watery green paddy fields waved in the breeze.

Debra felt overwhelmed by a sense of predetermined destiny as she gazed at these iconic scenes, sensing the inevitable forces that determined life and death. They made her aware of the need to embrace every moment she had, lest it be her last.

Jo checked the map in front of her and scanned the instrument panel. Gently nudging the controls, she banked so they could admire the view of sparkling blue ocean to the east. As always, being in tune with the elements was breathtakingly beautiful. Adjusting her headset, Jo pointed to a pair of White Bellied Sea Eagles, distinctive with their V-shaped wingspan as they dived and soared in the distance. Debra had seen them once before as they had circled and glided on thermals, skimming along the water to pounce on fish. But this pair were locked together, tumbling towards the earth.

'I've never seen them like this. Are they fighting? They look quite desperate.' Debra stared through the window as they continued to swoop and drop until, at the last moment, they both let go before gaining height again.

'It's part of their mating ritual. They risk their lives for love.'

Debra heard the tremor in Jo's voice before Jo coughed and cleared her throat. As Jo continued, Debra looked at her pale sweaty face. 'He sacrificed my job as well as his own to smuggle strangers across the border. I had such high standards. But he risked everything for people he barely knew.'

As she levelled the plane out and followed the coast once

more, the Cessna began to rattle and shake. The vibration spread to their legs, and Jo said she felt nauseous. Debra grabbed her a sick bag, concerned at Jo's emotional state. Her pale face turned grey as she vomited into the bag. Debra passed her a tissue to wipe her mouth.

'Oh! Jo, you've been through so much. It's just not fair.'

The morning's cloudy blue skies had developed a dark greenish tinge. Debra looked to the east where grey thunderclouds had gathered. She caught a brief flash of lightning, then five seconds later, heard a distant rumble. The dark clouds quickly thickened and the first few drops of rain fell on the windscreen. Jo turned the Cessna away from the coast and headed inland. As calmly as she could manoeuvre, she circled the townsite of Bandar Seri Begawan where the sloping rooftops of the palace and the golden-domed mosque came into view.

From there, it was a simple approach – over the water village of quaint wooden houses propped on stilts, through the cloudy haze, appearing as a Monet painting in a muted mix of light and shadow. Jo continued along the river, which appeared milky green, then onto the airport where she coaxed the aircraft into a smooth, gradual descent. By the time she touched down, she looked at Debra, wide-eyed.

'I'm going to leave Brunei and Gareth. Once this incident comes to light, I will no longer have a future here. I'll take Kali with me.'

'Oh, Jo, I'll really miss you, but I understand why you want to leave.'

For Debra, her own future looked awfully bleak right now. And like Jo, she had no idea what lay ahead.

***

Leaving the college was more difficult than Debra imagined. The teary eyes and subdued mood of the students provided some consolation. When her students first learned she was leaving, they were shocked. With no previous warning, they felt she'd abandoned them before the end of semester. On her last day, they presented her with a hand-tooled silver bangle designed by Brunei's traditional silversmiths. During the past year, she'd instilled in the girls a sense of self-belief; she had tried to give them the essential skills, and the knowledge they needed, hoping they would get opportunities to transfer those skills into worthwhile careers. The delicate silver bangle was accompanied by something that made her believe they had been listening to what she'd taught them. Using eloquent prose, and perfect grammar, they jointly compiled a letter of appreciation, with each student adding a personal touch.

Debra bit her lip, and stifled a tear as shy Fatimah, the girl with the face of a cherub, presented it to her.

'Thank you for teaching us. We will miss you.'

Her colleagues similarly presented her with words of love and heartfelt thanks. As promised, Rahim organised a morning tea to commiserate her departure from the college. Mike had just returned from the UK and his presence lightened what would otherwise have been a rueful event. Though his eyes said 'I told you so', he didn't refer to past warnings he'd offered or the cause of her demise. Forever the joker, he made light of the sombre occasion.

'I know of your fondness for poems, so I've quickly penned one for you. I'm going to miss you, Ms De Bra.' He hugged her and slipped her a piece of folded paper. She read:

> *Debra, you are the sun who lit up our room. Before you arrived, we were full of gloom. You were the one who shared my jokes. What will I do with all these blokes?*

'I shall miss you too, Mike. I don't want to leave the college, but I have no choice.' Despite his good-humoured intentions, she found it difficult to appear cheerful. He had teased them, admonished them, and predicted the fairy tale's tragic ending before it had begun. *I should have heeded his many warnings.*

'As I've said before, Grainger,' Mike reminded her, 'we are mere puppets. Someone else out there is pulling the strings.'

Rahim walked over to join them, his shoulders hunched, the weight of his bowed head seeming too heavy to lift. He insisted on walking her to the car after everyone else had left. They parted with a gentle clasping of hands, then he was gone. As she opened her car door, she glanced back to see him watching her. Wiping away tears, she wondered what the future would hold.

In the early bloom of their desire, they had sought out barriers within themselves they had unknowingly built against love. As they had devoured the passionate prose, it was like removing the lid from one of Rumi's fermentation jars. Such was their longing, they were empty vessels waiting to be filled. While omnipotent elements, ill-timed and unforeseen, had poignantly wrenched them apart, she hoped nothing could prevent them from sharing their prose or their love.

Seas of Blood

Come the wind may never again
Blow as it now blows for us;
And the stars may never again shine as now they
shine;
Long before October returns,
Seas of blood will have parted us;
And you must crush the love in your heart,
and I the love in mine!

Emily Bronte

Beams of sunlight streamed through the wooden shutters brightening the colourful exotic bedding and drapes. Debra sat up in bed admiring the rattan furniture, the parquetry flooring, everything that was now familiar to her. She reflected on what she would miss if she had to leave this place. Looking back, she remembered her reluctance at coming to Brunei, yet during this last year so much had changed.

She gazed around this house with its comfortable furnishings and lush tropical garden, a dwelling she now regarded as home. As she watched Alex lying peacefully, she smiled that he'd decided to stay on and make the most of life here. His new air of positivity gave her the reassurance and stability she needed. When she finally gathered the confidence to tell Alex the circumstances surrounding her dismissal, she'd been awed by his response.

'Good on you for sticking up for the girl. That Muhammad

sounds like a real bully; my father bullied me as a child so you know what I think about bullies. He can't treat employees like that. What's his excuse anyway?'

'I thought you'd be annoyed at me for sorting out other people's problems.'

'Well, it sounds as though Viola was powerless to sort out her own problems. At least with him sacking her, she's been able to find another employer. Let's hope her new boss treats her better.'

Debra had also been tempted to make another confession, about the possibility that his number plates may have been recorded by the Sultan's bodyguards. She pondered long and hard for about two minutes before making her decision. *No! One confession is enough for now. The Sultan's bodyguards can wait for another time.*

The sounds of Sam chuckling in response to something Lena had said echoed up the stairwell. These sounds too were a familiar source of comfort that she'd come to appreciate, and the special bond of friendship Lena and Sam had formed was an unexpected bonus. Lena sang as she cooked, her face lit up with joy. The smell of fried eggs and bacon wafted up the stairwell, tempting Debra to climb out of bed.

'Don't get up yet. I just want to hold you,' Alex said, reaching out and grasping her hand. He draped his arm around her shoulders, and she rested her head on his chest. 'You know how much I care about you and Sam, don't you? You are my number one priority.' He gently stroked her hair. 'I couldn't stand it if anything happened to either of you. I don't know what I would do with myself.'

Debra looked up at him, surprised by this rare show of affection. 'I'm pleased you care about us, Alex. But nothing's going to happen to us. Everything will be fine. After all that's happened lately, it can only get better. We've had our share of bad luck, from here on everything's going to be great.'

Debra pushed herself up from the bed, but he reached for her again and kissed her slowly, making it last. She pulled away but he scanned her face querulously.

'When I get back from Manila, let's go to Hong Kong for a few days, just to get away from everything. I think we could all do with a holiday.'

'Yeah, that sounds nice. I'm sure Sam would enjoy visiting Ocean Park, especially the dolphins. Let's eat our breakfast before it gets cold.' She patted his arm before grabbing her clothes.

'I'm hoping for a good outcome from this meeting in Manila,' Alex said, climbing out of bed. He stretched his arms above his head and walked towards the shower. 'We're going to be discussing new business ventures for maintenance contracts. It may lead to an increase in salary. We can pay off our mortgage. Perhaps I can get a red BMW like Gareth.' He forced a laugh. 'We might even look at doing a second contract.' There was a new lightness to his voice, a trace of enthusiasm.

'I'm glad you're relaxing, enjoying your job. I'd been worrying about how stressed you were. It's great to see you looking happier.' Debra pulled on her jeans, and as she buttoned her shirt, she felt more buoyant, lighter than she'd been in days.

Yesterday she'd received a phone call from Rahim asking her to meet him at their secret place. He had something to tell her. Her heart raced at the prospect of what lay ahead. When she had last spoken to him on the phone, he'd suggested she consider tutoring individual students now that she had spare time on her hands. There were plenty of students who would be glad of one-on-one English tuition.

She had weighed the merits of what he'd suggested – it would certainly give her the mental stimulation she needed, and the satisfaction of doing something productive. It would also take her mind off the one person who occupied most of her waking thoughts. When he'd talked about the advantages of being able to write more poetry with her additional spare hours, she knew he was trying to cheer her, to find positives instead of the despondent thoughts that had threatened to overwhelm her.

Previously, she'd looked at studying poetry appreciation and creative writing. *Maybe I might delve into that more deeply now. Then there's the sailing course at the yacht club. Learning to helm will keep me occupied.* Before long, she had loaded her life with a variety of activities to fill the hours of each and every day.

Alex and his colleague, Jim Lyons, were taking the morning flight to Manila for a business meeting. They would stay overnight in a hotel before flying back the next day. Gareth had been scheduled to go with them but now needed to stay and face the consequences of his recent transgressions. Besides, he was probably the last person Alex wanted to accompany him on a business trip.

Debra and Sam drove him to the airport, so he didn't have to leave his car in the car park overnight. After parking outside, they hugged at the car before he walked towards the terminal.

'Let's go upstairs and watch Daddy board the plane,' Sam insisted. 'Daddy said he will wave to me.'

So they stood on the viewing balcony facing directly above the aircraft departing for Manila, on a breezeless, stifling day. A Filipino family with three small children paused on the aircraft stairs to wave at an older woman standing next to Debra. Two Malay businessmen with briefcases followed, and a young European couple holding hands followed behind them.

Eventually, Alex climbed the passenger boarding stairs, the last to board before the ground crew removed the stairs from the aircraft. As he turned and waved, Sam waved his GI Joe and shouted goodbyes above the engine noise. The aircraft taxied along the runway and lifted into the clouds; Sam rammed his fingers into his ears to block out the noise of the revving engines.

They waved again in case Alex was watching through the aircraft window.

'How long will Daddy be away this time?' Sam asked.

'He'll be back tomorrow,' Debra replied, wrapping her arm around his shoulder.

'I don't like him going away. I want him to stay here with us.' He stared at GI Joe as if expecting the toy to answer him.

'He'll be fine, darling. It won't be for long. He'll be back soon, I promise. He may even bring you another present,' she reassured him, knowing Alex had already asked what he should buy Sam.

Sam's face screwed up in a grimace.

Later, in the afternoon, Debra quickly showered and massaged shampoo into her hair. Her skin tingled as she remembered Rahim's touch. It had been weeks since she'd enjoyed having his body next to hers, but she remembered it as if it was only yesterday. Convinced it was going to be a perfect day, she bounced out of the shower, pulled on a white skirt, and slipped on a blue silk blouse, a favourite of his. She generously sprayed on perfume before adding her string of pearls. From her bedroom door, Gareth's shrill voice brought her running down the stairs.

'Debra! I tried to ring you but the phone's not working. I'm afraid it's Alex.' His stony face and grave tone warned he was the bearer of bad news.

'Oh my God! Alex?' She gripped the stair rail to steady herself. 'What's happened?'

'I was supposed to go with him, Debra. It should have been me!' His eyebrows lifted and his eyes widened as he stared into space. Gareth had just come from the airline office in town where Jim Lyons had phoned from Manila. 'Alex collapsed soon after arriving there. According to Jim, they found him unconscious.'

'No! Not Alex. He just left a few hours ago. How could this

happen?'

Debra watched Gareth, and his eyes moistened as he retold the story. She'd never seen him so visibly overwrought. His lips trembled as he struggled to speak.

'Apparently, an ambulance rushed Alex to Manila General hospital.'

Debra frowned, staring at Gareth, trying to make sense of what he was saying. *He knows more than he's telling.* She tried to process what she'd just heard, but felt numb, despite the blood pumping through her veins. Her head spun with every imaginable scenario, but her brain had trouble comprehending this information. It had only been five hours since she'd dropped Alex at the airport.

'So, how is he?'

'They're not sure at this stage, but it sounds serious. Life threatening. He's in intensive care.' Gareth's hands mirrored his emotions as they clutched theatrically, wringing out the pain. Slowly he muttered, 'They think someone may have drugged him. It's my fault.'

'Drugged him? What do you mean … it's your fault?'

'Never mind! Just get Sam ready … pack a few things so we can leave as soon as possible. I've arranged tickets for the evening flight to Manila and will come back to get you at 6.00 pm.'

The shock of it all slowly sunk in. *Only a couple of hours? It's way too final.* A huge weight crushed down on her, and she couldn't breathe. *How can I make decisions like this with only a few hours?*

'You must hurry. It's important you get to Alex as quickly as you can. He should be your number one priority.' Gareth shook his head and babbled on. 'Lovers only hurt you. It's not worth the pain. Believe me, I know.' His speech quickened, his contorted face and hands became more frenetic as they clenched and twisted.

Her thoughts muddled but her pulse raced. *I must go to Alex, but I need to say goodbye to Rahim. How can I determine the ending of a dream that hasn't yet been lived in its entirety? Or has that dream already ended? I must at least try to say goodbye.* She raced to the phone; dialled the number she'd memorised by heart but an echoing emptiness prevailed on the line, confirming the phone was dead.

Leaving Sam with Lena, she grabbed the car keys from the sideboard and headed out. In heavy traffic, her car crawled towards Rahim's house. She pulled into his driveway, but his car wasn't there. The shutters were closed, his house locked up. Debra hoped he'd left for the museum, that he was waiting for her there. She forced her way back into the traffic once more, and veered off onto a back road. The car accelerated and so too did her pulse. She slowed down to manoeuvre between bollards where roadworks blocked off sections of the road. She was already late, so pressed her foot heavily on the pedal.

Up ahead, around one more bend, stood the museum on the hill and she started the slow, painful climb to the top, finally pulling into the car park at the back of the museum. No other cars were in sight. *He may have arrived earlier and thought I wasn't coming.* She walked up to the bronze cannon, willing herself to touch the smooth mound. *Perhaps he's left me a note.*

Underneath was the intimate, concealed receptacle, guardian of their secrets, keeper of promises, entrusted with their longing, of hearts filled with love, a portal into another world where nothing else mattered. She looked around before sliding her hand into the cold black recess. *Nothing.* She plunged her hand in further, stretching her fingers to the limit.

She peered underneath then looked around again. This time her fingers fastened onto something like paper. Butterflies fluttered in her chest; fluttered loudly in her ears. She withdrew her hand, slowly uncurling her trembling fingers. Something dry and brittle. She looked down at the spent petals from another season. *Bunga kertas, the paper flower.* Her heart sank. The butterflies scattered, leaving an emptiness in her gut. She stood waiting, twirling the rings on her finger. *He might still come, and I can't afford to miss him.*

Pacing up and down the gravel path, she crunched the small stones underfoot, prowling like a puma hoping to pounce on the first sign of car headlights drawing near. But there were none. The surrounding jungle grew darker, came alive with the eerie sounds of dusk. She listened but all she heard was the clicking of cicadas and fruit bats swooping low around the trees. She looked again at her wristwatch knowing she would not be able to wait much longer.

The museum exterior lights switched on automatically and thrust her into the spotlight. She slipped back towards the shadows, not wanting to be centre stage or attract the wrong attention. As she looked up the road once more, she listened to the disquieting sounds of silence – a dreaded sense of foreboding. Then came a whistle, followed by a faint imperceptible whisper. Then a thud as a hard object hit the back of her head. Another hit her back. *Someone's stoning me.* Frowning, she turned; saw a red cigarette glowing in the dark. This time a stone hit her forehead, and the warm copper taste of blood trickled down her face onto her lips. She ran towards her car, but the red butt chased her, accompanied by taunting laughter. She thought of the pepper spray sitting on the sideboard at home.

There were two of them, dark menacing strangers blocking her way. A couple of angry men, sneering, taunting, threatening her. As she moved towards the driver's door, one lunged at her, grabbing at her breasts, ripping her blouse. She landed against the car's wing mirror, whacking her ribs. *These are not harmless threats. I'm in trouble.* She smelled her own fear, the bitter taste in her throat. Kicking out at them, she lost her shoe as she struggled to reach the rear car door. The second man followed, grabbing her skirt, his foul mouth muttering obscenities as she wrestled from his grip and reached for the door handle. As he grabbed her leg, she kicked, but his hands ripped her skirt. Her pulse throbbed *Danger!* in her ears, and she feared for her life. Here, at this time, no one would hear her screams. No one would protect her from these savage thugs.

Her fear doubled. She wanted to scream but a hand clamped over her mouth. *It's over! It's over!* Then she heard a faint voice from somewhere deeper within. *Fight! Fight hard. Fight for your life.* With one last effort, she drove her fingernails into the eyes of the face in front of her. As he jerked back, she shoved with all her might to push him off, and slid to one side of the car. As she braced, wincing from the pain in her ribs, she dragged herself along the car, lunged to open the back door and slammed it on her foot. Locking the doors, she clambered over the seat and searched for the keys in the ignition.

She heard the faintest snap, then a cascade of pearls scattered down her chest, onto the seat, spreading pools across the floor of the car. Her heart pumped faster as she thumped the horn loudly. They were now jumping on the bonnet, throwing stones at the windscreen.

She slid down into the driver's seat and, as she turned on the engine, car headlights shone through her windscreen, brightening as a car stopped in front of hers, blocking her exit. The driver leaned out and waved at the two thugs, shouting, threatening them. They leapt from the bonnet and ran off into the night.

The driver dipped his headlights before parking his car in the space next to hers. It was not a car she recognised, and she wanted to escape from this place as quickly as she could. With her foot pressing the accelerator, she glanced at the man walking towards her car, and burst into tears.

Rahim tapped on her window.

She opened the passenger door to let him in beside her, then locked the doors again. Rahim reached out, grasped her hand, held it tightly as he repeated over and over, 'Are you okay?'

No words would come, the shock of the attack still reeling within her. Unable to tell him coherently through her sobs, he fathomed what had happened, his mouth agape as he stared at her, as he scanned her face and body. He stretched his arm behind her shoulders and drew her into him, nestling her head on his shoulder.

'I'm so sorry.' He stroked her cheek ever so gently. 'My car wouldn't start. It had to be towed away. The mechanic at the garage lent me that car but he is waiting for me to return it.'

Between sobs, she managed to relate, 'Alex … Alex is …'

'I already know about Alex. I called into your house before I came here. Jo told me what happened to Alex. I left a note for you with Jo. I am so glad I found you; that you are safe. It is my fault for asking you to meet me here.' He muttered over and over, 'I am so sorry.' He soothed her with his voice.

'It's not your fault.' She peered at his face in the darkness and heard the tremors in his voice. Locked in their sad embrace, they lost all sense of time. At some point, she glanced at her wristwatch. 'I have to leave now if I am going to make the Manila flight. Oh, Rahim …'

Like a terrible wrenching apart of two magnets that didn't want to separate, he turned her head, kissed her ever so gently for fear of hurting her bruised body. Taking out his handkerchief, he dabbed gently to wipe the blood from her face. Despite his best attempts to soothe her, it was a sorrowful farewell and his eyes moistened with tears.

'Life will not be the same without you. I know you will be back soon, but I will miss you.' He smiled, trying to reassure her. 'Just stay safe and never forget me.'

'And don't ever forget me.' She reluctantly eased herself from his embrace and he walked away towards his car. *Dear God please let everything be okay.*

Tears clouded her vision and sobs wracked her body as she swerved perilously onto the main road, her hands slipping on the steering wheel. In lighter traffic, with the bollards removed, she sped along the poorly lit road. As she pulled into their driveway, Lena stood waiting, Sam by her side. At the sight of Debra's torn clothes, stained with blood, Lena wailed. Debra limped towards them, leaning heavily on one foot with one shoe missing. Sam ran to her, crying hysterically.

'Oh, Mam, what have they done to you?' Lena cried, and threw her hands to her face.

Jo appeared with suitcases packed for Sam and Debra. She put them down. 'Oh my God. What on earth has happened? It's okay, Lena, I'll take care of her.' She ushered Debra into the house and bathroom. Briefly, Debra related the details of her attack as Jo ran water in the shower. She helped to dry her with a towel, avoiding the painful areas Debra pointed out to her. Bruises and swelling appeared around her face, foot, and ribs as Jo tried to soothe her with words of comfort and clean clothes for her to change into.

'Gareth has booked extra tickets for us. Kali and I are going with you to Manila.'

As Jo gently guided her into their car, Gareth turned on the engine. She tried to prise a reluctant Sam from Lena's arms, but the two were inconsolable.

Aware of shadowy moments where her body disconnected from her brain, Debra closed her eyes, trying to fathom the chasm that had swallowed her. While her mind was stuck in this foggy mythical underworld, her body throbbed with pain. She took one last look back as she climbed the aircraft steps. *Perhaps he will come to say goodbye.* But only the red taillights winked back at her.

Everything after that was a blur. Cold and numb, hours of

sitting on an aircraft seat did little to assuage her physical pain or the wretchedness of her mind. She remembered a taxi ride in Manila. Horns tooting, lights flashing with the four of them squashed together in the back seat. She remembered Sam's warm head nodding gently against her chest as loud heavy metal music screamed through the car radio speakers. The driver sped through endless traffic, fiddling with the radio, switching channels. Debra listened as the soulful chords from a melancholy guitar echoed her own pangs of sadness. As Mark Knoffler reached his final heart-wrenching crescendo, Jo reached out for her hand, and they both sobbed. Their cries were of pain, regret, and despair as they released them into the sultry Manila night. She'd left behind the one she loved. Who knew what lay ahead?

Journeys End

In secret we met -
In silence I grieve,
That my heart could forget,
Thy spirit deceive.
If I should meet thee,
After long years,
How should I greet thee!
With silence and tears.

Lord Byron

Jim Lyons stood in the hospital reception area waiting for Debra, having stayed with Alex until she arrived; he looked concerned but happy to hand over the responsibility of this unfortunate event.

'I'm sorry I can't shed any light on what happened,' he said as they hurried down the corridor to where Alex lay in intensive care. 'The taxi driver dropped me off at the hotel to check in while Alex went straight to the office for the meeting. When I arrived at the meeting, they told me Alex had been rushed off in an ambulance.'

'What do you think happened? Gareth said something about him being drugged.' She scanned Jim's face for clues, her thoughts whizzing around with endless possibilities.

'I think it might have been the taxi driver. He offered us some sort of fruit drink. Alex took one but I declined. It must have been the drink. He must have slipped something in the drink.'

'The drink? I'll ask the doctors … find out if they know any more.' Desperately, she wanted to sit but sharp stabbing pains assaulted her ribs each time she tried to breathe deeply.

As they reached the nursing station, Jim's eyes scanned her, but he didn't comment on her appearance.

'I have to go, Debra, to catch my flight back,' he said, then he turned and hurried towards the door.

A nurse stared at the bruise on Debra's forehead, the dried blood on her face, but directed her to the intensive care ward without mentioning it. A doctor stood by Alex's bed.

'He might be here for another day or so,' he told her. 'Then we will transfer him to a normal ward.'

'But what happened to him?' she pleaded. 'Do you know?'

The doctor scanned the chart on the clipboard he held and shook his head. 'We are waiting for further test results.' Leaning on Alex's bed, stroking his hand and whispering words of encouragement, she had little strength to give. She longed to stretch out, to rest her aching body against his, but the doctor peered at her over his clipboard. 'He is in a coma but may know you are here.' Depositing the clipboard on the end of the bed, he left Debra standing, looking down on Alex's ashen face as she listened to the monitors bleep and ping, no closer to knowing what had happened.

Eventually, a nurse encouraged her to get some rest, and she returned to her hotel room where she tried to sleep, but her mind roiled with menace as negative images competed for space in her head. Her endless prayers helped only a little to suppress the horrific memories threatening to rise to the surface.

***

As the days passed, Debra's prayers of supplication changed in purpose but not in intensity. They began with 'please let him come out of his coma' then 'please let him survive. Please let him breathe on his own and recognise us. Let him make progress today.'

Jo and Kali took turns keeping vigil at the hospital or minding Sam to give her a break. On the second day, Jo sat with Alex while Debra took some time out with Sam and Kali. When she pumped the doctors for more information as to what had happened, they simply said that he collapsed; that they found a large quantity of drugs in his blood. On further investigation, she found that his wallet and gold Rolex watch had been stolen, but his airline ID was left attached to his shirt.

'Your husband is a lucky man. The amount of drugs he was given was enough to kill him.' The doctor shook his head.

'Why would anyone do something like this?'

'Who knows why people act the way they do?' He shrugged. 'But there is a lot of poverty out there. Bad people will stop at nothing. You need to focus on helping your husband to get well.'

She spent many hours going over it in her mind, asking the same question, becoming more befuddled. *Was it someone who knew him or was it a matter of being in the wrong place at the wrong time?* She could only hope it was the latter. *Alex was agitated about having offended people over the contract for the new hangar. Surely not! Gareth also appeared distraught about what happened to Alex.* She replayed the conversation in her head.

'What did Gareth mean when he said it should have been him?' she asked Jo when she met her later.

'He was supposed to be going to the business meeting with Alex. He may have felt guilty that he wasn't there. I don't really know,' she shrugged. Jo had much to consider regarding her own future. It wasn't easy for any of them.

One morning as she stepped into the hospital elevator, a young Filipino doctor rushed to leap in, his stethoscope swinging at his neck. He brushed a strand of sleek black hair away from his sweaty brow before thrusting his hand into his pocket. He looked at her absentmindedly. It was not only his gesture that sent her heart racing. A trace of his aftershave wafted around the elevator, evoking tender memories of happier times. She wanted to inhale the evocative mix of citrus and musk blended with salty sweat, but reluctantly averted her eyes and nose.

As they raced through each floor, the lift climbed higher while her disappointed heart sank heavily to the bottom.

'You're Mrs Grainger, aren't you?' the doctor asked as the doors opened. They both exited at the same floor. 'I was treating your husband in ICU. He should be out of there soon. I guess you're looking forward to taking him home.' He checked his watch, eager to move on.

She wanted to ask him questions but didn't know where to begin, her thoughts were so muddled. So she simply nodded. He was already on the move. *Besides, he probably doesn't have the answers I need.* 'Thank you for taking care of Alex,' she said quickly, 'thank you for keeping him alive.'

She cupped her face in her hands. *There are so many questions I want to ask but I'm exhausted from these endless thoughts and quest for answers.* Indeed, most nights she couldn't sleep and therefore dragged herself through each day trying to stay awake. When she finally succumbed to sleep, it was troubled and restless, and full of weird dreams.

In her dreams, sunbeams landed in the palm of her hand. She watched dust motes transform into magical beings as the sun caught them at the right angle. Rahim lay there languishing on a fluffy cloud of fragrant flower petals, as she plucked each blossom, like tiny snowflakes dancing on a breeze. High above the clouds, she reached for the golden orb that had entangled them in its web, but she could no longer feel or touch it.

As she placed each of the tiny petals on this huge man far greater than her, he decreased in size, smaller and smaller until he was a mere mortal. Then her fingers were shrinking, and she could no longer reach out. As he floated past, her hair softly brushed against his smooth skin. When he looked at her, his eyes spoke to her of love.

But his eyes then changed, becoming that of a stranger with a jeering face and rotting teeth. As the red cigarette butt loomed menacingly closer, her screams wakened her once more, and she relived the terror and shame.

Drenched in sweat and tears, she watched the full insomniac moon shining through chinks in the slatted blinds, forcing her to keep it company. As her aching body tossed and turned, her restless mind continued to search for answers.

She turned to meditation, but nothing worked.

Though Debra prayed for miracles, she didn't believe she deserved them. No amount of cleansing would make her clean again. As Alex slowly recovered, her prayers were those of gratitude. *Thank you for saving him and me, for I too have been through hell and survived.* Focusing on Alex occupied all her waking hours, she didn't have to think about what had happened to her the night she left Brunei.

When not visiting Alex, she limped along the nearby Manila streets, aimlessly but forever vigilant. Since their lives had been threatened, she felt nervous, never straying too far from the hospital or hotel.

One day when she and Sam arrived at the hospital, Alex was not in his room – the nurse had taken him downstairs for more tests. To fill in time, they walked to a nearby café. The interior was light and airy with views of the hospital and a small children's playground. Debra sat at a window seat with her back to the cashier's desk watching a man push a small girl on a swing.

As she observed the pair, she envied the shared intimacy between father and daughter. The man's face shone with devotion as the girl lay back on the swing, her long black hair floating in the breeze. Debra's thoughts inevitably shifted to Rahim and his daughters, and her eyes filled with tears as the man handed his daughter a piece of fruit, peeling it for her. It may have been a rambutan, but it didn't matter. It was a tiny gesture of love. Everything reminded her of him.

As she sipped the last of her cappuccino and dabbed the froth from her mouth, a man spoke to the cashier behind her, asking for directions. But it wasn't what he said that attracted her attention: his charming Oxbridge accent was like music to her ears. She turned to see the back of his sleek black hair, his pale aqua shirt. She fumbled with her handbag, grabbed Sam by the hand but, by the time she reached the desk, he'd gone. She thrust a handful of money at the cashier, and didn't wait for the change. As she looked down the street, she saw a flash of aqua shirt, and her pulse raced. She charged after him, dragging Sam and her throbbing foot behind her. He crossed the road. They started to follow but the lights changed to red. They were stuck. As the the lights flashed green, they set off again just as the figure disappeared around the corner.

She wanted to cry out, to tell him to wait for her but he couldn't hear. Instead, they pounded past the shops, dodging busy commuters, mothers with prams. Round the corner, they dashed to where the street ended in a row of bus stops. A bus pulled in front of the queue where he waited, ready to jump on. She limped towards the bus, but he moved forward in the queue, turned his head towards her. Her heart sank like a rock in a deep dark pool. He was only a teenager and looked nothing like Rahim. She looked down at Sam who was whimpering – it was much too hot to be rushing around in the heat.

Dejected, they trudged back to the hospital, retracing their steps, the return journey seeming far longer. Breathing heavily, she knew she needed to let go of him, to move on with her life, but her senses still craved any tiny trace of him. Any glimpse of a white Fiat threw her into a frenzy and, if she fell asleep exhausted, she would be jolted awake by the frightening memories of the last few days. A menacing voice told her to wake up and remember what had happened when it was the last thing she wanted to do.

With Alex now free of most of his tubes, the nurses had propped him up on pillows and were adjusting his covers as they walked into his room. As they moved aside, Alex turned his head and looked at her

'Debra, you're here? I never thought I'd see you again.' He took a shallow breath before wheezing out a sigh.

'Yes, I'm here, and so is Sam.' She pulled Sam in closer; lifted him onto the edge of Alex's bed, the familiar gnawing pain stabbing her in the ribs. She kissed Alex's cool cheek, reached for his wrist, careful to avoid the canula in the back of his hand.

'How are you, buddy?' Alex smiled at Sam with half-closed eyes. Sam looked at his father warily before launching into a summary of what he'd been doing for the last few days.

'I really missed you, Dad,' he added exuberantly.

'Me too, buddy.' Then he muttered to Debra, 'I've missed you too.' Then he looked exhausted and, after a few minutes, his eyes started closing, his jaw dropped onto his chest. They left him to rest before going upstairs to meet Jo and Kali in the hospital cafeteria. Apart from three nurses sitting close to the counter, they were alone.

Debra sat at the nearest table to wait for Jo. Sitting on the chair closest to her lay a book someone had left behind: *A Practical Guide for Healing Body, Mind and Spirit.* She flicked open a page to familiar words from a Sufi tradition known as *A Mile from Baghdad.*

> *In the meditation you are asked to close your eyes, to imagine walking down a desert road.*

Debra continued reading.

Feeling the hot sun and sand beneath your feet, you are tired, overcome with thirst. You rest for the night near a rocky outcrop, letting yourself experience the desolation. As you watch the sun set, you feel your body slowly coming back to life. A smattering of lights twinkles in the near distance. From the sounds of soft music, you discover a city filled with people is quite close by, within easy walking distance.

The words on the page blurred as Debra's eyes filled with tears, but she continued to read.

While you thought you were in the middle of a barren desert, you were only a mile from Baghdad.

The meditation suggested you give a brief prayer of thanks, acknowledging that help is not far away. Debra gave thanks for being reminded of the Sufi prose and the mysterious elements that left the book there for her to find. While she'd experienced desolation, she was slowly crawling away from the barren wasteland. But there was still a long way to go.

When Jo arrived, Debra told her about the meditation, moving her chair in closer so she could lower her voice as Sam and Kali played with puzzles at a table nearby.

'What you experienced the night we left was horrendous. If you're ready to talk about it, I just want you to know I'm here to listen.'

Debra shook her head, knowing Jo only wanted to help … but how do you talk about an event that now seemed so unreal? – something she didn't fully comprehend or wish to acknowledge. Once she'd pushed the memory down into the deepest depths it was hard to release it again; it was an image that was so painfully unspeakable, it hurt to describe it. And repeating the words, she would have to relive it in her mind.

'It's so hard, Jo. I can't fathom what or why it happened. I don't know where to begin. All I recall are the emotions, the powerlessness, the pain, but mostly the guilt.'

'Perhaps that's what you need to focus on …what you're feeling right now.' Jo reached out and held her hand.

'It's so demeaning. I feel vulnerable and ashamed, angry that someone could treat me like that. But the overwhelming emotion right now is shame. The woman I used to be died that night. I've been left with an empty shell.' She took out a tissue to wipe her eyes.

'You did nothing wrong, Debra. It shouldn't be your shame. It belongs to the cowards who assaulted you. Those brutes are the ones who should be punished.' She gently stroked Debra's arm.

'They were strangers who didn't even know me. But I feel guilty and responsible in some way … as if it was my fault … that I didn't heed the warnings.'

'What do you mean? Attacking a powerless woman makes men powerful. They don't care about their victims. They are just gutless bullies. They threaten women because they think they can get away with it.' Her voice rose and her face flushed in anger.

'When I look back, I remember Mike tried to warn me. Perhaps I should have listened. He said it was a dangerous path I was treading.'

'You couldn't have known this would happen, Debra. You are not to blame. You are the innocent victim.'

Debra heard the conviction in Jo's voice as she stared into her eyes. If there were threats, she hadn't been paying enough attention; her thoughts were always occupied with him. And what of Rahim? Had he suffered too? What was he going to tell her that night? Did he, in his quietest moments, think of her as she was thinking of him now? Or was it simply the slow sultry days and exotic tropical nights that had fuelled such passion? She had not expected love in this faraway land. Nor had she imagined the complexities it would bring.

***

Free of the tubes and the machines that had kept him alive, life for Alex became easier. He could now eat and talk but felt groggy and struggled to get out of bed.

'Do you remember much about the day you arrived in Manila?' she asked.

'No, it's all a blur. The last thing I remember was dropping Jim at the hotel and getting out of the taxi a few blocks from our office. That's where they tell me I collapsed.' Alex propped himself against the pillow.

'Luckily you were wearing your airline ID. The stranger who found you rang an ambulance and the airline office.' She helped him to adjust his pillow. With his mind still a blur, he didn't notice her restless state, the dark rings around her eyes from sleepless nights. Most of her swellings had healed, and she concealed her bruises with clothing or makeup.

Alex focused on getting well enough to leave the hospital and, the next time she entered his room, two doctors were present.

'I am worried about your last test results,' the young doctor told Alex, 'so I have brought in a nephrologist, Dr Rojas.'

The specialist also looked at Alex with concern. 'Yes,' he nodded, 'you have blood in your urine so we did further tests. Your kidneys are damaged, my friend, and you will soon need dialysis. Are you able to get this medical care in Brunei?'

Alex shook his head slowly; looked across at Debra. 'I doubt it. The closest specialist care would be in Singapore.'

'Then we need to arrange this,' the nephrologist said. 'You will need future ongoing treatment as your condition is much more serious than we previously thought. You might even want to consider going back to Australia.'

Both doctors nodded in agreement as they added comments to Alex's medical chart.

'Yeah. That's probably a good idea,' Alex said.

Debra listened to Alex, trying to make sense of his words. *What? Are we going back to Perth? How long for? Will this affect his job?* She felt suddenly cold. *Is he intending to make it permanent, to cut all ties with Brunei?* There were so many questions she wanted to ask but didn't know where to begin.

Tired now, Alex closed his eyes again. Suddenly breathless, she let him rest and went to find Jo, Kali and Sam.

'We might have to go back to Australia,' she blurted out, her fingers tightly hugging her head.

Jo studied her face, her tight, pale expression. 'At least you know there are good specialists in Australia. Alex wouldn't get that quality of medical care in Brunei. You would spend all your time travelling overseas to specialists, and he may not always be well enough to travel or to hold down a job. Hey, and I'm going back to Australia … we could meet up,' she said trying to distract Debra from panicking. 'I've already booked flights to Sydney and I just need to arrange schooling for Kali …' Jo sounded keen to move on.

***

They made the most of their last few days together before Jo and Kali flew back to Australia. When the day arrived for them to leave Manila, Debra was a mess of mixed emotions.

'I don't know what I would have done without you, Jo. You've given priority to Alex when I know you had problems of your own to sort out.' She hugged her, held her for as long as she could. 'How are you coping?'

'I'm managing okay. But you too have been focusing on Alex.

Perhaps it's time you started looking at your own issues. Spend some time healing yourself.'

Debra sighed deeply. Jo was right but how could she heal herself when she didn't know where to begin? Not being able to see Rahim lingered like a festering wound.

She and Rahim believed they were part of what Cummings described as *"the sky of a tree called life, which grows higher than soul can hope, or mind can hide"* but the tree was now about to be cut down, the branches chopped, the leaves left to wither and die.

'I will focus on my own healing one day, but right now Alex needs me. I owe it to him. I feel guilty that it was my fault.' She released the hug, and eased away.

'Maybe Alex is not the saint you think he is,' Jo said, also stepping back.

'What do you mean?' She scanned Jo's face looking for clues.

'You shouldn't blame yourself, Debra. It's not always one-sided. Nor are relationships that simple.' Jo lowered her eyes, returned to her packing, and threw some last-minute items into her case.

Numb with shock, words froze on Debra's tongue. After the doctor's dramatic news, Alex's talk of going back to Australia, she felt stunned, defeated, full of disbelief. And Jo's suggestion shocked her. Debra's face felt cold and clammy but, before she could ask more questions, Jo handed her an envelope.

'I'm sorry I should have given you this earlier. I didn't think it was the right time. Now it probably is. Rahim left it for you when he dropped in that night.'

Debra looked at Jo and mouthed the word, 'Why?'

Day and night she'd tortured herself with questions of whether he thought of her at all. Was he suffering sleepless nights and restless days as she was? Did he lie awake tossing and turning with the same exhausted dreams? Did he care about her in the same way she cared so deeply about him?

Throwing her hands to her face, Jo whispered, 'I'm sorry I didn't give it to you sooner. I thought it might upset you.'

Debra tore open the envelope, and drew out a fragile mottled piece of writing paper. Instinctively, she lifted it to her nose, savoured the faint fragrance of camphorwood that lingered. Some of the words were smudged where the letter may have rested on dampened blossoms or sheltered under leaves.

She pictured him resting the pen on the Chinese rice paper as he leant against the camphorwood desk before pushing open the shuttered French doors at Mike's house. She could smell the rain, the dank tropical air as he stepped out into the courtyard. Water trickled into the wrought-iron grilles on the drains, as she visualised him staring into the night garden past the clumps of rustling bamboo and beyond, watching until the moths bombarding the light bulb collapsed in a lifeless pile on the mat, before slowly closing the shutters in on himself.

My Darling

What is this wonderful special feeling we have? It is difficult to put into words. But I think I can describe it in this way. When we first came together as lovers, we created a spark that lit a tiny light that now burns day and night for us. It burns in our eyes and anyone who saw us together, would see it burning ten times as brightly.

Without this light, couples stagger round in darkness, hopefully travelling a parallel course but alas, very often not. Neither of us knew about this light until we found one another and yet strangely, any two people in love, I'm sure, could have told us about it. Once we discovered it together, we knew we were on the same path. We knew we would always travel it together no matter what distances would ever separate us. That is the best way I can explain it to you.

We were so sure and determined, willing to risk everything for a future together. Whatever happens to me, to you, to us, together or apart in time to come, I know with a calm and utter certainty that in the final recollective moments of old age, I will look back over all those intervening years and I will say, 'Yes, you were worth it. You were worth every moment of anguish, sadness, self-doubt, longing, and frustrated separation that we had to endure. Oh, yes, you were worth it all right.'

All my love always

Rahim

She folded the note and put it back in its envelope. She'd waited so long for this, to read the comfort of his words. Now that she knew loss so well, she understood there were many reactions to love and loss. *Grief is something you eventually work through, but love stays with you forever.* She looked up at the blood-red tropical sun. The same radiance that often warmed her heart, illuminated her being. She remembered Rumi's words as if it were yesterday:

'If the sun were not in love, he would have no brightness.'

When their hearts collided on a ferry crossing in an ocean far away, their lives were inexplicably linked forever. He cared and that was all that mattered. He cared.

ॐ

Other Books by Moira Yeldon

Chasing Marigolds

About the Author

Moira Yeldon lives in Perth, Western Australia, but spent twelve years living in Brunei, Southeast Asia which inspired her to write this book. A love of writing motivated her to complete a course in creative writing and she has been writing ever since. This life-affirming journey has taken her along winding paths and off beaten tracks, to many exotic locations such as the tiny Shangri-La of Bandar Seri Begawan where this story is set.

As a member of the Australian Society of Authors, the Romance Writers of Australia, The Society of Women Writers of Western Australia, and the South Fremantle Writers Centre, she regularly contributes articles and participates in writing workshops.

After graduating with a Bachelor of Arts from Murdoch University, she completed a Graduate Diploma in Education at Curtin University and lectured for many years in English language, communication, and literacy. She has taught Indonesian and Malay language and is also a qualified yoga teacher.

Where Sunbeams Fall is her second novel, and the sequel, *Where Dragonflies Dream,* set in the same location twenty years later is soon to be released. Her first novel, *Chasing Marigolds,* a memoir inspired from travelling to India, was released in 2019.

She also publishes a blog that you can follow on her website at https://moirayeldon.com and has author profiles on most social media platforms.

Printed in Great Britain
by Amazon